FAMILY MATTERS

Vera Berry Burrows

Family Matters

It went without saying that John Hawthorne was extremely proud of his children. They had survived circumstances under which others would have crumbled. To bring up three girls without a mother had seemed a daunting task at the beginning, but with Nellie's help, they'd pulled through. He often thought of the times when he was at his wits end trying to fathom the workings of the female mind and now Meg was a mother herself, he couldn't help but hark back to the past.

"Meg?" he'd asked tentatively one day soon after her eleventh birthday when they unusually had the house to themselves for the afternoon.

"What, Dad? Have I done something wrong?" Meg looked at him quizzically, recognising the ominous, unfathomable expression on her dad's face. It was always the same when he was about to take her to task.

"No, you've not done anything wrong as far as I know, but..." he hesitated and fiddled with the buttons on his waistcoat. "I think we ought to have a chat."

"What about? Have Patty and Abi been doing something they shouldn't, because I try to keep an eye on them, but I can't be there all the time and anyway, Gran sees Abi more than me while I'm at school, so it's probably her you should be talking to, not me..."

"Just shut up, Meg and give me a chance," he urged feeling the sweat trickle down the back of his neck. "Oh heck, Meg, this is hard!"

"What is, Dad? For goodness sake, just say it, whatever it is. You're making me nervous."

"Well, I'll try. Er, well...er, well you know that now you are growing up, you'll soon be a teenager and the next step is being a woman..."

"I know all that, Dad. Girls grow into women and boys grow into men. I'm not stupid!"

FAMILY MATTERS

Vera Berry Burrows

A Wings ePress, Inc.

Historical Novel

Wings ePress, Inc.

Edited by: Jeanne Smith
Copy Edited by: Rosalie Franklin
Senior Editor: Leslie Hodges
Executive Editor: Marilyn Kapp
Cover Artist: Trisha FitzGerald

All rights reserved

Names, characters and incidents depicted in this book are products of the author's imagination or are used fictitiously. Any resemblance to actual events, locales, organizations, or persons, living or dead, is entirely coincidental and beyond the intent of the author or the publisher.

No part of this book may be reproduced or transmitted in any form or by any means, electronic or mechanical, including photocopying, recording, or by any information storage and retrieval system, without permission in writing from the publisher.

Wings ePress Books
http://www.wings-press.com

Copyright © 2013 by Vera Berry Burrows
ISBN 978-1-61309-851-6

Published In the United States Of America

Wings ePress Inc.
3000 N. Rock Road
Newton, KS 67114

Dedication

For my family, close and extended, especially those who have supported me through the good times and the bad. I love and appreciate you all, because family matters.

Prologue

The war bred children of strength, children whose upbringing had been aimed at providing as normal an environment as possible. Even though Belford was sheltered from the fighting and the air raids, several of them had experienced a death in the family and almost every week there was news of yet another telegram arriving at someone's door with sad news from the Front. Children were resilient and, despite their inexperience, they developed an understanding of each other's emotional needs way beyond what was considered normal for those of such tender years. The agony wrought by war made men and women out of boys and girls and had no respect at all for age.

For three children left without a mother in the middle of World War Two, survival was all they could hope for. Their father struggled as a single parent, but he always instilled into his children, determination, ambition and self-respect so that they might succeed in post-war years and achieve everything which he had been denied during his life.

This is their story.

One

"Don't tell me about complications," John snapped, abandoning his usual reserve. "My wife is dead! Why didn't you see what was happening?" He was becoming angry. He needed to hit out at everyone and everything. The naturally quiet and considerate young husband and father was behaving very uncharacteristically.

~ * ~

October 11th 1941 was a cold wet Saturday, much the same as any other autumn day in the north of England. Belford, situated on the edge of the West Pennine Moors, was snuggled between Winter Hill and Rivington Pike, sheltered from the ack-ack anti-aircraft fire that was lighting up Manchester to the south and Liverpool to the west. This little northern village was almost at peace when the rest of the world was at war—well, almost—because husbands, sons, sweethearts and friends were doing their bit for King and country and many Belford homes were manless, save for the old men and the Home Guard.

John Hawthorne was on duty on top of Rivington Pike that day and Siegfried Sassoon's words in his poem *Attack* went round and round in John's head, eerily filling him with an indescribable sense of foreboding. *Anybody who can talk about faces masked in fear floundering in mud must have witnessed the horrors of hell,* he thought. *I hate the dawn watch, especially today.*

He had joined the Home Guard as soon as he learned that he was unfit for active duty because of the comparatively unhealthy condition of his thyroid gland. "It says A Four," he complained to his wife. "That's nowhere near good enough. I'm devastated, Mary. I thought I was fit enough to do my bit. I could understand it if I were ill, but I'm not ill, am I? What a bloomin' mess!"

"What do you want me to say, John? As far as I'm concerned, I'm glad you don't have to go to war. God knows we've seen some who've gone to the Front and never come home. Don't sit there moping about what you can't change. Get off yer backside and do something about it. I don't like to be so blunt, love, but you just needed a push in the right direction. Bob Holden has joined the Home Guard and Sally says he's loving it. Can't wait for his watch to start, she says. We all need to feel we're being looked after, even if we're miles away from the fighting," Mary told him.

"To be honest, love, I never even thought about that. I know I've been a bit of a pain the last few days."

"That's an understatement if ever there was one."

"I was so sure the RAF would sign me up and I haven't given anything else any consideration at all, but it's a grand idea," and within a couple of days, he was out doing the training at Bolton TA Barracks in Fletcher Street and totally committed to the cause, his disappointment soon forgotten.

Standing at the top of Rivington Pike on that particular Saturday in October, he couldn't concentrate. His thoughts were full of Mary, who had gone into labour with their third child two days before. The ambulance had arrived in the early hours of Thursday morning.

"I'll be all right, love," she had told John as she lay on the stretcher, her fists clenched when a strong contraction wracked her body. "You see to our Meg and Patty. They'll need you in the morning. They'll be shouting for their breakfast at seven o'clock, so make sure you don't fall asleep in front of the kitchen fire. Mam'll look after them whilst you're on watch. Don't worry. I'll be okay," and she tried desperately to keep the strain out of her voice. Her thoughts were more direct. *If only he knew what the pain was like. There'd be no more babies, that's for sure.*

"It's not as though it's new to you, is it, pet?" John joked lamely. "But if you're sure, love..."

"Go on in," Mary urged, "I'll see you tonight when it's all over. Thursday's child has far to go. That's a good sign, isn't it?" She smiled lovingly at her husband as the doors of the ambulance closed on the cold, wet world outside.

John watched the ambulance pull away and then went inside. He poked the fire to warm up the kitchen in the two-up, two-down cottage. The cast iron range shone black and silver. *Mary had been black-leading the grate when her pains had started. I hope this one's a little lad, even if we have to move house. He won't want to share wi' two lasses!* He smiled at the idea. Meg was nine and Patty nearly three. *They're my pride and joy,* he thought proudly.

~ * ~

Mary thought of her two girls as she lay in the ambulance, remembering when she had given Meg a hug as she helped to bring in the washing only the day before. "I'm really grateful to you, my big girl," she said. "You've been so helpful to me now that I'm finding it difficult to bend and lift. Your little brother or sister is a big lump to carry around at the moment."

"Can I bath the baby when it comes?" she asked her mother.

"You can help," Mary told her, "and you can give it a bottle too."

"Can I?" Patty asked, eager not to be left out. At two and a half, she was such an inquisitive little soul and needed answers immediately.

"Of course you can, Patty. We'll all look after it together," Mary said. *It?* she had thought afterwards. *Poor little thing. I wish I knew what it was, then I could give it some identity. William Thomas if it's a boy and Abigail Marie if it's a girl.* She had patted her bulging midriff gently. "Won't be long now, little one," she whispered. "Won't be long."

~ * ~

John stared into the fire and thought of his dear wife going off in the ambulance. "William Thomas," he said out loud. "I like that. It uses both our fathers' names." *With both my parents gone, it's a very special way of remembering them. Typical of Mary to choose those names.* "And Abigail Marie." Smiling to himself, he slowly shook his head. "Where on earth had Mary found the name Abigail?" he said out loud again. "It must have been the name of the heroine in one of her books, as had been Margaret and Patience." *Mary always identifies with the characters in her novels and I know she hopes our children will aspire to great things as they do in the stories.* "Margaret Elizabeth and Patience Christine...such fancy names," he continued, "but my girls are worthy of them." His mind was filled with pictures of his children...the dark haired, brown-eyed Meg, kindness and consideration oozing from every inch of her and the fair-haired, blue-eyed Patty, quietly eager and enthusiastic in everything she did. *I'd challenge any man who wouldn't feel such fatherly pride.*

~ * ~

Mary clung to the side of the stretcher as the ambulance ambled along the tree-lined lane towards the Cottage Maternity Home. Her uncomplicated pregnancies enabled her to have her babies in the Cottage as opposed to Townley's Hospital in Bolton. The Cottage was only a couple of miles from her home and she found it preferable to a home confinement, especially with the other two little ones there. It also meant that John could walk the short distance to visit once the baby was born. She felt every bump on the road as the old vehicle chugged on its way and she gritted her teeth as they turned into the gates of the Cottage, but the driver didn't rush. Mary silently urged him to get a move on. *But look at him. I suppose he thinks he's seen it all before. I know that childbirth takes its time. My pains are stronger this time and not much time between them. This is far worse than I remember.* "Oh God..." She braced herself for another agonising contraction. Her whole body felt tense and the relaxation the midwives talked about was proving impossible.

"Hello again, Mrs Hawthorne," Sister Markland greeted her as they wheeled her into reception. Jane Markland had been the midwife in Belford for fifteen years. She was a buxom woman. Everybody knew she was fussy and particular, a stickler for the rules, but the most caring and proficient nurse who inspired her patients with confidence at the most vulnerable of times.

"I'm here again," Mary managed to say between wincing and writhing. She felt a warm surge of security when she saw the midwife's smiling face. "I feel all the better for seeing you, Sister."

"How long between?" Sister Markland asked so she could make a quick assessment.

Mary looked at her wrist-watch and managed to smile when she realised she was wearing Meg's Mickey Mouse Timex and his little arms were at ten past three.

"Ten minutes now, but they're strong. I don't think I'll be long this time, but ..."

Sister Markland sensed the tension in Mary's voice. "What's wrong?" she asked.

"It's nothing, Sister. I'm just anxious to get on with it," Mary told her and silently told herself, *And I'm just imagining things that aren't there.*

With ablutions complete, Mary was made comfortable in the Labour Ward. She lay on her back and stared up at the ceiling, whitewashed, clean and sterile. A couple of beds to the right, a young woman groaned and thrashed around, arms flailing and her deep breathing exploding into heart-rending screams. Mary turned her head sideways. The girl was very young, seventeen at the most. Her flaxen hair was plastered to her head, dripping in perspiration and her face was red and swollen with crying. *Poor thing,* Mary thought. *She's only a little girl. This war's got a lot to answer for. So many young men have been called up and have made the most of their last few days at home. Look at my friend Annie. She discovered she was pregnant a week after her Eddie had been posted to North Africa.* Mary winced. *These pains are making me feel sick. I can't remember feeling like this when I had Meg and Patty. I've got a pain in my chest too, or is it in my stomach? I can't tell. Perhaps it's because I had no breakfast. Funny the things you remember when they don't matter. Mam never allowed me to go to school without a slice of toast and a warm drink inside me. She didn't want me fainting in assembly.* She breathed in deeply and blew out strongly through her mouth. *I can still remember the routine clearly even though it's two and a half years since I had Patty.* Nausea swept over her: no eating during labour...she knew that. "Nurse! May I have a sip of water?" she asked as the ward nurse in crisp, white apron and cap, came to check her pulse.

"Just to wet your lips mind," the nurse told her and concentrated on her watch as she counted. She signalled to Sister Markland to come over to verify her observations. "Do you feel hot?"

"No, but I feel sick," Mary managed to tell her, "and I'm so uncomfortable. The pains are getting stronger and more frequent."

"I think we'll take your blood pressure again," Sister Markland told her as she joined the junior nurse at Mary's bedside. "Just to keep a check on you." *I think I'm experienced enough to make an educated judgment that all is not well.* Mary, propped up on several pillows, lay limply as Jane Markland pumped up the equipment, her expression remaining calm and unmoved belying what she felt inside. Slowly, she walked to the foot of the bed to record her findings. *I will definitely have to call Doctor McNeill.*

Mary said nothing, leaving her well-being in the hands of the experts. She could see the clock on the wall in front of her. Lunchtime already. *How many contractions have I had since I arrived in the labour ward? I've lost count. This little one must be a boy,* she thought. *They say boys are harder to part with!* and she raised a smile at the thought of William Thomas Hawthorne making his appearance at Number Nine Hillside Terrace. *How the girls will mother him—or smother him more like.*

"Now then, Mrs Hawthorne, how are you?" Doctor McNeill's soft Scottish brogue lifted Mary out of her reverie. He was the young GP who was assisting Doctor Lassiter at the local surgery. He was similar in age to Mary herself and she felt a deep admiration for his down-to-earth way of making everybody feel comfortable.

"Hello, Doctor," she whispered. "What are you doing here?" She managed to raise a half smile as she thought, *Some doctors are abrupt and supercilious, but Doctor McNeill isn't like that. He's not the typical dour Scot you'd expect in his position. I have every confidence in his judgment and I know he'll make me feel better. He's going to bring my baby into the world and it's going to be soon; it has to be soon.*

"I've come to have a look at you," the young doctor softly

explained and then, making sure she understood, "You don't seem to be making much progress." He kept quiet whilst he examined her and Mary continued with her deep breathing, hoping that William Thomas would be born before midnight. *Thursday's child; I've promised John.*

"I think we had better transfer you to Townley's Hospital, Mary," Doctor McNeill told her, "Your blood pressure is higher than I would want it to be and your heart rate's a bit rapid. Better to have you where the equipment is. Just a precaution, mind." His warm smile belied what he was thinking. *I don't wish to worry her with specific details, but I'm more than a little concerned that her heart rate is dangerously high. I can't understand why I didn't detect it during her visits to the surgery. Her readings were always so normal, so this has to be something that has come on in the last few days and developed quickly.* He took a deep breath while he collected his thoughts.

"Will you let John know? I don't want him worrying about me when he has our Meg and Patty to see to," she said wearily. She tried to cover her feelings, but ... *I really don't want to go to Townley's, but I have neither the energy, nor the inclination to argue,* she thought wearily.

"I'll tell John what's happening. Dinna you worry. He'll be able to come to see you this evening?" It was a question that didn't get an answer and didn't need one.

The journey to Townley's seemed to take forever. Mary felt wretched, in pain, short of breath and fast becoming weary struggling with her labour. The attendant nurse held her hand and wiped her face with a cool cloth. Mary found some relief and comfort in the nurse's attention and concentrated on managing the contractions as they rose in the small of her back and pierced agonisingly through her abdomen, bringing her baby into the world. Soon it would all be over.

~ * ~

Doctor McNeill himself rode his bicycle to Hillside Terrace to see John. "Mary's struggling this time, John. We've moved her to Townley's. You *will* be able to go see her tonight, won't you?"

"Aye, of course I will," he answered sharply, unreasonably irritated that the doctor should intimate that he might not be able to make the journey across town. "I'll go even if I have to walk it!" he snapped and, with a rushed apology for his curt manner, "Sorry, Doctor," he excused himself, realising that he would have to see the duty officer in order to switch his watch.

John stood before his commanding officer like a man asking for the moon. His whole demeanour displayed a proud man. *I hate myself for succumbing to feelings of inferiority. It's totally contrary to my nature and yet I'm beholden to this man to give me time off to visit Mary.* He took a deep breath, trying desperately not to show his anxiety, "...so you see, sir, I really have to go to Townley's. If necessary I'll make up the time later," he reasoned as he thought, *I don't want to belittle myself by pleading, but by gum, I will plead if that's what it takes.*

"No problem, Johnny. You go. I'll give Corporal Green time off to drive you there in the jeep. He can wait while you go in to see your wife. I hope you find her feeling better."

"Thanks very much, sir." He sighed with relief. *Duty officers are sometimes too full of their own importance, but not this one. Now I have to make sure that Mary's mother is able to stay with Meg and Patty until I get back.*

"You go off and see our Mary," Nellie Walmsley urged. "I'll see to the little 'uns," and John climbed into the jeep, thankful that Corporal Green didn't expect him to make polite conversation during the journey. He needed to be alone with his thoughts until he was able to see Mary and his new baby.

Townley's Hospital was an old Victorian building, a large part of which had been the local workhouse and orphanage during the1800s. Its black, sombre exterior did nothing to inspire confidence in the visitor, and inside, its long corridors smelled of boiled cabbage and pine disinfectant. John looked urgently at the ward signs: stiff, lifeless notices hanging precariously from the ceiling on white painted chains. D4 was straight on along the seemingly endless passageway. He walked briskly, completely oblivious of all the other visitors whose needs must have been as urgent as his own and he prayed silently that the air-raid siren wouldn't go before he reached Mary's bedside. His prayers were answered and he stood quietly at the door of the ward, a single side ward, gazing forlornly at his beloved wife whose face was flushed and beads of perspiration dappled her brow. "Hello, love," he whispered, moving forward to take her hand and squeeze it gently.

She breathed heavily. "Hello," she said. "This is a mess, isn't it?"

"No! No, it isn't! It's all right. They'll make you feel better. You're in the right place now." He tried to sound reassuring for his wife, but somehow his words were unconvincing. *I hate to see her like this.* He mopped her forehead gently and squeezed her hand with every contraction, whilst the nurses hovered and kept a caring eye on what was happening. Little was said, but words were unnecessary and their stoical attempts to shield each other from their anxious thoughts, were tacitly accepted. Even though the nursing staff moved about quietly and efficiently, John felt totally and ominously alone. *I don't understand why Mary should be having all this bother this time around.* When visiting time was over, he was quite desperate. He bent to kiss his wife's feverish head and whispered, "Hang on in there, sweetheart. I'll be back tomorrow night. If we don't get Thursday's child, Friday's child will do—loving and giving. Perfect!"

"I'll do my best," she murmured and closed her eyes on her hot tears as he left the room. "Please God," she prayed, "let's get this over and done with."

John did an early watch on Friday and then went to the hospital again. Mary still hadn't given birth and the doctor was talking about a Caesarean section when John left after visiting time. "We'll wait until midnight and then we'll decide. We are concerned about her blood pressure and heart rate. We need to stabilise them before we can make a decision. Mary seems a lot calmer now and the baby is not in danger. Perhaps when you come tomorrow, your baby will be here. Please don't worry, Mr Hawthorne. We'll keep a close watch on her," the doctor reassured him.

John decided to do the dawn watch when he arrived home. His section leader had been very amenable and allowed flexibility in John's duties. *Good mates are a godsend and I sure do appreciate their support,* he contemplated as he climbed the hill to his lookout point. At daybreak, on that cold October morn, he gazed up into the sky, heavy with rain clouds that hung over the hills like a thick, black canopy. His thoughts were with Mary. *Please God, let her have it soon,* he prayed over and over again. Even when the screeching sirens sounded in the distance, he continued to plead earnestly with God to ease his Mary's pain.

~ * ~

Mary was wheeled into the delivery room soon after midnight. Miraculously, her contractions had become more regular and the birth had begun to look more normal. She was tired, very, very tired, but she was aware that she was soon to give birth to William Thomas. *How thrilled John will be,* she thought with pleasure as she was transferred to the delivery table.

"Just do as we say, Mary," the nursing sister told her, "and you'll be fine."

Mary nodded. Her whole body felt like lead; her arms were numb and she wondered where she would find the energy to push when the time came. The pains seemed to be somewhere far away, starting at the top of her head and moving slowly and purposely down her whole body. In the distance, she thought she could hear the sirens and the sound of bombers overhead. *They must be after Manchester Ship Canal, or Liverpool Docks,* she thought as if in a dream, *and here I am, having a little war of my own.*

The delivery room with white tiled walls and floor, sterile and airy, felt like paradise. Angels in blue dresses, starched aprons and haloes, scurried around, seemingly, to Mary, in slow motion. Voices echoed a long way away and Mary somehow knew when she needed to push out the little life within her, without being told.

~ * ~

On watch, John stared somewhere beyond the distant hills through the dawn mist, unable to dismiss the words of Sassoon from his troubled mind. *'And hope with furtive eyes and grappling fists, Flounders in mud. O Jesus, make it stop.'*

Amidst the distant voices, the wailing of sirens, the far-away explosions and the pitter-patter of the rain outside, Abigail Marie Hawthorne made her noisy entry into the world. Her first cries were her contribution to the relief and celebration of her long-awaited appearance. She was placed in her mother's arms, her curly hair brushing Mary's cheek. Mary looked down and smiled at her beautiful third daughter. She sighed slowly, deeply. When the nurse went to take the baby to the nursery, she discovered Mary, still smiling, was still and lifeless. After her Herculean struggle with the most natural occurrence in a woman's life, she had relinquished her hold on her earthly existence.

Abigail Marie Hawthorne was asleep. She had worked so hard to come into this world, a world at war, a world in which success would not be achieved without Saturday's child's destined hard work.

Two

Life without Mary

John Hawthorne was inconsolable. He sat in the doctor's office at the hospital, shaking with grief and sheer disbelief. "What went wrong?" he asked over and over again.

The doctor looked at the devastated young man in front of him. "It happens sometimes. Women are naturally strong, strong enough to withstand the stress the human body takes during childbirth. Occasionally, complications occur…"

"Don't tell me about complications," John snapped, abandoning his usual reserve. "My wife is dead! Why didn't you see what was happening?" He was becoming angry. He needed to hit out at everyone and everything. The naturally quiet and considerate young husband and father was behaving very uncharacteristically.

"Mary's heart had not been as strong as we thought," he explained to John. "Somehow it managed to keep going until the baby was born." The doctor remained calm. He sat behind his desk, shrewdly concentrating on John's demeanour. He could see the hurt and devastation in his eyes, but there was no panic, no hysteria. He silently assessed that he was dealing with a strong-willed, gentle man who would go through the grieving process and come out stronger at the other end. *These times are never easy,* he thought. *How could any doctor not feel the pain and heartache in imparting such devastating news?* He stood up and walked over to where John was sitting, straight-backed, rigid, tense, eyes looking straight ahead, but apparently seeing nothing. He put a firm hand on the distraught man's shoulder and it was as if John had been given a signal to let go, to allow his grief to pour out. He slumped forward, tears rolled down his face and he sobbed uncontrollably.

An hour passed before John felt he was able to go to see the baby. His thoughts were slowly becoming untangled. His mind was beginning to make sense of what had happened, but he couldn't yet get beyond his anger. *I hate myself for getting Mary pregnant again; I hate Mary too for leaving me. Why did you do it, Mary? I hate the child for causing her mother so much agony—the final agony in bringing about her destruction.* He shook his head slowly. *Hate? It is such a strong, powerful word, a word so often misused, a word I have hitherto had no use for.* He sighed deeply. *Yet, my mind is full of it; hate for my life left in ruins.* He rested his head in his hands. *The devastation left after Manchester's bombs had been dropped is nothing compared to this. Perhaps if Jerry dropped a bomb to obliterate Belford, me and my two...but then reality registered ...three little girls could join Mary and be a family again.* He shivered violently and almost immediately regained his composure with the realisation that he had three children to care for. *My three little girls need me more than ever. With the war going on all around us, I need to be strong for them, but most of all, I need to be strong for Mary.*

He walked slowly along the corridor towards the nursery. Nobody spoke to him and he just walked as if in a dream until he reached the cot labelled 'Hawthorne.' He looked down at the tiny bundle whose delicate curls were tumbling on to the sheet on which she lay. There was an unusual quiet around him. He didn't notice the cries of the other babies waiting to be fed. He felt an overwhelming feeling of love surge through him, a momentary spiritual inspiration making him catch his breath. "She's beautiful, Mary," he said without thinking. "She is absolutely beautiful." He looked around for a nurse to gain permission to pick up the baby. He didn't speak. He simply nodded in the baby's direction and the nurse gave her approval. He held Abigail Marie in his arms for the first time and his tears fell onto her head, seemingly baptising her with the Hawthorne family name. "Hello, little one," he sobbed, "I'm your daddy and I am going to make you and your sisters the happiest children who ever lived on this earth. The war won't last forever and we'll live life to the full. I can promise you that."

John had to leave Abigail in the hospital when he went home to Meg and Patty. His next ordeal was to break the news to them and he felt sick at the mere thought. *How on earth am I going to tell them?* he agonized silently to himself. *They're only babies themselves. They have no idea what's going on. How could they? I have no way of letting them know other than asking Constable Bradley to call and I couldn't do that. The sight of a policeman at the door would alarm my mother-in-law and frighten my children.* So he delayed the inevitable until he arrived home. As he walked up the garden path, the girls ran to meet him.

"Have we had the baby? What is it? How's Mammy?" they shouted, excited at the prospect of having a new baby in the house.

Nellie Walmsley looked at her son-in-law's face. "What is it, John? What's happened?"

Instinctively, the children went quiet and John ushered them into the house. "Come on in and I'll tell you all about it," he said, his outward appearance belying the turmoil that was going on inside his head. Indoors, the fire in the shiny grate was cosy and welcoming. He flopped into the armchair, momentarily remembering he was in the place where he sat when Mary had left last Thursday. The children sat on the thick, knotted-rag, hearth rug at his feet. Nellie couldn't sit. She stood in the doorway waiting for what John was obviously struggling to say. The words he'd planned for the last couple of hours stuck in his throat. He took hold of his children's hands and gently pulled the little girls onto his lap. He nuzzled their heads and talked quietly. "Your Mammy had a very hard time when she had the baby," he said with forced calm, "She was very, very tired and God decided that she should go to stay with him so she could have a long rest."

"Oh no, no, no," Nellie cried and hid her face in her apron so as not to frighten the children as she wept. She moved forward and held on to the table for support, dropping heavily onto a chair in shock and disbelief. "Oh God," she whispered, "Please let it all be a big mistake. Don't take our Mary away from us."

John continued stoically. "You have a baby sister, Abigail Marie. She's the most beautiful baby you have ever seen. We are going to love her and cherish her for your mammy." He stopped, unable to say any more as the huge lump in his throat threatened to choke him.

Meg was the first to break the silence and she sobbed loudly as she tried to control her emotions. "I don't want Mammy to live with God. I need her here," she cried, hot tears streaming down her flushed cheeks and onto Patty's tiny hands. Patty was much too young to understand and she looked forlornly at her wet fingers. With her bottom lip quivering, she cried too. Even though she was unaware of the circumstances at that moment in time, she knew something had made them all cry, but she couldn't possibly imagine the terrible effect it might have on their young lives. John, Nellie, Meg and Patty huddled together and wept until they could weep no more.

"You don't expect to see your children go before you," Nellie said as she and John later tried to make sense of what had happened. "'er dad 'ad a weak 'eart, but we never thought 'e'd pass it on to our Mary. She was always an 'ealthy child. Our pride and joy. We couldn't 'ave any more after we'd 'ad 'er… 'er dad…" She paused briefly. "I know one thing though. She'll want us to carry on as normal, but God knows it's 'ard. It's bloomin' 'ard." And her voice broke as she fought back the tears that had flowed freely and frequently during the past few days.

~ * ~

The next weeks were more difficult than John could ever have imagined. St Peter's Church had been crowded when the funeral party arrived with Mary's coffin covered in flowers. John and Nellie walked hand in hand with Meg and Patty. Jane Markland, the midwife, nursed Abigail whilst the rest of the family paid their last respects to the wife, mother and daughter whom they had all loved and lost.

With the funeral over, the baby gave them all something upon which to focus their attention and the family tried to pick up the pieces of their shattered life. Nellie looked after the children while John continued his watch on Rivington Pike. Meg bathed and fed Abigail as she had promised Mary before Abi was born and little Patty held the soap and the baby powder and fetched a clean nappy when it was needed. Both girls were forced by circumstances to grow up very quickly and yet John Hawthorne was determined that they wouldn't miss out on their childhood. There were lots of love and cuddles, enough for the whole village.

Emotionally, they relied on each other and when little things reminded them that Mary had gone, things like home-made jam tarts and finding a hairpin down the side of a chair, it was hard to stop the tears from flowing.

"We've got to cry if we feel like it," he told Meg when she tried to hide her grief and found herself heaving and sobbing inside. "You must never be ashamed of crying, Meg. You wouldn't be human if you didn't cry from time to time."

Every night, Meg cuddled up to Patty in the double bed they were sharing.

"Tell me a story, Meggy," Patty murmured.

"Okay, but just a short one." Taking a deep breath, she calmly began. "Once upon a time," she whispered in the gathering gloom, "there were two little girls; one was called Patty and the other was called Meg..."

"Aw thanks, Meggy. I like stories about us," Patty said eagerly.

"...and they wanted a sister. They wished with all their hearts that they could have a baby girl to play with, not a boy who would want to play football and cowboys and Indians all the time. And guess what; their wish came true. But one day, God said that by having a baby girl, their Mammy would have to watch over them from Heaven..." She had no idea how she was going to finish the story. Maybe she had ended it already, because Patty was fast asleep in her arms. "Please God," she prayed quietly, "Look after our Mam..." and as the tears ran down her cheeks, she held Patty close to her until she too drifted off into oblivion for a while. Eventually however, Meg decided to explain to little Patty. "I don't think Mammy is coming home again after she's had a rest in Heaven. We'll just have to manage and we will, Patty, we will."

At school, away from the house, Meg was able to laugh and play with her friends without feeling guilty about being happy. The war had bred children of strength, children whose upbringing had been aimed at providing as normal an environment as possible. Even though Belford was sheltered from the fighting and the air raids, several of them had experienced a death in the family and almost every week, there was news of yet another telegram arriving at someone's door with sad news from the Front. Children were resilient and, despite their inexperience, they developed an understanding of each other's emotional needs way beyond what was considered normal for those of such tender years. The agony wrought by war made men and women out of boys and girls and had no respect at all for age.

Meg had her tenth birthday the following July. "I'm in double figures now, like you and Gran, Dad!"

"Yes you are, pet, but you'll never catch us up. We've got a head start on you!" John replied, noticing that Meg had gradually begun to shed the darkness of grief that had shrouded her young life for the past ten months.

She had divided her time between Abigail, Patty, Grandma and school without complaint.

She had been forced to grow up a lot in the past few months. She couldn't, or she wouldn't, say anything to her dad about the ache she had in her heart, because he thought she had adjusted well to her new role and for the most part, she did enjoy what she was doing, but sometimes, deep down inside, she wanted to run away and leave it all behind. She was weighed down by the notion that as the eldest, she had responsibilities to fulfil. "So you see," she told Millie, a rag doll in a gingham dress and with yellow wool hair that had long ago lost its curl, "I have to stay here, otherwise Patty and Abi won't have anybody to look after them. I'm the mammy now."

"For your birthday, we'll go to Moss Bank Park and have a picnic. Your gran will make a cake. She's saved her sugar ration so you can have a birthday to remember," John told her.

"Oh Dad, that will be brilliant! Can we take a bat and ball? Patty has learned to catch and I'll be able to run around with her. She'll love it in the park!" John was amazed at the way Meg handled everything and, with pride oozing from within his very soul, he hugged her tightly until she could hardly breathe. "Flippin' 'eck, Dad! I can't breathe!" she said, pushing him away. "We'll let you and Gran play too, if you like."

"Your mam would be proud of you," he continued and he smiled. "You know, Meg, I've just noticed that we can talk about her now without getting upset."

"I've noticed too," Meg replied, "I know Mam wouldn't want us to be sad all the time. I want her to look down from Heaven and see that we're all right." She preferred not to think of the times when she had locked herself in the outside lavatory, away from the rest of the world and broken her heart. "I need you, Mam, I really need you," she had frequently sobbed. "Gran isn't the same as you, even though she tries. Why did you have to leave us, Mam? Why? Why?" and as the tears somehow relieved the tension, she drew solace from the thought that she had at least survived thus far. With her dad always there and her gran not so far away, she thought she ought to be thankful. "Stop it, Meg Hawthorne!" she regularly chastised herself. "Don't be such a wet blanket and just get on with it."

"I'm that proud of you, my Meggy," John unashamedly told her again, but she looked down at the floor, embarrassed by her own selfishness in that occasionally she felt trapped and desperate to escape her demanding life. *It has to be my secret,* she determined, *and I will never tell anybody about it, not ever.*

In the summer of 1942, the news on the radio wasn't good. British fortunes in the war had reached their lowest point. The latest news reported that at the Front in North Africa, the British army was ready to face its enemies. Even though people tried to make their lives as normal as possible, they couldn't escape the fact that Hitler was making everybody miserable. John and Nellie sat in silence as they listened to the sombre, measured voice of the newsreader on the wireless as he informed them, *"On July first,*

Rommel attacked and was hammered by British artillery. Montgomery waited seemingly too long until he was ready to launch his attack, even though Mr Churchill urged him to go sooner..."

"What do you reckon, John? Should Churchill be interfering with Monty's plans? I don't know if politicians should be telling the military what to do," Nellie said, voicing her own concerns. "This is two wars now for me, yer know. My father never came back to us from the Battle of Ypres." She pronounced it as 'Eepress,' which added a sense of pathos to the situation. "I were twenty-four at the time," she continued, "expecting our Mary and worried in case 'er dad was called up, `is `eart being weak an' all. Our Willy were only ten and every time I 'ear of little 'uns being left fatherless, it wreaks 'avoc in me 'eart."

"I know, Nellie, and it's always a sad day when the dreaded telegraph boy rides his bike up somebody's street, but he's an experienced soldier, Nellie, is Churchill, so he must know what he's talking about. I'm not so sure I agree with his politics, but we have to trust these men to run the country and hope they do what's right for us. God knows we have need of somebody who can defeat Jerry, and Churchill is our only hope just now. I don't know if I'm right or wrong, but like every other man in the street, we need some sort of hope in order to look forward to peace, however long it takes."

By November, Britain had a resounding victory to cheer, the defeat of the Desert Fox. In addition to that triumph, the Hawthornes had survived their own ordeal and Abigail Marie was a year old - smiling and laughing, a joy to them all, her whole future before her.

Three

Family adjustment

Nobody could pretend that time passed quickly during the war. Everybody knew that each day brought new problems, but the first flowers of spring, a warm summer's day, even a day without distant explosions, encouraged people to smile and forget it for a little while. With the war still raging in the North Atlantic, Belford was like a port in a storm. The villagers went about their daily lives, surviving as best they could on meagre rations and hand-me-down clothes. There was a national appeal for people to grow their own vegetables and the old men in the village spent most of their waking hours on their allotments. The Hawthornes had a large garden and John was able to grow potatoes and carrots, cabbages and onions and still leave enough land to have a lawn for the children to play on and a little flowerbed for Patty to grow bluebells and pinks.

The church played a big part in keeping the community together. St Peter's Church was always full at morning Eucharist and Evensong alike. The afternoon Sunday school was well attended and gave the children some focus in their lives. Very few families rejected what the church offered, and like most of the children in the village, Meg, Patty and even baby Abigail loved going to Sunday school. *Learning about Heaven and God and Jesus helps a bit,* Meg thought as she pushed Abigail's pram through the village. "Our mam must be happy up there, but I don't know how happy she'll be without us all to keep her company," she tried to explain to the little ones. For her young mind, it was difficult to accept that her mother would be happy at all without her family around her. Only the sensitive Meg understood that, but she did feel a sort of confused contentment when she had been to St Peter's on Sundays.

Meanwhile, John Hawthorne lavished his girls with all the love and attention he could muster. Slowly, he was learning to live without Mary and, although she was never far away from his thoughts, he had begun to make his life normal again. With the two older girls at school and Nellie taking care of Abigail during the day, he was able to take a job at the Bleach Works, keeping himself in the Reserves for the Auxiliary Fire Service in case of another national emergency. He was a self-effacing sort of chap, but the day he got the job, he could hardly contain his enthusiasm.

"Nellie! Meggy! Patty! Everybody! I've got good news!" he announced breathlessly as he rushed in through the back door.

"It must be good too, 'cos it's put a smile on yer fizzog like the cat that's got the cream!" Nellie beamed. "Ee John, it warms the cockles of me 'eart to see yer smile again."

"I've got a job at the bleach works and it means no more shifts and you know what that means? No more weekends! And Christmas is coming up too. It's about time we had a bit of time for ourselves." He grabbed hold of Nellie and swung her round in his excitement.

"Gerroff, yer daft thing," Nellie said, laughing with him. The children beamed at the thought of their dad being home more often than they had known during the past few years.

"Yippee!" squealed Meg and as she grabbed hold of little Patty, they skipped around the kitchen with her teddy. *"If you go down to the woods today, you'd better go in disguise,"* they sang excitedly, swinging Teddy back and forth until his little arms were ready to break away from his much loved body. *"If you go down to the woods today, you're in for a big surprise."* John and Nellie grinned at each other. It was good to hear the children singing and it filled the house with joy after so much misery had swamped them. With cheerful hearts, they allowed the girls to finish: *"For every bear that ever there was, will gather there for certain because today's the day the teddy bears have their picnic—And our dad doesn't have to work weekends anymore!"* Meg continued jovially, yet unsuccessfully trying to fit the words to the tune. "Oh well," she declared with a shrug, "How about this? *Dad doesn't have to work, Dad doesn't have to work, Ee Ay, Addio, Dad doesn't have to work!"* she sang out loudly and enthusiastically. The sun was beginning to shine again on the Hawthorne home.

~ * ~

Thinking back to Christmas 1941, it had been very quiet. Meg and Patty had had a present each and John had put up the tree, but, only three months after Mary's death, it was all they could do to survive. Only time would heal their wounds and fill the great chasm that had been left in their lives, but at that stage, every second was a minute, every minute an hour and trying to see beyond the next meal was like conquering Everest in the bleak winter weather.

However, the days, weeks and months did pass and life took on a more optimistic view. A man on his own with three young children was inevitably bound to be targeted by the young war widows in the community who needed masculine presence in their lives, someone upon whom they might focus their attention in their war-affected world. They considered John Hawthorne to be a very attractive object of their affections, a very good catch, considering that his three little girls would need a mother as they were growing up. John himself, had not really contemplated that another woman should enter his life.

"You know, Nellie, I don't think I'm ready yet to go a-courtin' again. You're always there if I need you for the girls," he confided, "and, you know..." He blushed "...I'm comfortable being alone in my bed at night." He paused pensively. "Actually, I haven't totally dismissed the idea of walking out with a lady when I feel the time is right, but not with any of the brazen hussies who flaunt their assets in my face when I'm out for a quiet pint with Bob."

"Any 'ussy in particular?" Nellie smiled and understood her son-in-laws attempts to justify himself. "You don't 'ave to explain to me, John. You'll know if and when, so don't worry about it." She smiled knowingly to herself. *He's an amusing chap at times.*

Friday night was John's night out with his friend, Bob Holden. "Just you look at 'er, John!" Bob whispered behind his hand, trying to hide the big, cheeky grin across his beaming face, "She's 'ad you undressed and done three rounds with you already! War or no war, she's giving you the come-on, by 'eck she is!"

John blushed to the roots of his chestnut hair. "Get away with you, Bob. You've got too vivid an imagination and a dirty one at that!"

Gertie Barrow, however, was persistent and continued to give him the eye across the bar in the Black Dog. She had lost her husband early in the war. Harold Barrow had been one of the three hundred pilots of Fighter Command lost in August 1940. Gertie had grieved publicly for a short time and then had set out to snare every single man in Christendom, well in Belford anyway. John always thought, perhaps a bit too piously, that she sullied the name of her hero husband and wanted nothing to do with her, but that was no deterrent to Gertie. She flirted shamelessly with him all the same and it unnerved him greatly. "Life goes on," she would say loudly to nobody in particular, "There's nothing wrong with trying to make the most of what's left." Thus undeterred, she set out on a mission. "Hello, John," she whispered huskily, eyelids fluttering fifteen to the dozen, her false eyelashes hanging on for dear life. "How are you and how are those lovely girls of yours? Why don't you bring them round for a piece of my homemade sponge cake? I've saved up all my egg and sugar rations to make it specially, just for you, because you are one of life's gentlemen," and she would pout her full lips and blow a red lipsticked kiss to him in front of the amused pub regulars.

John wanted to - indeed needed to stop Gertie thinking she might get her claws into him. *I just have to think of something that will stop her in her tracks, but I've always found it very difficult to be blunt. I hate...that strong word again...to hurt her feelings, especially when Gertie hasn't really committed any crime against me.* He struggled to think rationally about it. *I should be flattered, but I'm not. Mary was my first and only love and the handling of pushy women is so alien to me. I don't like the thought of being rude, especially to a woman.* Finally he decided, albeit reluctantly, that he must act in order to regain his sense of composure and peace of mind. Eventually, he plucked up the courage one Friday night and agreed to walk Gertie home from the Black Dog. It was a spur of the moment thing.

"Go on, John, get on with it," Bob urged him, "There's only you can put a stop to it if that's what you want."

"It *is* what I want!" He took a deep breath and said, "I'll walk you home, Gertrude. We can't have you walking up the high street on your own at this time of night."

Gertie was flushed with delight. She clung possessively onto his arm, her high heels clip clopping on the pavement and her pillbox hat perched at a jaunty angle on her peroxided hair as they walked down the high street. He chatted to her about his children and about Nellie, about his job and generally about the war. As they approached her front door— "...and our Meg is a proper little lady these days."—they stopped and Gertie, true to form, went to put her arms around him, pushing her voluptuous bosom close to his chest. John was taken aback as he unwittingly allowed her bright red lips to brush his cheek before he grabbed her arms strongly and holding her at arms' length, he breathed in deeply, filling his lungs with the cold night air and said firmly, "Gertrude, please don't think me rude, but I'm really not interested in forming a relationship with anybody, not just yet anyway." He turned away quickly before she could react and in his eagerness to escape, he tripped over the empty milk bottles on the doorstep, sending them clattering into the porch. Hastily, he picked them up and clumsily replaced them. He called out a panicky "Er sorry...oh, er, goodnight," as he fled down the garden path, desperate to reach the safety of his own home. Once there, he permitted himself to feel a little pleased, smug even, that he had been forceful enough to make his point. *I didn't think I had it in me. I really ought to be more assertive in future. Am I a man or a mouse?* He knew he was gloating, but reassured himself that he was justified in doing so. *Regardless of my inexperience with women, I know in my heart of hearts that if and when I feel the need of a woman in my life, I'll choose one for myself.*

"Oh Mary," he said, grinning up to the ceiling as he lay in bed that night, "I bet you've been laughing your wings off up there! You did a pretty good job on me, love. Gertie wouldn't come anywhere close to you in the wife stakes. But I'm okay, sweetheart." Then more softly, yet confidently, "I'm okay," and he went to sleep with a satisfied smile on his face.

Gertie, on the other hand, had merely sighed deeply and loudly, shrugged her ample shoulders at the retreating John Hawthorne and returned to her lonely bed yet again.

~ * ~

Christmas 1942 was different for them all. John's job at the Bleach Works had helped him to save a few coppers and Mr Abbott at the corner shop in High Street had managed to obtain some chocolate. John diplomatically didn't ask how, or from where. He was just grateful to be able to have it. On Christmas Eve, Nellie had appeared with a rabbit to make a pie. The tree was in place and behind the black-out curtains, the Hawthorne family sat in front of the fire, roasting potatoes in the glowing embers and singing carols. War, or no war, Christmas would be celebrated and their hearts would be lifted with the festive spirit.

When they'd finished eating the potatoes that tasted delicious in spite of the fact that they were speckled with gritty black bits from the burnt skin, Patty announced contentedly, "I love Christmas." She was generally the quiet one, but always eager to follow Meg to learn how to do things. "It's all cosy and warm and there are no bombs going BANG over the hills."

John gave her a hug. "Yes, Christmas is nice," he agreed, "Now come on, you three little ladies. Up to bed and then Father Christmas can bring your presents!" Dutifully, they climbed the stairs to bed. Meg carried the sleepy Abigail and placed her in her cot, but Patty and Meg were too excited to go to sleep. John could hear them chatting and giggling long after he had turned out the light. As he placed the presents under the tree, he thanked God that he had been able to find what his children wanted. It hadn't been easy with the war still going on, but he'd managed a fountain pen for Meg and a doll for Patty, dressed in clothes that Nellie had made from remnants of fabric she'd picked up at the market. There was a red fluffy ball for Abi that would dangle from the hood of her pram. He smiled as he pictured his children scrambling under the tree to find their presents. *And the biggest surprise of all will be the chocolate*, he thought happily.

On Christmas morning, John lay in bed staring up at the ceiling. "The children are quiet and it's already seven o'clock," he whispered. "Keeping them up a bit later than usual last night seems to have worked."

In years gone by, he'd known Meg to be wide awake at three o'clock in the morning, asking if Father Christmas had been. Now, at least, he could relax a little before the Christmas rush. Within seconds of that thought, his bedroom door burst open and two excited little girls jumped on to the bed shouting, "Come on, Dad! It's time! It's time! Get your slippers on and come downstairs!"

The happy smiles on his children's faces that Christmas morning were the best present John could have wished for. When Meg produced a little parcel wrapped in green crepe paper, he was more than delighted. "I saved my penny pocket money," she told him excitedly, "and I bought it all by myself. I hope you like it."

John opened his present eagerly. "A stick of shaving soap!" he announced, "Just what I wanted! Thank you, sweetheart."

"Here's mine!" Patty shouted, jumping up and down in her excitement and she produced a paper lantern she had made at nursery school.

"Oooh, it's lovely, Patty! Thank you very much. I'll hang it on the tree. Just look at that!" he enthused. "Doesn't it look nice?"

Baby Abigail sat in her high chair and clapped her hands, shrieking with delight. John looked around at his tiny home and counted his blessings. "And you, little one, are a present in yourself. Every day you give us something new—a word, a smile, everything that you learn," he said to the curly headed baby.

"Da-dee! Da-dee!" she cooed and Meg tickled her affectionately, making her chortle with glee. When Nellie arrived, their family was complete.

"Here's your present, Gran." Meg went to hug her grandmother warmly and handed her a tiny package wrapped in the same green crepe paper as John's had been.

Nellie was overcome with emotion. She held her granddaughter tight and whispered in her ear. "You're a good girl, our Meg. Thank you, but yer shouldn't 'ave bothered about spending yer pocket money on me."

"I didn't spend much, Gran, but open it and I think you'll like it," Meg told her eagerly waiting for Nellie to see her surprise. "I found it in Mam's drawer and I thought it would suit you."

Nellie carefully unwrapped the package, taking care not to tear the crepe paper. "I'll save that for next year," she said folding it neatly. Inside was a tiny cardboard box that contained an ornate silver pin. Attached to the box was a gift card. She opened the card and read what was inside.

> *You'll always be my grandma forever and a day,*
> *I know you're always there for me when I'm working or at play.*
> *Sometimes when I'm cheeky, or don't do the things you ask,*
> *I don't blame you for being annoyed and taking me to task.*
> *I hope you know I love you heaps and I'm grateful that you're here.*
> *Thank you Gran for being YOU and all that I hold dear.*

"Did you write this, love?" Nellie asked through her tears.

Meg nodded shyly. "But I did ask my teacher if I'd got it right and she helped a bit. Do you like it, Gran?"

"I love it," Nellie replied. There was no need to say more.

"Now, see what I've got for you. I've bought you something that we 'aven't seen much of while this blessed war's on. I'm not sure our Patty's even 'ad one, but 'ere you are...an orange each." Nellie handed out the fruit to the wide-eyed children and she winked at John. He knew that she had probably obtained the oranges in the same way he'd got the chocolate, so it was best not to ask.

They sat down to a dinner of homemade leek and potato soup, rabbit pie with vegetables and plum pudding with real custard, surely a wartime feast fit for royalty. At three o'clock on the dot, as Big Ben summoned the nation's attention, they savoured the smooth, dark chocolate whilst they listened to the King's speech.

Patty woke up with a temperature on Boxing Day and it wasn't long before she was covered in red blisters that she scratched vigorously. "Don't scratch, Patty. You'll make them sore and then you'll have scars all over you," Meg told her. "When I had chicken pox, Dad told me they'd have to fill up the hole on my nose where I'd scratched a spot and guess where they'd get the skin to fill it...from my bottom!"

Patty's little face broke into a smile, "He didn't mean it, did he, Meg?" she asked with some uncertainty and trepidation.

"No, but it stopped me scratching and I had to wear gloves so I wouldn't make a mess of my skin. Please try not to scratch, Patty. I'll dab your spots with calamine lotion and it'll help," Meg reassured her. The following day, Abigail was covered in spots too, so the magic pale pink lotion was put to full use and Nellie sensibly took over the nursing duties from Meg.

"Goodness me, it never rains, but what it pours," she commented, "but it's better that they get rid of the chicken pox before they start school."

"I already go to school, Gran," Patty pointed out indignantly.

"I know, love, but I mean when you go to the big girl school like our Meg." Nellie didn't think of the nursery as proper school, more of a child minding service to give the mothers a break.

Soon after Christmas, Meg arrived home from school with a very important letter. "Miss Rothwell says I'm clever enough to take the scholarship," she said as she handed the letter to John, "Can I, Dad? Please."

John opened the letter and read out loud: *"Dear Mr Hawthorne, We have been preparing Class 6 for the Scholarship examination for places at the Great Moor Grammar School in Bolton. As Margaret has the required academic ability, we duly ask your permission to submit her name for consideration."* He looked at Meg, her eyes shining with expectation. He sighed and her expression changed instantly, her enthusiasm being replaced by anxiety. "Well, love," he explained as gently as possible, "you can do the exam, but you've got to understand that I can't pay for you to go to the grammar school if you don't pass." He knew that there were still fee payers at the school, those whose parents were well-off enough to buy education for their children, even though some of them weren't really academically inclined. "With two other children to consider, I can't, nay won't, set a precedent with you, Meg. It wouldn't be fair if I did and I have to treat you all the same."

"Oh, Dad!" she cried, "I'll try my best, but I promise I shan't be upset if I can't go to the grammar school. I can still work hard at the secondary modern, but thanks for letting me try." She threw her arms round John and hugged him tightly, planting a big kiss on his cheek.

"Just do your best, love. That's all I ask."

In February, Meg went along to school one Saturday morning to sit the scholarship exam. For all ten and eleven year olds, it was the event of the year and going to school on a Saturday was a treat, rather than a chore. Meg was very excited and, before she left home, she needed the toilet three times in fifteen minutes. "I'm really nervous," she informed Patty over breakfast, "but if I pass the exam, I'll be able to help when you have to do it." Left alone with her thoughts when she made a final visit to the lavatory before leaving for school, she sat contemplating her situation. *I wish I had somebody to show me things,* she brooded. *I always have to do everything right so that the other two will know what it's all about. Oh flippin' 'eck! What if I don't pass?*

"Don't forget your gas mask," John shouted from the kitchen as she left.

"Got it already, Dad! It's always with my coat on the peg." she called and with a nervous, "Ta-ra, Dad. Wish me luck," she closed the door behind her before her Dad had time to answer.

"Good luck, sweetheart," he said anyway. "Let's hope the sirens don't go off in the middle of the exam. It'd be just like Hitler to mess with your future." But John didn't want to think about that.

She had to do three papers: English, Arithmetic and Intelligence. Her dad had given her two pencils sharpened at both ends in case she broke the lead. She had some homemade shortcake biscuits in a bag. Miss Rothwell had told them all to have a little to eat between each paper. "To keep your strength up," she said. Meg felt very important and wouldn't have admitted to anyone, not even her friend, Dorothy, that she had butterflies in her tummy and was worried that she might need the toilet in the middle of the test.

Dorothy, on the other hand, made no bones about it. "I'm shaking like a leaf," she gabbled nervously. "'urry up, Meg, because I might just wet meself if we don't get to school soon." She grabbed hold of Meg's arm and the two girls walked quickly into the playground. When they saw the rest of their class, together with pupils from other local primary schools, their fears were forgotten and eager excitement took over.

~ * ~

When the letter landed on the doormat in May, Meg ran to pick it up. *"To the parent, or guardian of Margaret Elizabeth Hawthorne,"* she read, handing it to John.

"Don't forget what I told you, will you, about not being able to pay?" John really didn't know what to expect when he opened the envelope. He wanted to let Meg down lightly if needs be.

"Open it, Dad! Open it, *please*." Meg couldn't stand the suspense. She watched John's face as he silently read the contents of the letter. "Well? Well? Come on, Dad. How did I do?" she asked, hopping from one foot to the other as she waited in eager anticipation.

John scratched his head and looked wide-eyed at Meg. "You've..." He hesitated dramatically, "...passed!"

Meg squealed with delight. "Have I? Have I? Really? Oh Daddy." And tears of joy swam in her eyes. She hadn't called him that for a few years. John held her close to him for a long time, savouring the contentment brought about by her success.

This is just the beginning, he thought, *then on to better things.*

~ * ~

By the end of the following year, Meg had established herself in her new school with her friend, Dorothy, who seemed to have overcome her bladder problems. The whole new experience broadened her outlook in many ways and she was so full of enthusiasm when she arrived home after her days at Great Moor Grammar.

"We had history and geography today," she told them. "Did you know that cavemen drew on the walls of caves and that's how we know about how they used to live? Archaeologists have discovered their tools and pots and things and guess what, Dad, I learned a new word—*palaeontologist*." She said it slowly and precisely in order to show that she'd pronounced it properly.

"That's a good word," John marvelled. "What does it mean?"

"It means...just wait..."

"Come on, Meg," Patty encouraged her sister. "I've never heard of it. I bet you made it up!"

Meg giggled. "I didn't make it up. I'm not that clever, Patty, but shut up and let me think... er...it means...er...a person who studies fossils."

"What are fossils?" Patty continued.

Meg tutted loudly. "Oh you tell her, Dad. I've got to do my homework. I have to write an essay about the Suez Canal. I think I'd like to visit Egypt one day!" she enthused. Meg had been impressed with the geography teacher's description of the man-made structure of such worldwide economic and political significance. John realised her young mind had been opened to things she had not previously even thought about.

"And I hope you can afford to go there when you're older," her dad told her, "but in the meantime, just go and do your homework so you'll know what to expect when you get there! I hope Hitler doesn't get to Egypt first."

Patty was progressing well in primary school. She was truly the studious one and was rarely seen without her nose in a book. It was amusing to see her washing the dishes with a book balanced precariously on the taps, reading as she carried out her chores. Every now and again, a sudden irritated *"TUT"* followed by the splashing of soapsuds and dirty dishwater let everybody know that Patty's book had fallen off the taps again. Nevertheless, there would never be any doubt that she would follow her big sister to Great Moor Grammar and John watched with great interest as she continued to shine.

Abigail, with the other two to guide her, learned very quickly. At two, she could dress herself and doggedly stuck to learning a new task until she mastered it. Her fierce determination to succeed was clear even at that early age. She watched and listened and imitated and copied. Just before her third birthday, she learned to write her name and was able to recite all the nursery rhymes without any prompting. Every Sunday afternoon, she stood on a stool in the middle of the living room and gave a rendition of *Baa, Baa, Black Sheep*, or *Humpty Dumpty* as the rest of the family dutifully listened and applauded. None of them dared mention roast beef and Yorkshire pudding until Abigail had finished her recitation.

"Flippin' 'eck, Abi," Meg groaned one Sunday just before dinner time, "I'm starving and we all know that Jack and Jill went up the hill. Please can we have our dinner before I faint from lack o' nourishment?" Abi looked dejected, but stood defiantly eyeing them from her pedestal whilst her family eagerly encouraged her to "Get on with it!" and "Hurry up, Abi!" or "That's a good one!"

She gabbled through *Mary, Mary* and Patty commented pointedly, "Yes, you are like contrary Mary. Do you think our Abi is going to be a politician, Dad?"

John laughed. "I have no idea, love, but whatever she decides to do, we'll back her all the way, won't we?"

Abi raced through *Ding Dong Bell* before she jumped down from her stool and with an impish grin said, "Okay, time to eat! Come on, be quick, I'm starving!"

By the end of 1944, she too began to look forward to starting school herself.

Four

Life goes on

Every mother knew the traumas of taking a child to school for the first time. Fathers were usually spared the testing time of leaving one's baby in the hands of a complete stranger, but John felt duty bound to take Abigail to school on her first day. Nellie had offered to take her. "I can walk to school with our Abi, John. I took our Patty when you were on watch, yer know. You don't need to take an hour off work to get 'er to school on time."

"I know you can, Nellie, but I need to take her. It's my job. I'm her dad and I have to do it." He declined Nellie's offer in favour of making sure for himself that Abi was safely inside the school before he went to work. Patty had run on ahead, not wanting to be seen going to school with her dad.

"Dad!" she called to him pointedly. "I'm nearly eight years old and in the junior department now, not the babies' class! I don't need to walk to school with you."

The short walk through the village down to The Square gave him time to reassure his youngest child that everything would be all right. He smiled to himself. *I'm becoming like a mother hen and I dislike myself for it, but I've got to be both mother and father to my children.* He was totally lost in his thoughts as he held on tightly to Abigail's hand. *With our Meg and Patty already settled at school, I know Abigail has had good children around her,* he thought. *Our Meg never seems to get tired of helping and takes her duty very seriously. She's had a lot of responsibility thrown in her direction. I'm sure she must find it a strain sometimes. I wouldn't be a proper dad if I didn't understand that. I'll try to remember that next time she gives her lip to her gran. Not that I've heard it very often, but she can be a bit uppity at times. And what about our Patty? She never ever gives up on anything...a quietly determined little Miss, is our Patty. And I think she's made our Abigail the same without realising it.*

Patty had recently joined the library and she wanted to read each book as soon as possible so she could go back and spend ages choosing another one from the vast collection. "I love it, Dad," she told him. "I can hide myself behind the big, wooden shelves that reach right up to the ceiling and it's like...er...when I read a book, it's just like pretending to be in the stories," she tried to explain to John, "because it's all quiet and peaceful. Just imagine being able to look over Lewis Carroll's shoulder when he was writing about Alice in Wonderland. Why does it feel like that, Dad?"

"You're a proper little bookworm, aren't you?" he said and then thought for a moment or two before he answered Patty's question. "I suppose you feel like that because the authors wanted you to know that they were writing just for you. They are encouraging their readers...and you're one of them...to feel what they felt when they were writing their stories. They are trying to help you to paint pictures in your imagination to make the characters real."

"Does 'characters' mean the people in the story?" she asked innocently. John smiled and nodded enthusiastically. "It's lovely, Dad, and I'll never get tired of reading." Patty adored the old building with its quiet atmosphere, the smell of leather-bound tomes and furniture polish and the wonder of browsing through hundreds of books until she found what she wanted. She giggled as she related her experiences to John. "Sometimes when the old men reading newspapers cough, the lady behind the desk glares at them and taps on the desk to tell them off, because you can't talk in the library, you know."

"And does that make you laugh?" John asked.

"It does," Patty continued, giggling even more, "but I try not to laugh out loud, because the lady..."

"The librarian," John interrupted.

"Yes, the librarian...she scowls at me too for giggling, but I don't want her to send me out for making a noise."

"You won't get sent out, Patty," John reassured her. "You're too good to get into trouble." As he recalled the conversation with his middle child, he looked down at his youngest daughter skipping along beside him and smiled to himself. *This one's a resolute little madam too, almost to the point of stubbornness. I think she must have been born with commitment etched into her brain. Even at this age she sets herself impossible targets. I'll never forget that Saturday morning and not just because it was teeming down with rain and I couldn't peg the washing out.*

~ * ~

"I'm going to tie my own hair ribbons today," she announced with an air of childish pride. John knew every detail of that event and treasured it in his heart.

Patty had looked at her pointedly. "I don't think you'll be able to do it," she said gently so as not to deter her little sister, "It's hard not to get your hair knotted in the ribbon and you'll cry if it gets stuck," but she went back to reading her *Famous Five* book, involving herself in solving the *Mystery on Treasure Island.*

Abigail's hair ribbon task was momentarily forgotten as she immersed herself in the immortal words of Enid Blyton. She loved them all, especially *The Famous Five* and *The Secret Seven*.

Undeterred and contrarily spurred on by Patty's lack of confidence in her, Abigail pushed a tall, solid dining chair with a padded seat in front of the sideboard and climbed up so she was able to see herself in the mirror. Her tiny hands gathered up her long blonde curls and she dexterously laced the silk ribbon underneath with one hand whilst she held up her hair with the other. Time after time it slipped and she started all over again. For two hours she stood on that chair, until finally, her ribbon was tied in a bow on top of her head and her little arms literally flopped down, aching with the sheer effort she had had to endure in order to succeed.

John had been in the kitchen doing the weekly wash, his strong arms up to the elbows in soap suds. With steam billowing out of the boiler and his face dripping with sweat, he turned to see Abi framed in the doorway.

"How do I look?" she asked him, "I did it all by myself. Patty didn't help and Meg is upstairs doing her homework." She beamed with uncontrollable pride.

John had looked in on Abigail's endeavours several times during those two hours. He had smiled to himself as he furtively watched her struggle, but opted not to interfere. He had decided that the only way children would survive in this world was to be completely independent and focused on what they planned to do with their lives. Whether four, or fourteen, twenty or thirty, life was what you made it and John Hawthorne intended to make sure his girls were equipped to cope with whatever life threw at them.

"You look lovely, sweetheart. Well done!" he said to his youngest daughter, who went to give him a hug despite the soapy water dripping from his elbows. She wrapped her tiny arms round his legs, the silk ribbon sitting precariously on top of her head as John ruffled her hair.

"Don't do that, Daddy! My ribbon might fall out!" she giggled, but nonetheless determined to scold her father for his rash action.

"It won't," John told her, "You've done such a good job, it'll be there 'til next Sunday!"

~ * ~

John's thoughts ran riot in his head as he and Abigail walked towards the beginning of her new life in the big, outside world. "Thank God the war's over," he said out loud and then thought, *I don't think I would have liked leaving this little one at school on her own knowing that the sirens could go off any time even though our Patty would be there too to keep an eye on her.*

To the relief of everybody, 1945 had heralded the end of the war in Europe and John had run all the way home from work when he heard the news on the wireless, waving and shouting to everybody he passed. Nellie was putting plates on the table ready for tea and she stopped dead in her tracks when the door flew open.

"Whatever's to do, John? You scared the living daylights out o' me."

"Have you not had the wireless on?" John grabbed hold of her and swung her around and around. "It's over, Nellie. It's over! The war is over!" he said. "The bloody war is over!"

"Oh my lord! Oh my lord!" Nellie cried. "Oh my lord!" she said over and over again, "Oh my lord! Wait till we tell the children. Oh my lord!" and when they did tell the children, they cheered and ran excitedly into the garden.

"Hooray! Three cheers for King George! Hip, hip, hooray! Hip, hip, hooray! Hip, hip, hooray! God save our gracious King," they sang as they stood to attention and saluted the wonderful thought of a new and peaceful world.

In May of that year, VE Day was celebrated everywhere throughout the country and Belford was no exception. The High Street was alive with music and dancing, bunting and flags flying from every cottage in the village. The Hawthornes sat outside the Black Dog pub and watched the young men and women celebrating the end of six dark years of war and uncertainty. The old men puffed on their pipes and nodded contentedly as the youngsters cavorted up and down the street. Women leaned on their gateposts and shouted happily to each other. "Just look at that now!" called Edith Batty, "Canoodling like that and in broad daylight too!"

"Hey, what does it matter? They're enjoyin' 'emselves," Clara Pickersgill called back, "God knows we 'ave need of a bit o' pleasure after all that bleedin' misery! Stop yer moanin', Edie!"

"Ooooh 'ark at 'er!" her neighbour light-heartedly replied and they both dissolved into fits of laughter. Nobody was prepared to put a damper on things that day. Spirits were high and fuelled with a happiness that had been in short supply of late.

John lost himself again in his memories. That day, before the party began, he and the girls had picked flowers from the garden and taken them to Mary's grave in St Peter's churchyard. It wasn't a sombre occasion...on the contrary, but they had stood quietly, each with their own thoughts, hand in hand, to show Mary that they had survived and were looking forward now to a life in peace.

~ * ~

He was still deep in thought as he and Abigail arrived at the school gates. It seemed that his whole life had gone through his mind during that ten minute walk through the village. Abi was excited and she chattered away to her daddy, who roused himself from his reverie to ensure that his baby was ready to face her first day by herself, away from the bosom of her family. He looked at the mothers of the other children and realised that many of them looked like he felt. He was the only man there and just for a moment, he felt quite self-conscious, but he bent to kiss Abigail. "Go on in now, Pudding. Have a nice day. Eat up all your dinner and Grandma will be here for you when you come out."

"Ta-ra, Dad," Abi said, feeling very grown up. It was the first time she had used the word 'dad,' and she knew that she could, now that she was going to school. After all, this was the grown-up world.

Five

Pre and post-war adjustments for all, especially Meg

People were proud to recall that in spite of the war going on, Belford had remained a happy place and the children made the most of what they had. The fierce sense of pride that existed not only manifested itself in the attitudes of the man on the street, but also in the appearance of their houses, houses that were homes for whoever needed them, family and friends alike. Doors were open to all and strangers soon became friends. Cleaning and gardening were wartime occupations and not chores. Water, although not in short supply, had to be saved for fire fighting, but there was still that fierce pride amongst the village community. Doorsteps were donkey stoned regularly and net curtains dolly-creamed, despite the restraints of war. Everyone appeared to make the best of his lot. Back-to-back terraces in neat little rows looked out onto streets full of loving friendship and constant support. Somehow, a row of terraced houses symbolised a close-knit community. Community spirit was surely born during those years; open house was commonplace; the welcome mat was always out. People regarded themselves fortunate whatever their circumstances even though some harboured dreams of one day owning their own semi-detached homes with large front gardens to be kept neat and tidy and enclosed by privet hedges and wooden fences. Those dreams became the simple, modest ambitions for the survivors of a Britain that had had devastation thrust upon it by war.

Meg stood wide-eyed on the pavement with her friend, Dorothy, as the noisy farm vehicle was driven through the village. "Look at that, Dorothy!" she marvelled. "What's a tractor doing in the village?" It sounded like a lorry, but it had enormous, muddy wheels that seemed too big for its little body and the tyres were thick rubber, thicker than she'd ever seen. There were no doors on it, but it had a little metal frame that covered the driver and had a very dirty windscreen.

Dorothy looked at Meg in dismay. "Don't tell me you've never seen a tractor before, Meg."

"Yes, I have seen a tractor before, but not close up. What's it doing here in Belford?" she asked, "and there's a girl driving it!"

"I don't know, but look at all that muck it's left behind on the road. It looks like horse manure!" and they giggled as they wrinkled their noses more at the thought than the smell.

As soon as she said it, doors opened and men came out of their houses with buckets and spades, racing to shovel up the manure for their gardens, much to the amusement of the girls.

"Dad?" Meg enquired as they were clearing up after tea, "Why would a girl be driving a tractor through the village, and a dirty one at that?"

"Oh, I'd heard something about that. She must be part of the Land Army. Bob said that some land girls had been posted at Highfield Farm because old Farmer Grimshaw's lads had been called up and he needed help."

"But why girls, Dad?" Meg was curious. "I don't think I would want to be doing that dirty job. You should've seen all the muck it left on the road."

"Blimey! I wish I'd been there with my bucket and shovel. Our veggies would have tasted lovely with all that pure manure!" John said, grinning at his grimacing daughter.

Meg grinned too. "Yeah, all the men were there shovelling it up! Me and Dorothy thought they were disgusting."

"Dorothy and I," John corrected.

"That's what I said, me and Dorothy watched them scrambling on their hands and knees to see who could get the most. Ugh!"

"Okay! I give up, but in answer to your question, love, girls have had to do men's jobs while the men are away at the Front. From what I can gather, they love it. I'm sure we'll be seeing those girls around the village on a regular basis now. I bet they're from down south." John told her.

"P'raps they'll feel like all those children from down south who have had to go and stay with strangers to get away from the bombs," Meg contemplated. She'd heard it on the radio. "Some of them have gone all the way to Wales from London, haven't they, Dad?"

"They have, love, but I think the land girls won't mind so much. They'll enjoy mixing with us northerners. We're a friendly lot."

"Can I go out to play for a bit now, Dad?" Meg asked as she dried the last plate and put it away in the cupboard.

"Just for half an hour. It'll be going dark soon and our Patty and Abigail will be going to bed." He didn't want Meg to be out after dark.

"Okay. I won't be long. Dorothy and I..." she paused and playfully stuck out her tongue at her amused father. "Dorothy and I are learning how to play two balls. See yer later."

John stood looking through the window at his vegetable plot and at the neat little gardens at the end of the road. *Folks are happy,* he thought, *in spite of not having much.*

Nobody seemed to mind that there was very little money to go round. Poverty was the norm and there was no stigma attached to it. Whilst wardrobes were limited, there was a tacit acceptance that if a man's shoes were polished, he was reliable and trustworthy and even if Cherry Blossom was in short supply, spit and polish would do. A pair of highly polished shoes was kept for wearing to church on Sundays and regular attendance cleansed the soul in preparation for the following week's activities, whether saint or sinner. Church was, for most families, the hub of village life. Clogs with metal irons on the soles were the symbol of hard work and worn during the week. Boys who wore sparking clogs were popular with the girls and went through a performance of the sparker's ritual whenever a pretty girl appeared. They would throw their feet in all directions, scuffing the irons along the stone pavement and sending up a shower of sparks that might rival any firecracker on Bonfire Night.

"What're they doin' that for?" Meg asked the older girls, who never seemed particularly impressed with their flamboyant kicking routine.

"Oh, they think we'll fancy the pants off 'em if they show off like that!" Susie Shawcross who lived across the road told her. Susie was fifteen and wore lisle stockings and red lipstick.

"Why would you want the pants off 'em, Susie? It's a bit rude, isn't it?" Meg asked innocently, but couldn't prevent a broad grin appearing on her face as she thought of Sid Brooks standing there in his underpants and his flat cap.

"Oh, I'll tell you when you're a bit older, Meg. You're a bit too young. Ask me again when you're fifteen like me." Susie grinned and carried on watching with her mates.

"Does it work? Do you fancy Sid Brooks then?" Meg called as she ran off.

"Well, that's for me to know and for you to find out, isn't it?"

Meg ran off thinking, *I'm not that bothered one way or the other.*

In August 1945, the whole world had been able to rejoice in the fact that the war had finally ended when Japan surrendered. Whilst food supplies were initially still limited, other wartime constraints could be forgotten. There was no longer the threat of air raids so gas masks could be consigned to the cupboard and the children were no longer required to carry them to school each day.

"Thank goodness we don't have to drag these to school now. All we ever did was hang them on our coat pegs," Meg said. She had had a grown-up one, but Patty's and Abigail's were Mickey Mouse masks. None of them could claim to have worn them in a time of necessity, but they had played their imaginative war games at Hillside Terrace, when they would struggle into the tight, uncomfortable contraptions that smelt of rubber and of disinfectant because Gran had wiped them out with Dettol from time to time as a precaution against the germs that might have accumulated.

"Gran, what have you done to these?" Meg asked, screwing up her nose as she attempted to force the mask over her head, "It smells like something the cat dragged in!" and Patty heaved a pretentious "Yuk!" as their grandmother stopped sweeping and glared at them.

"Don't you be so cheeky, you two. You won't catch any germs from them unhygienic things while I'm around. Mucky looking things they are. Now go outside and play in the garden, there's good girls and take our Abigail with you." And off they went, swinging the gas masks round and round in the fresh air so that the obnoxious smell would be blown away.

"I hope them Germans can smell these things," Patty said, giggling at the thought of the enemy soldiers screwing up their noses with one whiff of the pong emanating from her Mickey Mouse mask. She had no idea what a German soldier looked like, but she'd seen pictures of Adolf Hitler in the paper and if they all looked like him, well, she could do without them, thank you very much.

"It'd be enough to kill 'em off, I'm sure," returned Meg whilst the little Abigail just looked up at them uncomprehending. "Let's leave them out here for a while and lie on the grass."

Lying on their backs and looking up into the sky as the fluffy clouds sailed by, Meg pointed out a white rabbit with its ears pointing backwards floating above their heads.

"Where? Where?" Abi implored. She could never see what her big sisters could see, even though she tried hard to make cloud pictures for herself.

"Just there," Meg explained. "Can you see that patch of blue and then something that looks like a big lump of cotton wool?"

"Yes, I can," Abi squealed excitedly.

"Well, just past that there are two pointy things...the rabbit's ears and then its nose and its body...can you see it?"

"I can, I can!" Abi was beside herself. It was the first time she'd been able see what her sisters could see in the sky and she was over the moon. "I can play your big girl games now, can't I, Meg?"

she asked excitedly, "and not be left with Gran when you and Patty go to play near the allotments."

But Meg and Patty, on the other hand, had different ideas.

"She's too little," they often said, "and she spoils our games."

"No, I don't!"

"You do, Abi," Meg tried to sound sympathetic. "You can play with us when you're a bit bigger."

"Come on, love," Gran would say, "let's leave them two to play on their own. We'll go and make some currant buns, shall we? And you can scrape the bowl." Abigail was happy with that and she would stand on a chair near the table and wait patiently for the baking bowl lined with the creamy mixture just asking to be licked clean.

Children's post-war daring escapades brought excitement into their young lives, especially when the exploits were forbidden activities. Rebellion became attractive for two otherwise obedient girls. There was an air raid shelter at the bottom of Hillside Terrace next to the allotments. It had always been regarded as a no-go area. John had given strict instructions that it was out of bounds. The Hawthornes had certainly not been forced to shelter in there, even when they could hear the sirens blaring out in the distance, so it had always been an object of curiosity to the two older girls. It was becoming derelict and overgrown with weeds, but it was still recognisable as a brick building with an open doorway at each end and totally black inside. Scary rumours, the sources of nightmares, were rife amongst the village children who furtively reported that the bodies of missing persons were hidden inside the shelter; that German prisoners of war had been tied up and left to die in the depths of the blackness. Meg and Patty had stood rigid, hearts racing at the mere thought of it when some of the village children had related the compelling tales.

"Keep away from that shelter," Dad told them, "it's pitch black in there and filthy dirty and goodness knows what's been left inside. It must be a haven for rats and mice, I'll be bound, so don't go anywhere near it." And with that, the topic of the shelter was absolutely taboo in the Hawthorne house.

One day as she and Patty were walking home from doing an errand for their Gran, Meg told Jimmy Smith, a cheeky, arrogant lad from the class above her at school that he was too cocky for his own good, so he had thrown down the gauntlet. "Oh yeah!" he challenged. "At least I've been in the shelter AND by myself. I bet you daren't go anywhere near the spooky place, Meg 'awthorne!" He bragged to her about having ventured inside with a torch and had discovered that it was made up of several, dark, eerie compartments with wooden benches round the sides..."where the Germans 'ad bin tied to 'ooks in t'walls! I saw skelingtons too," he graphically told the two wide-eyed girls. "Go on, I dares yer fot go in, Meg 'awthorne! I dares yer!"

"I'll show you!" she retaliated, her Hawthorne determination shining forth. "Come on, Patty." She had grabbed hold of Patty's hand and dragged her to the entrance. Patty gripped Meg's hand tightly and fearfully looked up at her big sister who had stopped outside the black hole and who was biting her bottom lip more in dogged determination than fear. Looking back at the smirking Jimmy Smith, she took a deep breath and shouted at the top of her voice, *"NOW, PATTY! RUN! RUN FOR YOUR LIFE!"* They raced along the passageway at full speed. They ran straight through, seeing nothing but the light at the other end which was their escape and shrieking so loudly that they scared themselves half to death when the echoes of their screams bounced back at them. *Oh heck,* Meg thought as they stood breathless at the far end of the shelter, knowing they had recklessly responded to the dare even though the strict instructions to keep out of the old building were firmly embedded in their minds.

On the way home later, Meg threatened Patty. "If you dare to breathe a word in front of Dad about running through that shelter, I'll tell him about you reading under the bed clothes until midnight when you're supposed to be asleep. And you know what will happen then, Patty?"

"Oh heck, I won't tell, Meg, honest I won't," Patty promised. "Dad will take my books off me and I'll never survive. I promise, Meg—cross my heart and hope to die."

When the shelter was eventually demolished to make room for bigger allotments, there were deep sighs of relief from the anxious youngsters and yet they still harboured that apprehensive uncertainty about what might have been lurking in the darkness. "What if we'd seen a ghost?" Meg whispered to Patty as they passed to ruins of the old shelter on their way home from school. They both shivered and the Hawthorne girls quickly forgot the terrors they had imagined when rows of cabbages and cauliflowers and wigwams of runner bean canes replaced the austerity of the cold, brick wartime eyesore.

"Will they put the railings back round the park now that the war is over?" Meg asked John one day whilst they were on one of their Sunday afternoon walks. The cast iron railings had disappeared early in 1940 and they were supposed to have been melted down to make Sherman tanks.

"I don't know, love," John replied truthfully. "Rumour had it that some people had to hand over their aluminium pans to make more aircraft, but nobody knew of anyone who had donated their kitchen utensils at any time during the war. It's one of those situations where it's unlikely that we'll ever know. Funny things happen in times of war and that's a fact," he said with conviction, knowing full well that half a story would not satisfy the inquisitive Meg. "I do know that they took down all the road signs in Bolton in case any German pilots had to bail out of their planes and parachute down into Bolton. They wouldn't have been able to find us in Belford, would they?" He winked at Meg. "They wouldn't know which way to go!" He made light of it, but the fact of the matter was, the signs had actually been removed to that end.

"I'll ask our history teacher...about the railings and things, I mean," Meg said, quite undeterred by John's vague answer. "She might know, because she seems to know everything about wars. She told us about Napoleon and how he became too ambitious in trying to fight the Russians. His soldiers didn't have enough food to keep them strong enough to fight in terrible weather conditions. Did you know that, Dad?"

"I did, love. I read about it in a book I borrowed from the library. I wish I'd gone to Great Moor Grammar like you. You are learning loads more than I ever did at your age. My mam and dad couldn't pay for me to go to grammar school and there was no scholarship exam when I was eleven."

Patty had been listening to the discussion. "How could they make tanks out of railings?" she asked naively. "And anyway, how will they be able to put the railings back if they've been made into tanks?" The world was a very complicated place, but she skipped off ahead of the others, considering her skipping rope much more important than stupid, old railings and tanks.

Once the war was over, everything had been rationed for a while, even clothes. Every household had a sewing machine and every girl tediously and very often unwillingly, learned to sew. The Hawthorne girls were no exception. They had a treadle sewing machine, a Singer which they considered was a step above the hand-operated ones. Painstakingly, Nellie had put Meg through her paces in learning how to co-ordinate hands, eyes and feet so they were able to control the machine and make it do what she wanted it to do. At times, the brain didn't tell the hands to set the wheel turning first before the feet felt the treadle moving in unison. The feet always wanted to push down on the treadle first, with disastrous results. The wheel would go backwards, the needle would get stuck in the fabric with the thread all knotted up in the spool under the plate that covered the shuttle as it moved back and forth with tremendous speed once the technique had been mastered. On numerous occasions, she had flounced off in frustration declaring, "This flippin' machine has a mind of its own! I'm not doing anymore, Gran."

"Don't be stupid, Meg." Nellie told her. "You'll thank me for this later when your wardrobe's full of nice frocks. You mark my words, young lady, you'll never regret learning to sew."

Meg reluctantly stuck at it and eventually became a competent seamstress. Nellie had collected scraps of material on which the girls, in turn, were able to practise sewing in straight lines. Once that was mastered, she could move on to greater things. At first Meg made a nightdress, a straight up and down garment gathered into a yoke and then she progressed to using paper patterns to cut out and make summer dresses for herself and her sisters. She learned how to make pleats and adapt patterns to make each dress different from the previous one. Patty and Abigail always had matching knickers, too and these were often displayed with pride when they did handstands against the wall in the school playground. Eventually, all the Hawthorne girls were able to add to their wardrobe frequently by making dresses that were fashionable and attractive from fabric that could be bought quite cheaply on the market. They eventually became very grateful for their grandmother's perseverance in making them master the temperamental treadle of that flippin' sewing machine.

By the end of 1945, the Hawthorne family had settled into their own peacetime routine. Meg was a grown up fourteen years old.

The days when she had misguidedly felt the urgent need to establish her independence had passed by. *I understand now that my silly, childish show of defiance was really unnecessary.* She sat pensively during the half-hour bus ride home from school and smiled to herself as the Mooney Street sign loomed in front of her, ugly and clearly wantonly vandalised. She wondered if she were becoming a snob, but shook her dark head, still smiling at the memory of her flirtation with the Mooney Street culture...

~ * ~

...Meg had always remembered the day when her dad had brought Abigail home. *I had waited ages to see the baby and when the tiny bundle arrived, I really wasn't disappointed. Abi was beautiful, still is. I genuinely wanted to look after my baby sister, but I needed Mam to show me how. Deep, deep down inside, I felt trapped and thought I'd been put in a position from which there was no escape. I couldn't please everybody all the time and sometimes my efforts to do that really got me down. I had to be the big sister; the shining example, when I knew I couldn't always be the perfect person Dad expected me to be. I always worked hard at school, because I liked my lessons, not because Dad constantly drummed into me that to get on in life, I had to prove my worth.*

She recalled vividly all the occasions when she had tried to make a stand.

"Why?" she frequently asked when she resented his instructions.

"Because I said so," her dad replied, "and don't be so impudent, Meg. It doesn't become you."

Dad always had a way of making me feel guilty just with a withering look and I always felt like I was shrinking into my shell. My head was full of thoughts of rebelling against what I thought was an impossible situation.

I loved my teacher, Miss Rothwell, and imagined what it would be like to have her for my mother. She blushed at the memory. *Miss Rothwell had a gentle manner about her that coaxed us all to do our best at all times and I liked that. I thought she was beautiful and clever and perfect. I even dreamed up stories of Dad and Miss Rothwell getting married and living happily ever after as a family with a mother and a father like in a normal family.* She smiled again at the thought. *I realise now that we have a wonderful family, and now I'm older, I don't think Dad will ever marry again. He loved our mam too much,* she mused, *but I was so disappointed after parents' evenings when nothing ever came of their meetings.*

Whilst she enjoyed her lessons and did her work well, Meg often looked in awe at the children from Mooney Street and listened to their exciting tales. They were rough and ready youngsters with a hardness about them that made them admirably daring in Meg's eyes. She longed to join in their dangerous games. They played out at night after dark; they fearlessly walked past the haunted house on Harper Street. They knocked on doors and ran away. Yet for Meg, her obligatory duties at home made it extremely difficult for her to cut loose and feel the freedom that these courageous characters from Mooney Street were at liberty to do without fear of punishment. She thoughtlessly abandoned her usual friends in order to taste the thrill of the carefree and careless life of the Mooney Street mob.

"I don't want you mixing with that lot from Mooney Street," her father told her when she arrived home late from school one Wednesday afternoon. "Where did you go after school yesterday? Your gran said you didn't get home until quarter to five."

"I was only dawdling, Dad." She didn't enlighten him further, but Bob Holden at work had told John he had seen Meg the day before at the corner of Mooney Street, talking to a girl... "with 'oles in 'er elbers and wearin' Wellingtons wit' tops turned down.

Yer should o' seen 'er, John. T'wellies 'ad rubbed rings round 'er legs, she were that dirty!"

"You must keep away from there, Meggy."

"Why?" Meg asked, her eyes wide with indignation. John was taken aback.

"Because I said so," her father replied, irritated that she had dared to question his wisdom.

"They're okay, Dad, the kids from round there. They play brilliant games and Annie Seddon said I can play with them any time."

John looked straight at Meg and saw that spark of resentment in her eyes. "See here, young lady. I never thought I'd have to speak to you like this, but I'll tell you once more and then that's an end to it. You do *not* play with those children from Mooney Street."

Meg said nothing. She belligerently snatched up her school bag and went to her room to do her homework. She sat there for a long time brooding. *After all the help I've given them with the little ones, you'd think Dad would allow me to play out with my friends.*

The following week, Annie Seddon challenged Meg to defy her dad and sneak out after dark. Meg thought about it deeply. "I'll try," she agreed, knowing full well that she would have to choose the night Dad went to his Union meeting and she would be able to hoodwink her gran into allowing her to go the corner shop for some sweets.

On Thursday evening, as John got ready to go out, Meg sat quietly reading her *Sunny Stories* magazine, but keeping a weather eye on her father's movements. She was ready to carry out her master plan as soon as he was round the corner at the bottom of the Terrace.

"Right, I'm off, Nellie," he said, "I'll be back by nine. Meg, you be a good girl for your Gran. Patty, up to bed as soon as I go out. Abi should sleep until morning, Nellie."

"John, just go. You tell me the same things every time you go out. Don't worry. We'll be okay. Have a good meeting." Nellie Walmsley smiled to herself as he left the house. *He's done well over the past couple of years since Mary went, but he does tend to fuss.*

"Gran?" Meg seized the opportunity. "can I nip to the corner shop for a penny chew?" Then she remembered—"Please?"

"It's dark outside."

Gran always states the obvious, she thought, irritated that time was being wasted. "It's only at the end of the Terrace, I won't be two ticks," she said, almost pleading. *She's taking too long. Hurry up, Gran, for goodness sake. Annie Seddon said they would go without me if I wasn't there for quarter to seven.* "Please," she begged again, "I'm ten now, nearly eleven and I've got to learn to go out in the dark ready for when I'm at the big school and it will be dark when I'm coming home from Bolton."

"Go on then, yer little madam," her gran declared. "You'll get me in trouble if yer dad finds out! Have yer got yer sweet coupon?"

"Mrs Abbott lets me have a ha'penny chew 'cos they don't take a full coupon," Meg convinced her gran as she grabbed her coat from the hook behind the door and called out, "See you in a tick!"

Now whether it was by good fortune, or sheer bad luck, Meg couldn't decide, but Nellie, sitting by the kitchen fire, closed her eyes almost as soon as Meg shut the door. The soothing warmth from the grate had made her very sleepy and she nodded off within seconds. The house was quiet, Nellie was tired and so she slept.

Once out of the house, Meg ran like the wind to the corner of Mooney Street. They'd gone! She stopped in her tracks, utterly disappointed that she had missed her opportunity to prove herself with the Mooney Street gang. Suddenly, someone grabbed her from behind and she let out a scream, scared that the bogeyman had got her. "Scaredy cat, scaredy cat!" sang Annie Seddon, "Shurrup, or yer'll waken t'dead! Where've yer bin? Yer late."

Meg grinned. "My gran was a bit slow letting me out, but I'm here now. What're we doin'?" she asked with eager anticipation.

She listened in mute admiration as Annie told her that they would go down Belford Road to the big houses. "They have bells on their doors, so we can ring and then 'ide behind the bushes in the garden and watch when they answer the door. Yer should see their faces when there's nobody there!"

They ran all the way down Belford Road and, breathing heavily in the cold night air, their breath steamed out of their mouths like smoke floating up into the sky from factory chimneys. They selected their prey...a big Victorian house with a thick carved oak door. Creeping stealthily up the garden path trying not to make too much noise as their feet crunched on the gravel, Annie pushed Meg forward and she quaked with a mixture of fear and excitement. She turned and looked at Annie, who was near the bushes, ready to dodge behind them as soon as Meg touched the bell.

"Go on!" Annie urged in a loud theatrical whisper. Meg took a deep breath and reached up towards the little light with an ornate label that said '*Ring me.*' Her hand trembled as she stuck out a determined finger and poised, ready to make the final thrust before she turned to run and join Annie in the bushes.

Inside the house, the Union meeting had been called off. "If we haven't got a quorum, it's no use us starting the meeting," the shop steward said, so the members prepared to leave. John Hawthorne opened the door just as Meg's outstretched finger was ready to press. She froze on the spot and stared in horror at her father's face. She couldn't read his expression. It wasn't surprise, not even shock, more mystified bewilderment. Meg turned to look for Annie, but she had gone. She turned back to see her father's realisation that his eldest daughter was out after dark and could have no valid excuse for being at this house at this time of night. She swallowed hard, unable to utter a single word in her own defence, knowing full well she had disobeyed her father who was roughly taking hold of her arm and marching her down the drive without saying a word. The tight grip on her arm and the military manner of her father spoke volumes to Meg and she acknowledged the silence with mute respect.

It seemed to take ages to walk back to Hillside Terrace, Meg's little legs hardly touching the ground as her angry father strode purposefully towards home territory. When the door flew open, Nellie woke with a start. John chose his words deliberately and with great care. To lose control would be fatal. To swear in front of his child and his mother-in-law would be despicable, but God knew that he had the ammunition to blast all the bloody hells from here to eternity. "I am not best pleased," he said with remarkable reserve, "In fact, I am angrier than I have ever been in my life." His eyes burned with the fury that raged inside him.

Nellie, who was totally confused having just wakened up, looked first at John and then at Meg who was silently sobbing and finding it difficult to look either of the two adults in the eye. "Oh, I see! You caught 'er at the corner shop," Nellie said, half smiling that the pair of them had been caught out.

"Corner shop? Corner shop?" John raged. "No I did not! I caught her at the bottom of Belford Road just about to ring on a doorbell and then run away, I presume." Those very words brought his almost violent ranting under control. He thought how mischievous it was and was almost tempted to laugh, but he could not be seen to be amused. After all, Meg had disobeyed him and Nellie had let him down.

Nellie caught the hint of a gleam in his eye and relaxed a little. "It's my fault," she admitted, "Don't blame our Meg. I said she could go to the shop. I thought she was old enough to do that without getting into bother."

"The shop doesn't come into it, Nellie. I trusted you to look after my child and you let her slip out and get into mischief."

Nellie looked embarrassed. "Aye, I did and I'm sorry. It won't happen again."

"And you, young lady, defied me. I saw that Annie Seddon run out of the bushes up to no good as usual. I told you I didn't like you playing with the lasses from Mooney Street and you did it anyway. What sort of a friend would leave you to carry the can when you were both in it together?"

Meg dared to lift her tear-stained face towards her dad when she heard the softer tone. "I'm so-or-orry," she sobbed, "I wanted a bit of fun," but her reasoning sounded weak and very selfish. John scrutinised her through squinting eyes. He realised at that moment that she had had to grow up too fast and had been given too much responsibility too soon. It was a hard lesson to learn, but one which Meg would never forget. When she had served her sentence—no pocket money for four weeks—she resolved that perhaps her dad had been right all along and realised that the kids from Mooney Street really did have nothing going for them.

Meanwhile, Patty and Abigail remained asleep, blissfully unaware of their older sister's exploits and as far as Meg was concerned, that's how it would stay. She determined that what they didn't know wouldn't hurt them and her big sister reputation would remain intact.

~ * ~

As the old bus climbed up the hill into the village, the straining chug, chug of the engine broke into her thoughts and the teenage Meg was still smiling at the thought of that doorbell. Growing up in Hillside Terrace had, for the most part, been a joy to them all. The childish arguments and sulks never lasted long and they eventually accepted their lot as independent individuals, all different, but in many ways the same. Meg got off the bus and wandered pensively to Hillside Terrace with a very contented smile on her face.

Six

Abigail growing up

The primary school in Belford was an old Victorian building situated halfway between Hillside Terrace and the Bleach Works. Built of grey stone from the local quarry, it stood tall and erect, a monument to that wonderful age when technology found its place in the lives of mankind. It was the epicentre of life for the village children, a place where they experienced stability during the war years, an extension of home, a place where they could feel safe amongst friends. The noble edifice provided the solid foundations upon which futures were built.

Abigail's first term in school went by very quickly. She soon adapted to the daily routine and her days were so full of everything that even her excitement didn't keep her awake at night and there were never any tears when John left her at the school gates each morning. Some of the children clung to their mothers' skirts when the bell rang. It was not unknown for a few of those mothers to walk away from the school with tears running down their own faces. The children were so small and the world so big. How difficult it was to turn a child out into the unknown!

Mornings were always spent on the three Rs and with a class of forty-two, Mrs Harrison organised her time so that each child received attention as required. The room was large with a high ceiling and long, high windows all along the wall opposite the door. Those who sat by the windows were able to see out into the playground and it was tempting to watch a game of football, or rounders when the junior classes were having their PT lessons. Mrs Harrison soon recognised the shirkers and moved them to desks where such distractions would not be a problem.

There were five rows of eight desks which stood on terracing and the desks at the back were reached by climbing up the eight steps between each row. The teacher's desk was near the window at the far side of the room, opposite the door and she had to step inside it to sit down. *Teachers must be very strong to be able to stand all day without getting tired.* Abigail was very impressed with her teacher and thought, *I might be a teacher too one day.*

Abi made friends very quickly and she was never short of playmates to play tag and skipping ropes and chasing, although she didn't like chasing much since it was usually the boys who instigated it and they tended to be rough and too boisterous. On top of all that, they called it 'kiss catch,' expecting to kiss the girls when they were caught and she had to outrun Billy Dawson so he wouldn't want to kiss her. *Boys are so horrible!* She preferred to be with Jean and Lillian and they just played together without hassle from the boys.

"Children's pleasures are so simple and uncomplicated, aren't they?" John commented to Nellie one Saturday morning over a cup of tea. "When I was taking Abi to school yesterday, I could hear their excitement a couple of hundred yards away. Just listen to our three now." He paused to listen as his children ran around the garden shrieking and laughing, not a care in the world. "They're never short of games to play, are they? I love listening to them, especially when they make up games for themselves."

"Let's play hopscotch," one would say.

"No, leap frog," another would argue and then to settle the argument they'd play something different like *one-two-three-a-lara*, or *piggy-in-the-middle* and the ever faithful *hide and seek* often came to the rescue when agreements were proving elusive.

In class they worked quietly, because Mrs Harrison didn't like them talking and she had a very loud voice when she told people off, especially when the boys misbehaved. Even in the reception class, pupils were meant to get on with their work and some of them found it really difficult to sit still even for five minutes. Every day after lunch, they would have to rest their heads on folded arms and sleep. Most of the children found this problematic, because they had long grown out of the habit of having an afternoon nap.

"Dad," Abi said pointedly at teatime one day after school, "I can't go to sleep at school, because it hurts my arms when I have to put my head down for all that time. Shall I tell the teacher?"

"I don't think you'd better do that," John told her, "Rules are rules and if the teacher says that's what you do, that's what you do."

"But what if I can't keep my eyes closed? She'll shout at me, but it's hard, Dad and I don't want to get in trouble."

"Just do as you're told, Abi and you'll not come to any harm. You'll just have to learn to be quiet and patient," John explained to the confused little girl.

"What's patient, Dad? How can I be it? I don't know what it means."

"It means waiting quietly without complaining."

"What's complaining...?"

"Oh Abi," John sighed, realising he was in great danger of becoming impatient himself. "Sometimes we have to do things we don't like, but usually it's for the best, so we just get on with it. I think you should be able to rest your head on your arms for half an hour when Mrs Harrison tells you to. It won't be long before you're in the next class and then afternoon naps won't be a problem."

"Why won't it be a problem?" Abi asked, still uncertain of the merits of keeping your head down for what seemed like hours to her.

"Because you won't have to do it when you're a bit older and in the next class."

"Okay then, if you're sure," she conceded. "I'll try my hardest, Dad, honest I will," but she wasn't sure about it at all and sighed deeply, grimacing at the thought of having to struggle through seemingly unnecessary, endless nap times until she turned six.

It was during the reading lesson one day that Abi was asked to read to the class. She stood proudly in her place and read out clearly from her *Janet and John* book. Her confident and eloquent style impressed Mrs Harrison, who soon recognised the potential in the child. "She's a pretty little thing with a sharpness about her that makes her stand out in the crowd," she informed her colleagues, "but that's not what makes her different. It's her vibrancy, her eagerness to learn, her strong will to succeed which is incredible for such a little girl."

The teacher smiled as Abi purposefully took a deep breath and began, "Here is Janet. Here is John. See Janet. See John..."

Pride goes before a fall they say and it seemed that others in the class weren't particularly impressed that Abigail Hawthorne could read well. As she sat in her place again, a missile flew from the back of the room and hit Abi on the shoulder. Innocently, she picked up the paper ball and turned to see which person was trying to attract her attention. She was only able to see a big girl at the back scowling and gesticulating wildly. Being careful not to let the teacher hear her, the big girl spat out words of jealousy and hate. "Big 'ead! Show off! Teacher's pet! Think you're good, don't yer?" she said and with that Abigail was ominously introduced to Betty West. In her naïveté, Abigail was uncomprehending of the malicious tone that emanated from the hissing and snarling of her classmate. She looked at the other children around her and every one of them was seemingly unaware that a minor confrontation was taking place. Their heads were down and they were all seriously concentrating on the open books on their desks without a single glance in her direction.

Betty West was a child who craved attention. She was tall and of large frame, had the loudest and harshest of voices and an evil, menacing grin. In short, she was the proverbial child from hell, but not unintelligent. Her fierce sense of competition was meted out with vindictiveness rather than a healthy display of rivalry. Her parents had instilled in her from a very early age that she should let no one stand in her way when achieving her goal. In primary school, her arrogance was already in place and by the time she reached her final year at the age of eleven, she had managed to accumulate a few lackeys who adhered to her every whim. The missile incident in the reception class was the first manifestation of Betty West's malice. She made it her business to keep a close watch on Miss Abigail Hawthorne and that did not bode well for Abi's life in school.

As Betty continually bombarded her with insults and ridicule, Abigail soldiered on, determined not to allow her antagonist to hinder her own progress. Every day brought a new challenge as far as Betty was concerned. She was a real pain in the neck, as Abi's gran would have put it and Abigail's reluctance to fight back was fuel to Betty's fire. There was something inside that was telling her to ignore the frequent tirades and Abi had lost count of the times she had had to close her ears to pointless insults. "Hey, 'awthorne! Who made your stupid frock? Looks like it came off the rag man. I'll get you after school, 'awthorne," and it was always completely uncalled for. Betty, ever cunning and furtively devious, was obviously not seeing the same person as everybody else when she viciously bombarded Abi with "Ugly mug! Pig face! Toad features!" It did, however, infuriate Betty when her words fell on deaf ears. "Cat got yer tongue 'as it? Can't stick up for yerself. Scared of getting in trouble, you softie baby."

Abigail fearlessly ignored her, even though at times she was crying inside. Often, in the early days, she had hidden herself away in the toilet cubicle as she fought back the tears and it was during those times that she determined to laugh in the face of adversity. At playtime, Betty and her cronies would stand a short distance away from where Abi was playing and frequently snigger and point in her direction. When the bell went at the end of the break, Betty's gang would run en masse and deliberately bump into Abi in turn, almost as if they had choreographed the moves to prevent Abi from getting out of the way. "Ooops! Not enough room for you and me," Betty told her pointedly as she shoulder-charged her resolute classmate. Abi stood her ground as Betty turned and barked at her like a yapping terrier. "Grrr," she growled, "Get out of my way!" and then, "Cowardy, cowardy custard; yer face'll turn to mustard."

For obvious reasons, Abi's friends, Lillian and Jean, were afraid of Betty turning her wrath onto them and Abigail very soon realised it was clearly something she was going to have to deal with all by herself. Over the next few years, she endured the regular onslaughts with the Hawthorne inner strength fortifying her resolve. In her childish wisdom, she decided it was one of those occasions where she had to get on with it on her own. She hadn't told her dad, nor her sisters about Betty West, because she wanted to deal with the situation by herself. She realised too that she shouldn't expect her friends to get involved with her problems, but for her own satisfaction, when they were in their last year at primary school, she decided to tackle her friends. "Why do you two always run away when Betty West appears?" she asked them one playtime. "You could at least stay with me when she starts her name-calling."

Lillian looked embarrassed, but Jean found the courage to speak up. "We're scared of her, Abi. We don't know how you can face up to her like you do and we think you're really brave, but we don't want her to start on us."

"Yes I know, but I wish you'd just stay with me. I can stand up for myself, you know," Abi told them. She didn't want to lose the good times she had with her friends either if she burdened them too much with the wicked witch of the West, so she accepted their stance. This was one battle she would fight alone and she was determined to win.

On numerous occasions, Betty West cornered her in the cloakroom and held on to the coat pegs at either side of Abi so she was trapped like an animal in a cage. She could feel Betty's hot breath on her face as she snarled threateningly, "Watch your back, Goody-Goody Hawthorne, or else!" and then she would take Abi's coat off the peg and spitefully throw it on the floor before walking away with her arrogant nose up in the air, followed by her sniggering hangers-on. Abi's initial fears were eventually replaced by frustrated efforts to placate her enemies with friendly gestures, but even offering them sweets at playtime was misinterpreted and inevitably seemed to make matters worse.

"Don't think you can be my friend for a measly pear drop, Hawthorne. I can have as many toffees as I like when I like, so clear off."

Out of the blue one day, Betty West asked Abi to help her clear up some black ink she had spilled in the cloakroom. Abi typically obliged, only to find that Betty disappeared as soon as she knelt down to mop up the offending ink with a paper towel. It was a very messy job and Abi struggled afterwards to wash the ink off her hands. It stained her fingers and was down the side of her fingernails. It would take several washes before her hands would be clean again.

A tearful Betty West walked into the classroom after playtime. She was carrying a bright pink coat folded over her arm. It was perhaps unfortunate for Abigail that the new teacher, Miss Robinson, on her first day in the school, was alerted to the tears of a seemingly distressed Betty.

"Whatever is the matter?" the teacher asked, concerned that the child would disturb the other children with such heart-rending sobs. The gullible Miss Robinson was completely taken in.

Betty continued to howl and held up the coat for all to see. The back of the garment was splattered copiously with black ink. "Somebody has thrown ink on my best coat," she bawled. "It was hanging on my peg in the cloakroom and I saw Abi Hawthorne cleaning ink up off the floor. Look at 'er 'ands, Miss. She's ruined my coat and my mam will clout me and it's all 'er fault."

"Abigail Hawthorne?" Miss Robinson looked around to make sure she was speaking to the right girl. "What have you got to say for yourself? Let me see your hands," the teacher demanded angrily.

There was no escape. "Please, Miss, I didn't do it," Abi implored, tears welling up in shocked eyes as she held out her hands that apparently confirmed her guilt.

"Yes you did," Betty goaded, her own tears suddenly dried. Miss Robinson glared.

"Enough of that," the teacher continued, but she swiftly convicted Abi without trial. "Go and stand in the corner until you have learned to be contrite. I'll have to write to your parents, Abigail. I think the least you can do is pay for the dry cleaning of the coat."

Abigail dejectedly looked down at her hands. She didn't know what contrite meant, but she knew that she was the innocent victim. She blinked vigorously to stop the tears from flowing. How could she convince the new Miss Robinson that she had only cleared up Betty's mess? Betty West had won this time and it was written all over her smug face. Miss Robinson had taken her side and Abigail couldn't argue with the evidence, especially with a teacher. When she was given the note to take home, she kept it hidden in her pocket. *I have enough money in my piggy bank to pay the bill for the dry cleaning,* she thought. *I can deal with Betty West myself.*

Abigail was always grateful that she had two older sisters with whom she could talk over anything that bothered her and she eventually told Patty about Betty West. She hadn't planned to say anything, but it just seemed to come out when Patty unexpectedly asked if she were all right. She hadn't wanted to worry Meg. Meg was at teacher training college in Liverpool and in Abi's view, she didn't need letters from a little sister whinging about a girl at school who was less than sociable. Meg was Abigail's role model in life. She had taught her everything possible and had passed on their father's advice that to get anywhere in this life, you have to work for it.

"Remember, love," Meg told her, "the world does not owe you a living. You reap what you sow and if you work hard, you'll get there in the end. After all, you weren't born on a Saturday for nothing!" and she smiled at the memory of Mary, her mother, planning her children's futures from the days on which they had been born.

Patty was the quiet one. Her name, Patience Christine, was perfect for her and most times, she was tolerance personified. She had followed Meg to Great Moor Grammar School and simply adored it. She generally got on with her life without troubling anyone and when Abigail eventually drew her attention to Betty

West, she listened, dismayed that Abi had not said anything sooner. "Why didn't you tell Mrs Tattersall? Or Dad? They could have done something to stop it," she said earnestly, trying to find a solution to her sister's problem.

Abigail, eleven then, looked at her sister with great awareness. "Because that would be playing right into Betty West's hands," she explained, "I'd worked that out ages ago. She's as wily as a fox. She'd use the fact that I'd squealed on her to her own advantage. Those friends of hers think the sun shines out of her backside…"

"Oooooh, Abigail Hawthorne! Wash your mouth out with carbolic soap!" Patty shrieked and they both dissolved into peals of laughter.

"Well, they do," Abi continued, undeterred by Patty's interruption. "Sometimes I can't even go to the toilet without one or other of them appearing to keep an eye on me. I mean, what do they think I'm going to do? Get an extra mark for washing my hands? Betty flippin' West is paranoid about our grades. She hates it if I get half a mark more than she does. I wouldn't mind, but she's really quite clever. She just hankers after compliments all the time, especially from Mrs Tattersall."

"And does she get them…the compliments, I mean?"

"Not often. I think Mrs Tattersall is irritated by her. She says, 'Sit down, Betty, and get on with your work. I'll check it with all the rest later'. I just keep my head down and try not to let her see I know what her game is. She only takes her work to the teacher so she can say she finished before me. She always smirks when she passes my desk."

Patty smiled. "I think you have already handled Betty West in the right way, Abs. Ignoring bullies like her is the most effective way of dealing with them. And she *is* a bully even if she isn't violent." Patty paled at the thought. "She isn't, is she? You haven't not told me anything?"

"No, I'll give her that. She may be aggressive and she's done some pretty nasty things, but she has never hit me. Do you think I should just carry on doing the same thing then?" She had become hardened to the regular onslaught and did everything she could to avoid confrontation with the class tyrant.

Patty felt her eyes burning with tears. "Don't cry, Patty," Abigail said gently, "I'm not made of paper and every time Betty West growls at me, I'll just think of the sun shining out of her..."

Patty giggled, her tears subsiding. "Oh, Abs, you'll get there. I know you will and next year you'll be at Great Moor Grammar with me. Now won't that be brill?"

Abigail grinned. "Can't wait, but I'm sure Betty West will go as well. Now that *is* a lovely thought."

In February 1952, King George VI died. Mr Armsley, the headmaster, called the whole school into a special assembly and gave the sad announcement. Some of the teachers were crying and the children sensed the seriousness of the occasion, even though living in the north of the country, they didn't feel the distress as it was felt in the capital. Very few of the children, if any, had ever been to London and as far as they were concerned, it could have been a million miles away. They had heard about the big Festival of Britain the year before, but no one from the village could afford to go all that way to London. They saved all year in the diddl'em clubs at work so that they could have a week in Blackpool at Bolton Wakes, but London? That was way out of their league.

Come 1953, the whole country was looking forward to the coronation of Queen Elizabeth II. In February of that year, Abigail and her classmates took their Eleven Plus exam and went to the church hall armed with a drink and chocolate much in the same way as Meg and Patty had done a few years earlier. Somehow, the significance of the examination had shifted and all the candidates seemed to take it more in their stride than had Meg and her school friends. The 1944 Education Act had paved the way to provide post-war children with an education to suit their needs. All children appeared happy to take the examination and many primary schools gained the paradoxical label of being 'Eleven Plus factories,' such was the drive and fierce competition in local schools.

When the results came, everyone in Class Six turned up early for school. Remarkably, twenty-five of them had been offered places at a grammar school, most at Great Moor Grammar, but one, or two were going to travel to Farnworth Grammar, which had been their first choice. The ones who hadn't been offered places were not in any way upset with their results. The war had bred children who accepted their fate with good grace. The secondary modern schools catered to the needs of their pupils and there were jobs for everyone when the time came for them to leave school at fifteen. Jean and Lillian were going there, so Abigail and her friends prepared themselves for going their separate ways. "We can still be friends though, can't we?" they all agreed, even though their lives were destined to take very different paths.

On a more enjoyable note, Abi, Lillian and Jean were chosen to be members of the school choir and thankfully, the tone-deaf Betty was excluded from the musical activities. As a special celebration for the forthcoming coronation, all the choirs in the area were going to give a performance in Queens Park. They spent weeks learning a specially written song called "Elizabeth of England" and a hymn called "Jerusalem," which was a bit of a mystery to them all, but it was a wonderful song about the Holy Lamb of God walking in England's green and pleasant land and among the dark satanic mills of Lancashire. The children were ready to give a rousing performance and the highlight of the rehearsals was a final practice in Great Moor Grammar. Abi was beside herself. She stood in the big assembly hall with the choirs from other schools and looked up at the balcony along three sides of the seemingly enormous room, feeling very small. Adrenalin pumped in her veins and she got so carried away that she sang too loudly, oblivious in the heat of the moment that she was causing a stir.

The children from another school who were lined up in front of her were turning round to see where the big voice was coming from. She blushed profusely as they stared at her, wide-eyed and open mouthed and one rough looking boy whispered loudly, "Who d'yer think you are? Vera Lynn? What a show off!" Abi was mortified. Lillian nudged her from the right and Jean nudged her from the left, both grinning at their errant friend.

Oh flippin' 'eck, she thought, and she stopped singing abruptly, looking down at her shoes to hide her embarrassment. She had unwittingly drawn attention to herself in her over-enthusiastic rendering of the songs so she resumed her singing quietly and as inconspicuously as possible, but she couldn't resist laughing at herself for her impetuous performance. Soon she would be a pupil at Great Moor Grammar in her own right and that made her thrill at the mere thought of it. Secretly, she hoped the boy in front wouldn't be there when she started in September.

June 2nd was Coronation Day and Belford joined in the party spirit with the rest of the country. The whole village was decorated with bunting and Union Jacks flew from every window and every flagpole just as they had in 1945. Some people had bought television sets especially for the occasion so that they could watch the spectacular event on a screen inside their own homes. There were street parties with tables set up outside and music blared forth. Everyone was dancing and singing and eating and drinking. The news of the conquest of Everest reached every part of Britain and made for an even greater celebration of the glorious day. Edmund Hillary and Sherpa Tenzing were the close friends of everybody in Britain for just one day. There was a display of public pageantry never known to the British people and it nurtured a wonderful feeling of well-being throughout the land.

The Hawthorne family was invited to watch television at the Wilkinsons' house. Meg had been courting Philip Wilkinson since she was in sixth form. Now that she had taken up her teaching post in neighbouring Astley Bridge and Philip was working as an engineering consultant in Blackburn, they were saving up to get married. Mr and Mrs Wilkinson were amongst the people who had bought their television set especially for the coronation and Abigail was really impressed. "It's like being at the pictures in your own home," she enthused and looked wistfully at her Dad, who merely shrugged.

During the following few days, the subject of televisions and their benefits had been raised at Hillside Terrace and discussions had always ended in disappointment for the girls. John told them he couldn't see the need of a television in their house when there were other more interesting social activities available to them. On Saturday morning they were sitting round the table at breakfast. The atmosphere was icy. Meg was glaring at the teenaged Patty because she had tried on her new blouse and left it on the floor. "You should have asked me before you touched it," Meg told her as she ran down the stairs and into the kitchen.

"Touched what?" Patty asked feigning innocence.

"You know very well what... my new blouse. I'm fed up with you, Patience Hawthorne. Every time I get something new, you have to try it on. My clothes are too big for you anyway, so keep your prying hands off in future."

"Ooooo! Who's rattled your cage this morning?" Patty was determined not to be browbeaten by her older sister. She always seemed to be piggy in the middle. She had decided ages ago that because she was the middle child, she had to learn to stand her ground, even if she were defending a hopeless case like she was then. She was guilty, but it wasn't a heinous crime, just a blouse on the floor. "Just because you're a teacher, it doesn't give you the right to boss me around, Meg. I'm not one of your pupils."

Meg was incensed. "I'll really smack you one in a minute, Patty..."

"Stop it!" Abi joined in. "I'm fed up with you two arguing all the time." It was a bit of an exaggeration. "You always start when we're eating, or when I'm trying to get to sleep at night. For goodness sake, grow up, the pair of you."

"That's rich coming from you, Abi. You're only eleven and I love you dearly, but your opinion doesn't count in this case." Her little sister had no right to pass judgment on her. She needed a bit of experience before she might do that. "You and our Meg always side together against me. I'm always left to fight my battles on my own and it's not fair." Her self-pity was showing and for once she didn't care. The usual tolerance at that moment simply wasn't on her agenda.

"Hey, hey, hey, stop it, the lot of you," John intervened. "Meg, don't ever let me hear you talking like that again. I won't have you using your fists to settle a dispute. Now get on with your breakfast. And Patty, go and pick up the blouse and put it back where you found it."

"Too late, I've done it," Meg put in belligerently, "But I'm telling you, Dad, I object to her rifling through my things."

"Enough," said John, 'I don't want to hear any more about it." He didn't think he'd ever master how to deal with girls affected at regular intervals by raging hormones, but in the meantime, he intended to stop the present fracas so they might have their breakfast in peace.

When the delivery van rolled up at the front of the house, curious eyes were drawn to the window and Meg said ironically, "That's Mrs Dawson getting something new again," and silently, moodily, the three girls went back to their tea and toast.

John had deliberated for days and eventually concluded that the new item of home entertainment would soon become an integral part of the modern home. With an eye on the future, he decided they shouldn't be left behind and his girls would love it. He kept his surprise until Saturday morning when he knew that they would all be at home.

When the doorbell rang, John made a point of saying, "I'll get it," and deliberately walked slowly in order to hide his excitement. "Come in, come in," the girls heard him say and then there were screams and shrieks of delight, their argument forgotten as the delivery man appeared at the door carrying a brand new television set with a fourteen inch screen and in a light oak cabinet which was going to look so luxurious standing in the corner of the front room. John grinned at them, a twinkle in his eye.

"But it won't go on until you've finished your homework."

When school resumed after the coronation, nothing had changed. The only consolation was that the end of term loomed and then there'd be five weeks of bliss before Abigail started at Great Moor Grammar. As for Abigail herself, she clung to the divine hope that Betty West would indeed go west so that she might settle into her new school quickly and without complication.

Seven

Great Moor Grammar School was everything Abigail had hoped. First year pupils were placed in forms according to alphabetical order of surnames, so she was free of Betty West during lesson time at least. The time flew by and there were so many new subjects on the timetable. The greatest novelty was moving from room to room for different lessons and meeting a new teacher for every new subject. During the first year, Betty West had very little to do with Abigail and she thought that perhaps she was rid of her for good. They each had their own circle of friends and it seemed that Miss Chip-on-her-shoulder West had at last learned to grow up. She didn't have the same clout there as she'd had with the minnows at Belford where she had paraded as a big fish in a very small pond. Nobody at Great Moor fawned after her like the simpering hangers-on she had accumulated in primary school. It must have been a rude awakening for her when she no longer wielded the mighty sword of authority amongst her peers. Abi presumed that the girls at the grammar school were too intelligent and too socially aware to allow Betty West to be lord and master of all she surveyed. Alleluia!

The school was situated on Great Moor Street in the town centre of Bolton. The main entrance opened from the street into a hallway that housed the Secretary's office which in turn led into the Head's room. There was a grand staircase up which pupils filed to their classrooms. The corridors seemed to be never-ending and there were science laboratories, a geography room, a music room and a wonderful library as well as numerous general purpose classrooms which were used for form rooms and subjects such as English and Mathematics. The only setback was that there was no gymnasium and the assembly hall had to double as the gym for physical education lessons. Nor were there any football fields, nor netball courts. Games lessons involved a short walk across town to Queen's Park and sometimes a bus ride to Leverhulme Park where the facilities were available to schools on particular days. All this made school life much more exciting for Abigail and her friends, who worked hard and played hard with satisfying results.

Abi and her best friend, Janet Kingston, sat in a corner of the canteen eating their packed lunches. "I can't believe how the time has flown," Janet said as she took a bite of an apple. With each term flying by, each school year seemed to end almost as soon as it had started.

"Nor me," Abi agreed, "It doesn't seem like two minutes since we were all lining up to be put into our first form groups, does it? Do you remember how nervous we were on that first day? I was dreading being in the same form as Betty West. And now just look at us...sweet sixteen and..." she giggled... "and never been kissed!"

Janet regarded her friend pensively. "Do you wish you had, Abs?"

"What?"

"Been kissed? What about that big chance you threw away with every girl's dreamboat?" Janet reminded her.

Abigail shrugged as she remembered the embarrassing invitation she'd had to go and see Elvis at the Odeon. "Oh shut up, Jan. You'll never let me forget that, will you?"

To onlookers, it did seem strange, though, that by the time Abi was sixteen, boys had never really featured in her young life. They had always been around in her class at Belford and in her form at Great Moor Grammar, but she hadn't found it important to become attached to any particular boy like some of the girls in her group. She had listened in awe when they described their first kiss and what it felt like to be held in an amorous embrace, two bodies touching and feeling the hot breath of passion on your face. She had gasped at the graphic accounts of groping in the back row of the cinema, but had not as yet felt the need of that experience. The mere thought of her dad finding out that she had even dreamed of going out with a boy, embarrassed her. In that respect, she was still very young and somewhat naïve and she was very much aware of her own inexperience. The acceptance of her own naïveté really contradicted her mature attitude to life in general. She still had an innocence about her that seemed so out of place.

"There's plenty of time for boys when your education is finished," her dad had told her when Brian Yates, who lived round the corner from Hillside Terrace, had called to borrow her biology textbook for the third time in two weeks. "Where's his own book?" her father asked when Abi had handed over her copy again.

"He's lost it and hasn't had the courage to tell Mr Ashton yet!"

"Well, I think he has ulterior motives." His thoughts were frequently full of concern. *My youngest daughter has grown into a beautiful young woman and I need to make sure that she won't be distracted by the attentions of adolescent boys.*

"Oh Dad.. Stop worrying. I know plenty of boys, Brian Yates included, but they're just friends and I'm not about to rush into marrying anybody just yet," she replied, laughing and feeling embarrassed at the mere idea of going out with any of the boys in her form at school. As far as she was concerned, they were all gawky, awkward individuals, full of testosterone and ogling the girls in their gym kit during games hoping to get a saucy glimpse at their knickers. One, or two of them were quite friendly without being overbearing and she tended to consider them as her friends without strings attached.

The truth was, she had only ever been asked out just that once and she had declined the invitation. Boys of her own age were afraid of her. She was extremely beautiful, sophisticated and very bright and they felt intimidated by her and they had told Janet that on numerous occasions. Abigail would have been mortified had she realised that at the time, and Janet saved her from that information, so she just carried on with her life totally unaware of the effect she had on those love-struck adolescents.

The young man who had dared to ask her to go to the Odeon with him had been in the Sixth Form when she was only in Lower Fifth. She blushed profusely as he approached her, acutely aware that a group of her friends was trying unsuccessfully to appear uninterested at the opposite side of the hall. "Hi Abigail," he said, very confident and self-assured and he didn't beat about the bush. "Can I take you out on Saturday night? *Jailhouse Rock* is on at the Odeon. Do you like Elvis Presley?"

Abi was embarrassed and didn't know how to handle the situation. He really was very good looking and not in the least bit awkward or gawky, she observed. She could see her classmates across the hall watching her silently, yet obviously urging her to say that she would go out with him. She twisted a strand of her hair nervously and looked up at this tall, dark and handsome young man looking down at her hopefully.

"Th-thank you for asking," she stuttered, hating herself for sounding so incapable of speaking coherently, "b-but I'm b-busy on Sa-Saturday."

"Another time perhaps?" the young man asked, disappointed that she had turned him down.

"I don't think so," Abigail said, regaining her composure. "I'm sorry." And thankfully she didn't have to give a reason as he made a hasty retreat to the sixth form common room.

As soon as he had gone, Abi breathed a sigh of relief. The other girls descended upon her, eager and curious, thrilled and excited, their shrill voices demanding to know what he had said. "Come on! Come on!" they urged, "What did he say?"

"He asked me out," Abi stated matter-of-factly.

"And?" Eager eyes stared at her expectantly.

"I told him I couldn't go," she said and not wanting to appear embarrassed again, she added quickly, "It's no big deal."

Her friend Janet looked astounded. "You did what?" she asked, her voice rising in a crescendo, "You're mad! Do you know who he is?"

Abi shrugged. She didn't know who he was; she'd had no reason to ask his name. She'd seen him around, but hadn't taken much notice and it really didn't matter to her if he were Paris wooing Helen of Troy. She didn't want to go out with him and that was that.

Janet was undeterred. "He's Alan Jackson, the Head Boy. All the girls in the Sixth Form are mad about him. My cousin told me. Why didn't you say you'd go?"

Abigail didn't know why really. She had been caught unawares. He was much older than she, she had never been asked out and she felt very silly and confused. If that was what fancying a boy was all about, she'd leave it alone for the time being. Who needed it anyway? As for Alan Jackson, he didn't go to see Elvis Presley after all. He knew that perhaps he should have waited a little while longer before he asked for Abigail Hawthorne's heart.

It seemed that in no time at all the teachers were advising them to start revising for the forthcoming General Certificate of Education exams. They were constantly reminded that Ordinary levels were the first rung on the ladder to success. "Don't become a 'wish-I'd-done-more' victim," Mr Pickering told them as the mock exams loomed. "I say this to my pupils every year and there are always people who think they can sail through O levels without revision. That's poppycock and I don't want to be saying 'I told you so' when it's all over. Is that clear Upper 5A?"

They mumbled "Yes, sir," quite oblivious of the seriousness of his words and some of the boys scoffed as he left the room at the end of the lesson. "Old Pickers has to say that to cover his back. If we fail, it'll look bad on him."

Abi went through the Upper Fifth blissfully unaware that she was the focus of attention for several of the boys in the Sixth Form. Unknown to her, they had taken bets on who would be first to go on a date with her and ultimately kiss her. Alan Jackson had left to go university, so he was out of the running. Abigail was concentrating on the forthcoming GCE exams and, although she still found her PE lessons and netball matches most enjoyable, her main aim was to remain focussed in order to gain good results for entry into the Sixth Form the following year. However, one particular young buck observed her from a distance. Tony Simpson was the school games captain and had fancied Abi for ages. He had watched her on the netball court and thought, *she is the most beautiful girl I've ever seen. I know Alan Jackson suffered a knock-back, so I'll have to wait and choose the right moment to ask her for a date. How athletic she is; how intelligent; how vibrant and absolutely gorgeous with it,* he dreamed. *It is my bounden duty to ask her out and I will. No doubt about that.*

Abi and Janet spent most of their time working hard in the lead up to O levels. When they weren't in class, they were generally in the library, or at netball practice. Their intention was to enter Sixth Form with the maximum O level passes and both were destined to achieve the best results.

"Have you finally decided which subjects you're going to do next year?" Janet asked earnestly one evening as they studied together in Abi's bedroom. With Patty away at Nottingham University, Abi had a room of her own. Meg and Philip had been married for a year and lived in Bromley Cross, so although Nellie popped in now and again, generally there were only Abigail and her dad in the house.

"I'm going to do sciences," Abi declared. "I really need to study physics, chemistry and human biology if possible."

Janet feigned disappointment, as she was more inclined to the arts and she wanted Abigail to do similar subjects so they wouldn't be separated in the sixth form. They had met on the first day at Great Moor Grammar and had been together ever since. It was Janet's intention to read English Literature at Oxford. "Sciences are a bit ambitious, Abi," she teased, knowing full well that her friend was determined to study medicine and was dogged in her resolve to do well.

"No more ambitious than you wanting to go to Oxford, Jan," and she smiled at her grinning friend who knew she would have to get used to the fact that eventually they would have to go their separate ways. "Lower Sixth Science, here I come!"

O level results came out in August and were as expected. Arriving in school to collect them during the summer recess was always a thrilling occasion. Nobody slept the night before and there was an air of excited expectancy which filled the entrance hall as pupils queued to go into the office. Even the school prefects were there to welcome prospective sixth formers and Abigail and Janet felt very proud to be joining the ranks of the senior pupils.

Tony Simpson was standing at the top of the stairs when Abi and Janet came out of the office with their results. The broad smiles on their faces advertised the fact that they had each gained the grades they needed to follow their dreams. He waved to them and leapt down the stairs two at a time to greet them. Directing his words to Abigail, he said, "No need to ask how you've gone on. I can see it in your smile. And you too, Janet; it is Janet, isn't it?"

"Yes, it is," Janet gushed, but she was only too aware that it was Abi in whom he was interested.

"There's a big celebration party tonight at St George's Youth Club. Do you think you'll both be able to come?" Speaking to both of them wouldn't make his mission too obvious.

The girls looked at each other. They had been working so hard over the past few months and almost read each other's mind in thinking they deserved a bit of fun. When the answer came, it was Janet who spoke for both of them. "Why not?" she crooned. "We'll be there. See you later then."

"Is he for real?" Abi asked her friend who was still smiling at the thought of the party. "What do you mean?"

"Well, '*I can see it in your smile?*' Come on, Jan, he sounds like he fancies himself as Frank Sinatra. God, what a creep!"

"I think he fancies you," Janet told her, "and he's trying to impress you with romantic words of love. It's a wonder he didn't come dancing down the stairs like Gene Kelly! *'I'll build a stairway to Paradise,'* she sang, "Abi Hawthorne's got an admirer. Look at her blushing!" Janet teased.

"Don't be daft, Jan. It was probably you he fancied and who's blushing now?" Abi retaliated.

Janet felt terrible and no wonder she was blushing. She had known about the party and hadn't mentioned it to Abi for reasons of her own, but she determined that they would enjoy the night out. Abi was her best friend and she had never kept a secret from her.

Tony Simpson couldn't believe his luck. *Abigail Hawthorne has accepted my invitation to the party. She's agreed to see me later—well, as good as. Abigail Hawthorne is going on a date with me, isn't she? I'm half way to winning the bet already.*

Standing in the shadows and eavesdropping on the conversation was Betty West. She had spent the last five years watching in the wings as Abigail Hawthorne had gone from strength to strength in all aspects of her school life. Betty, a big girl still, had been unable to compete at any level and at first it had irked her greatly. Gradually, she had grudgingly accepted the envied Abi Hawthorne was perhaps deservedly successful and consequently, Betty had kept her distance. Seeing Abi and Janet with a string of A grades between them, she bristled at her list of B's and C's. *Why do I allow this girl to get under my skin like that? she brooded sulkily, and to top everything else, the best looking guy in the school has invited her to the party.*

Abigail was so excited. She spent hours in the bathroom getting ready for her night out. Somehow, this evening was different to any of the socialising she had done previously. By comparison with her classmates, she was really socially inexperienced. She had gone to the cinema with Janet and occasionally skating at the Nevada in town, but had not been dancing at the Palais as some of her friends had. She and Janet had taught themselves to jive to Cliff Richard records. *I would be too self-conscious to jive in public,* she thought as she got ready for the big event. *I'm confident in everything else I know I can do well, but jiving amongst streetwise, trendy bee-boppers is another matte*r. Still, going to a party with all of her school friends was a thrill and she smiled at herself in the mirror as she put on her make-up.

"Anyone would think you were going to meet the Queen," her father joked as she came down the stairs looking absolutely radiant, "Just be sure you're in by midnight, Cinderella!" he said, "The last bus from town is at quarter past eleven."

"Okay, Dad, I won't be late. Janet is going to stay over so we'll come home together."

"All right, love. I'm going round to see your gran. You know how tired she's been lately. I've told her to put her feet up and not worry about us. She's run around after us for long enough and she's getting too old to be fetching and carrying for us all the time. If we had the room, I'd bring her round here to stay with us. Anyway, have a good time and I'll see you later."

John watched his youngest daughter with pride as she left the house for her first real teenage party. She was wearing a pale blue halter-neck dress with a full skirt under which she wore the fashionable frilly net petticoats. Her tiny stiletto shoes were pale blue to match the dress and with her skin tanned from the August sun, she looked exquisite. As she walked to meet Janet at the bus-stop, her skirts swayed and her hair shone in the evening sun. Her blonde curls had been swept up into a ponytail which fell in natural ringlets on to her shoulders. Little wisps of hair framed her face and even Janet gasped when she saw her. "Wow! You look lovely, Abi! No need to wonder who you'll be with tonight!"

"Janet!" Abi scolded. "I'm going out to enjoy myself, not to get hooked up to a boy all night. You look great too. We should get dressed up more often."

"We'll see," her friend chided. "You won't be short of dancing partners, that's for sure!"

St George's Youth Club building was a converted air raid shelter on the school grounds. The Church Council had put in windows and extended it at one end to afford a coffee bar and a cloakroom. Big French windows opened on to the playing fields beyond and tables and chairs had been put outside to accommodate the lively crowd of teenage revellers. It seemed that the organising committee had ordered the weather specially and the setting sun lent a balmy atmosphere to the occasion, adorning the merry-makers with a rosy glow. When they arrived, Janet went to buy lemonades from the bar whilst Abi made her way to an empty table outside on the grass. No sooner had she sat than Tony Simpson was by her side.

"Hi!" he beamed, his smile so charming and endearing, "I'm glad you could come. Would you like to dance?"

Abi smiled, not so much at Tony, but at the thought of Janet's earlier comment about not being short of dancing partners. Now that she was seeing him for the second time, Simpson looked quite acceptable. Momentarily, she chided herself for being too judgmental earlier. This was a new experience for her. Dancing tuition in gym lessons had not been the ideal practice for sharing the dance floor with the partner of your dreams; more the nightmare situation of sweaty palms, halitosis, stiff, awkward side-together-walk forward in waltz time performed with the utmost embarrassment and the urgent desire for the music to finish almost before it had begun. She stood slightly nervous, but she accepted his invitation in the hope that she wouldn't tread on his toes and ruin his winkle-picker shoes. Tony took her hand and led her towards the dance floor. His hand was cool, his grip strong without being aggressive and this stirred a new feeling within Abi, a sensation she had never experienced and she liked it. He turned to face her as they reached the dance floor and she smiled at him, looking into his brown eyes for reassurance. He smiled back and placed his arm around her waist. He was in heaven, he was certain, and making sure that he did nothing to offend this beautiful creature in his arms, he allowed enough space between them to move with ease. No need for words!

Abi was impressed with his dancing skills. "You're a good dancer, Tony. Who taught you to dance? It surely can't be as a result of the lessons in the assembly hall that we all suffered before the Christmas party in our first year!"

"My mum taught me. She said it would come in useful. I didn't realise just how much until now," he admitted, bristling with pride and he gasped audibly when she moved closer to him so that their bodies were almost touching.

The music gently guided them...They listened to the words of *'Can't help falling in love.'* Elvis Presley definitely had a way with words. At the end of the dance, Tony took Abi back to the table and Janet was talking animatedly to Robin Baker, their heads close together, their hands touching across the table.

"Oh, I see," Abigail said to her friend, "I go away for two minutes and you take up with a stranger." They all laughed, but only Abi noticed Janet's embarrassment, even though at that moment, she didn't know why her best friend should react in such a way.

Trying to make light of the situation, Robin spoke up, still hanging on to Janet for fear she might run. "We're not exactly strangers, Abi," he explained, much to her surprise. She looked quizzically at Janet and realised immediately that this was not a spur of the moment thing.

"I'm sorry, Abi. I wanted to tell you, but we were so pulled out with our studying recently and I knew you didn't want any distractions, so I didn't say anything." Why Janet hadn't spilled the beans during the summer holidays, Abigail was at a loss, but what did it matter? Tonight was a celebration and she didn't wish to spoil the moment for anyone, most of all herself. Janet continued unabashed, "Robin and I got together at the church choir practice. He was always waiting round the corner from Hillside Terrace when I left your house after we studied together, to walk me home."

Abi allowed her jaw to drop dramatically and then gave her friend a hug. "No wonder you always left on the dot of nine o'clock! And you, Mr Baker, don't you dare do anything to hurt my friend, or you'll have me to answer to." She playfully nudged his chin with her fist. "And," she continued, "please don't get in the way of her Oxford dream."

"I won't," he told her, "I've already done my Oxbridge paper, so we have that in common at least."

Abi's disappointment in her friend's secrecy didn't last. She was having too much fun. Tony Simpson stayed with her all evening, much to the annoyance of the other suitors who were all waiting to ask her to dance. All too soon the last waltz was announced and dreamy couples wended their way to the packed floor. Abi was at ease. She liked Tony after all and had enjoyed his company. In the middle of the dance floor, she reached up to drape her arms around his neck and he held her close. Feeling her lithe body close to him made his senses whirl. Her head was on his shoulder; he could smell her delicate perfume and they shuffled in time to the music, swaying in unison, lost to the world around them. Abi looked at the handsome young man who held her close. Seized by the moment, he tilted her chin and gently let his lips meet hers. Abigail caught her breath, closed her eyes and was transported to another world. Her lips parted and she allowed him to gently probe with his tongue until she could hardly breathe. Her legs were weak, her heart racing and she knew then what falling in love must be like. This was her first real kiss and she didn't want it to stop.

When the party was over, Tony walked Abi to the bus-stop and they kissed some more while they waited for the bus to arrive. Janet and Robin were too pre-occupied with each other to notice a figure lurking in the shadows, watching and waiting for the right moment.

Betty West had watched them all through the evening. She was consumed with jealousy. *Nobody offered to walk me home,* she brooded, *and the only boy I've ever kissed is my dad and that doesn't count. Now, I can impart the information that will be my final snipe at Miss Goody-Goody Hawthorne. I'll wait until we get off the bus later so that Prince Charming can't deny anything. You wait, Abigail Hawthorne,* she thought, *I'm going to have the last laugh tonight,* and she smiled to herself, the same evil grimace she had displayed as far back as the reception class at Belford Primary School.

The bus journey home was a very quiet one. Abi linked her arm through Janet's, all hurts forgotten, each deep in thought. Janet thought about her time with Robin and decided that he was the kindest and most considerate boy in the whole world. Abigail was in a dream. She had never contemplated what it would be like to kiss a boy, but now that she had, she thought it was the most delicious experience of her entire life. She tingled all over. She felt like she had just awakened out of a deep sleep and discovered that the world had become Paradise overnight. She squeezed her best friend's arm as Janet smiled knowingly and all the while, unnoticed, Betty West sat at the back of the bus waiting to burst their bubble.

They all got off the bus at The Black Dog in Belford and Abi and Janet had a short walk up High Street to Hillside Terrace. West was off the bus before them and took them by surprise when she spoke. "Enjoy yourselves?" she asked, sounding almost pleasant for Betty West.

"Brilliant," Abi replied, determined that she would not allow anyone to spoil her dream, not even her old arch-enemy, Betty West.

"Well, enjoy it for now, 'cos it won't last. He's no good, that one," and she cocked her stubby thumb back to where they had just travelled.

Curious as to what West's ploy was this time, Abigail stopped abruptly. "Why?" she asked, trying desperately not to let her irritation show. "What are you saying now, Betty? I thought you might have grown out of your childish behaviour. Can't you ever leave me alone?"

Janet felt uneasy. "Come on, Abi. Ignore her." But Abi stood her ground.

"Oh, I'll leave you alone when I've delivered this *pièce de résistance*," Betty gloated. "I've got a job with my dad so you won't see me for dust after tonight. I'll have money whilst you two are poverty-stricken students and who'll have the fellas then, eh?"

"So that's what this is about, is it?" Abi questioned, almost feeling sorry for this big girl who obviously objected to the attention she and Janet were getting from the boys, but who wasn't ever likely to impress any young man with her inborn intolerance of other people.

"Well, Miss Fancy Knickers Hawthorne, hear this and listen good. Your precious Tony Simpson only went with you for a bet. I heard them all planning it at the end of term. He's in for a bob or two, because not only did he ask you for a date, but he kissed you as well, which will double his winnings at least. What do you think of him now, eh?" and with the evil grin on her fat face, she turned and laughed out loud as she walked away, out of Abigail's life for good.

Abi stood quite still for a while and Janet took her arm gently. "Take no notice of her," she coaxed. "She's just jealous and I doubt very much if Tony is involved in all that nonsense." *How can I tell my best friend that Robin had informed me of the bet? I really hope with all my heart that he will refuse the cash, or at the very least give it to a worthy cause.*

Abigail, on the other hand, had already decided not to allow Betty West to ruin her evening and whether it were true or not, she still had the wonderful, lingering memories of that first kiss which she would treasure for the rest of her life. Tony Simpson, bet or no bet, had awakened her body to sensations she could savour until the time was right to unleash the passion that lay dormant within her soul. *Nobody will have access to that until I'm ready.* From the ashes of Betty West's fiery obsession would rise Abigail Hawthorne's resolve to succeed.

Eight

When the two girls arrived at Hillside Terrace, John Hawthorne was at the door waiting for their return. He looked flushed and agitated and Abigail hastily looked at her watch to see if they were late. She hated letting her Dad down. He had never prevented her from doing what she wanted to do, not that she had ever shown the defiant streak that had materialised in her older sister, Meg, but he had always been there for her and had never given her cause to doubt his wisdom. "We're not late, are we, Dad? It's only quarter to twelve and you said to be in by midnight," she asked, uncertain why he was so anxious.

"It's your gran," he said, desperate to control the trembling he felt inside and not to break down in tears in front of Abi and her friend.

"What about Gran? Is she all right?" Abigail was becoming increasingly agitated. "Dad, tell me!"

John could restrain himself no longer and he burst into tears as he tried to tell Abi what she already knew. "I went round like I said and she was ready for bed. She said she was going to watch television for a while and then have an early night. I left after about half an hour and she said she was fine," he sobbed. "Alice Higson came round here after she'd been in to check on your gran. She died about an hour ago," and his youngest daughter went to hold him as they wept together. Janet tactfully went inside and put the kettle on. The old Lancashire custom of brewing a pot of tea in times of stress went a long way to easing the burden. Nellie Walmsley had simply gone to sleep in her favourite armchair and when her neighbour had called to make her usual nightly check on her, she couldn't waken her. "We had to call the police as she'd been on her own when she went. I feel so terrible that I'd left her by herself, but I had no idea..."

"Dad, it's not your fault. Surely you know that." Abigail tried to console him.

John did know, but he had lost his best friend. Since Mary's death, he had relied on her to guide the girls through their growing up, shedding feminine light upon female problems and just being there when she was needed. Now she had gone. The seventeen years since Mary's demise had taken their relentless toll on the old lady who, at almost sixty five, wasn't really old at all. She had looked very tired recently though. She had shared the ups and downs of their family life before, during and after the war. She had never complained when Meg, Patty and Abigail had played their childish pranks nor when John had left her to cope with feeds and nappies when he had been on watch. *Nellie was an angel in disguise,* he thought, taking comfort in the knowledge that there was another star in heaven that night.

~ * ~

After the funeral, Patty had had to go straight back to Nottingham and Meg and her husband offered to stay at Hillside Terrace, "Until you feel able to cope," Meg told her father.

"Nay, lass, we'll be okay, won't we, Abi? Your gran wouldn't want to think that we were moping around after her. I've to get back to work and earn some money for our Patty's and Abi's education. Once I've got them settled, I'll be happy," and he gave a telling sigh which only the astute Meg noticed. Her dad was covering up how he really felt and was too proud to admit that he had sometimes found it difficult to play the part of two parents. Now, his main ally had gone and Meg wasn't sure how it would affect him long term.

The weeks flew by for everyone, particularly for Abigail and Janet. Life in the Lower Sixth was both demanding and enjoyable. They were in different forms for the first time in five years, but they spent their breaks together and occasionally they were free at the same time, so were able to meet in the common room.

Tony Simpson made sure his friends knew he hated himself after the party. He really did fancy Abigail Hawthorne, but someone had told her about the bet. As a result, she had refused to go out with him again. She was very polite about it, but she had made it abundantly clear that he had blown his chances of kissing those luscious lips ever again. As school games captain, he had played out his frustrations on the football field and had been spotted by the Bolton Wanderers' scout as a potential professional when the time came for him to leave school. Some stories had a very odd twist at the end.

Sixth Form studies left little time for social life, at least for Abigail. Her inherent ability to work when others were at play gave her the advantage when it came to exams, and she sailed through with comparative ease, gaining the results she required. Her friend, Janet, respected Abi's drive and commitment, but felt she was fast becoming obsessed with the will to succeed. "All work and no play," she quoted one day as they returned from netball team practice.

"How can you say that?" Abi retorted, "We've just been playing netball for the past hour! And anyway, my name isn't Jack and I'm not about to become a dull boy under any circumstances!" She grinned and Janet had to smile at the failed attempt at analogy. "Do you really think I'm boring then, Jan?"

"No, silly, I don't, but you've always got your nose in a book and I can't remember the last time we had time for a girlie chat."

"Ah," Abi detected that wistful, forlorn look in Janet's eyes, "You want to talk about Robin?" She looked questioningly at her friend who clearly wasn't very happy and she hated herself for not noticing earlier. "What is it, Jan?"

Janet, half pleading, smiled weakly at her best friend, the friend whom she knew would always be there for her. She hoped she didn't show the desperation she felt inside, but she had to tell someone, she just had to.

The common room was empty. Not many students stayed behind much after half past four, so Janet was relieved that she had the privacy she needed to talk to Abi. Warming their hands on their mugs of coffee felt like heaven after the netball session in the freezing cold. "Right then, what's this pressing problem, my friend?" Abi asked airily, trying to make Janet feel relaxed. She could see that Janet was extremely tense about something, but she had no idea why.

"I think I'm pregnant."

Stunned silence filled the room. Abi just stared, unbelieving.

"I've missed a period."

"Oh, goodness is that all? I've missed periods too occasionally. Our Meg says it's through stress sometimes and with looming A levels, we're bound to be stressed," Abi reassured her.

"No, Abi, you don't understand. I've missed a period and Robin and I have..."

"Oh Jan," Abigail was nonplussed. "I didn't think you would do it before you went to Oxford. What can I say? I want to sympathise; you're my best friend, but what an idiot you are! I am so determined not to put myself in a position like that. You know my opinion already. The thought of having a baby scares me to death, not because of actually giving birth, though God knows I have more reasons than most to be afraid of that, but it would totally shatter my dream and I can't allow any boy to do that for the sake of ten minutes of fun. Have you told anyone else? Does your mum know?" She couldn't believe Janet had been so stupid. Robin had gone up to Oxford in October. It didn't take a super brain to work out that this was his leaving present.

Janet's eyes filled with tears. "I haven't told anyone, not even Robin. I can't upset him when he's just settling in Halls. Oh, Abi, what if he finishes with me when he finds out? I think I would die if he did."

Abigail didn't have the answer to that question. What she knew of Robin she could write on a thre'penny bit, as her gran would say, but she felt she had to give Janet her support. "Robin wouldn't do that, Jan. He loves you. He made love to you and he knew what might happen. Try not to worry. We'll talk again after the weekend and I'll be there for you when you need to tell your mum and dad. Don't do anything yet. Let's both think it out and then pool our resources."

~ * ~

Janet was relieved to have shared her problem and went home, hoping that mother hadn't noticed her period was late. She rightly assumed that as nothing had been said, she was safe. Her mother was out at work all day, so she was hardly likely to notice. Weekends were different, however. Her mother was at home, but Janet resolved to stay in her room to study and appear only at meal times so as to keep a low profile. Her mother would accept the need to study, especially with the Oxbridge exam due in a couple of weeks. *Oxbridge? Will I be able to go now?*

~ * ~

Abigail was perplexed. *How on earth could Jan have been so idiotic?* She recalled the sensation she felt when Tony Simpson had kissed her...the stirrings deep within her soul, the butterflies fluttering in her loins. Those memories made her thrill even then, but she pushed them to the back of her mind and resolved not to allow anyone to take her virginity until she was ready. *Only when I have met the man of my dreams will I give myself totally to him and that will only be after I have achieved my goal. Janet has recklessly allowed Robin to venture into the realms of desire and he has probably ruined her future. What a fool she has been.*

To become mentor, mediator and social worker had not been on Abigail's agenda and she felt way out of her depth. She had no idea how to help Janet and she pondered on it all weekend. She went to the churchyard and quietly knelt at her mother's grave, inwardly pleading for inspiration, but none came. She walked over the moors towards Rivington Pike and stood where her father had stood on the day she had been born. She looked up into the skies and prayed earnestly that she might help to resolve her friend's dilemma, but she felt no divine intervention and was left devoid of all feasible remedies. It went totally against the grain for her to admit defeat, but she had to concede that Janet would have to tell her parents and face the consequences. The least she could do as her best friend was to be there when battle commenced.

~ * ~

Janet was restless. She lay on her bed staring at the ceiling. She wanted to write to Robin, but each time she started to open her heart, the words would not come. She turned on to her side and closed her eyes. The visions of babies and nappies and prams and night feeds haunted her. She wasn't ready for it and the whole situation was a complete nightmare. Perhaps she would wake up in the morning and realise it was all a dream. She passed her hands across her belly. It was flat and taut from regular exercise.

Soon it would be big and bulbous. Her body would become distorted and horrible and she would have to hide it under voluminous, hideous clothes. Hot tears seeped from beneath her eyelids, tears of despair, of loneliness and of shame.

In the middle of Sunday night, Janet woke up racked in pain. The pit of her abdomen twisted and knotted in spasms and she felt violently sick. She struggled to the bathroom trying not to groan too loudly and locked the door before she sank to her knees, her head over the pan of the lavatory. "Please God, if I'm going to be sick, let me do it now," she prayed, "I feel so awful." She rested her arms on the edge of the pan and put her head in her hands. Looking down at her nightdress, she saw red wetness where it ought to have been white silk. She was covered in blood and she laughed out loud, almost hysterically, until her laughter turned to tears.

"Jan? Are you all right?" Her mother was at the door. "I heard you crying. Open the door, then I can help you, whatever it is."

"I'm okay, Mum." Janet desperately tried not to sob between words. "I've been sick," she fibbed, "but I'm fine now. Go back to bed. I'll see you in the morning." Eve Kingston stared quizzically at the bathroom door, but trusting that her daughter would say if she were needed, she shrugged and shuffled back to her bed so that the disturbance wouldn't waken her husband.

Stripping herself bare, Janet filled the bath and lay in the warm water, allowing the heat to penetrate her aching body and supply the relief to her tormented mind. Finally, relaxed and refreshed, she returned to her bed and slept, ironically, like a baby.

~ * ~

On Monday morning, Janet didn't attend school. Abigail was worried and felt she had let down her best friend in not having found a solution to her problem. Mr Hallam, the Sixth Form tutor, wanted to see her. "Janet has been sick all night," he informed her. "Her mother telephoned the school to say she wouldn't be in and to ask if you might take any homework for Janet after school." Abi went to see Janet's tutors and obtained the necessary work so that she might go quickly to Astley Bridge as soon as she finished her last lesson.

Being careful not to appear anxious, Abi tentatively rang the doorbell expecting to see Mrs Kingston when the door opened and mentally prepared to stand by Janet when she had to impart the delicate news. She was surprised, nay shocked, when Janet herself opened the door, beaming and looking like she hadn't a care in the world. "Come in," she sang and Abi entered the house in utter dismay and confusion.

"Janet?" she asked, not knowing quite how to react. *Has my friend flipped under the strain? Has she become deranged through the stress of her pregnancy?* "Are you all right?" a pathetic question under the circumstances. "I tried my best to find a solution to your problem, but drew a blank, I'm afraid. I'm so sorry."

Janet looked at Abi's worried face and went to hug her. "Somebody's prayers were answered," she said, grinning widely. "My period came in the middle of the night. I felt dreadful and then I felt wonderful! I was so exhausted this morning. Mum said I could take the day off. Oh Abi, I feel like I've been let out of jail and won the Pools all at once!" And reading the expression on Abi's face, she added, "Yes, I have learned my lesson. If you play with fire, you can expect to get your fingers burnt. I vow to tell Robin and if he really loves me, he'll understand when I say no. Oxford, here I come!"

The two returned to their studies with added enthusiasm. Before their exams started, they had both been offered places at university with the proviso that they obtained the relevant grades, Janet at St Hilda's College, Oxford and Abigail at Manchester. The Medical College in Manchester offered Abi everything she wanted and her desire to become a doctor fired her determination to succeed. *The past few weeks have emphasised the necessity to focus on the job in hand,* she contemplated. *Distractions are out of the question for us both. Aiming high is our priority. We intend to reach the top, however many mountains we have to climb on the road ahead. Come on, Janet! We can do it.*

Nine

Meg, the adult

Meg felt that she had led a charmed life in spite of the little indiscretions that she knew were all part of growing up. During the year of 1950, before she had gone to Liverpool to train as a teacher, she had enjoyed life to the full. She had been made a prefect at Great Moor Grammar and even at seventeen, she coped with the fact that her dad was openly proud of her achievements and she totally understood why. He had always encouraged her and helped her with her homework, in spite of his lack of educational qualifications. That fact had always been a thorn in his side, yet when presented with algebraic problems, he solved them by using arithmetic, a marvel in itself according to Meg. He learned to conjugate Latin verbs and memorised the process of osmosis as well as discussing all manner of English essay topics so that she might absorb some of his vast, varied self-gained knowledge and experience. Now that Patty and Abigail were both following in her footsteps, he was well equipped with the knowledge gained from his firstborn's time at grammar school.

When young men from Sixth Form came calling for Meg, John was taken aback. Meg had grown up before his very eyes, but he seemed to have buried his head in the sand. Strangely, he had never considered that Meg was a young woman and not his little girl anymore. "Is it all right, Dad, if a few of my form come to study with me? We won't make too much noise and if we stay in the front room, we won't disturb your forty winks after tea!" She grinned at her dad who was trying to read the expression on her face. *Is the little madam testing me?* he wondered.

"All right, love, but make sure they don't stay too late. You know your sisters go to bed early and they'll play up if they think you're staying up with your friends till all hours."

"Thanks, Dad. I'll make sure they're out of here by nine. Some of them live at the other side of town so they won't want to be too late," Meg told him. "Apart from that, knowing how our discussions usually go, we'll have had more than enough after a couple of hours."

At first it was a just case of doing homework together, a mixed group of eager teenagers happily arguing some point of political history, or sitting with heads close together poring over Hamlet's soliloquies and trying to decide why his relationship with his mother had affected his love for Ophelia. John loved those discussions and would listen intently in the next room without participating. These boys and girls were friends and scholastic rivals and that was a healthy situation that John freely and easily accepted.

Then the inevitable began to happen. Meg began to act mysteriously. On certain evenings soon after tea, she started to make excuses to go to the corner shop. She would sit by the window around the same time on Mondays, Wednesdays and Fridays and as soon as the young cyclist had passed by, she decided that she needed some ink for her pen, or some sweets to help with her revision. "It helps me to concentrate having something to chew," she explained and oddly, nobody questioned it. With sweets not rationed, it was easy to buy them without a problem; more sorts than you could choose and as many as you wanted.

It was a few weeks later when John called in the corner shop for some groceries on his way home from work. Normally he would have asked one of the girls to collect them, but on this particular day, they all had things to do and would be late home from school. Even the eight-year-old Abigail was going to her friend's house for tea. "How are you, John?" Mrs Abbott asked, "I haven't seen you for ages."

"I'm fine, thanks, Joyce. I haven't got my helpers today. They're all busy doing something so I've had to do the shopping myself! You can't get the staff these days!" he joked.

"Well, I'm glad I've caught you," Mrs Abbott continued, "Do you think you might ask your

Meg's young man to stop banging his foot on my wall when they're talking? He props his bike up and leans on my gable end knocking his heel against it non-stop. It's usually just as we're closing. We can't concentrate on the telly when he's there and after being on me feet all day, I need a bit o' peace." She spoke quite earnestly, but without animosity.

"Oh right. I'll see what I can do." John hoped he didn't look as surprised as he felt.

The teenaged Meg arrived home after her trip to the library in town. She'd bumped into Patty as she approached Hillside Terrace and so they went in together.

"A word, Meg," John said as soon as she had taken off her coat and thrown it over the back of the settee.

"Whoops, sorry!" and she quickly grabbed her coat to hang it on the hook behind the kitchen door, knowing that she'd get told off for being untidy.

"Who's this young man of yours?"

Meg cast a quick, irritated look at Patty and was convinced it could only be Patty who had told her dad about Phil.

"Patty!" she chided, her heart suddenly beating nineteen to the dozen, "I told you it was a secret!"

Patty looked indignant.

"It's nothing to do with our Patty," John assured her. His voice was soft, his tone reasonable.

Meg knew from past experience not to come up with excuses. "His name's Philip Wilkinson. He goes to Bolton School and I met him at the tennis club."

Bolton School, eh? Well, he must be all right then, John thought and he continued, "Well, the next time you go to the shop for some sweets, you bring him back here. If you are meeting a young man, I want you to welcome him into our home. Don't let him annoy Mrs Abbott when he can't keep his feet still!" and he winked at Patty, who grinned impishly at him. From then on, Philip Wilkinson became a regular visitor to the Hawthorne's house and it didn't take long for John to realise that Meg had found her soul mate.

Little Abigail had been quite puzzled at first with Philip's appearance. She giggled a lot when he spoke to her and tried to hide herself in the big armchair when he was sitting on the settee close to Meg. She dramatically covered her face with her handkerchief as she pretended to blow her nose and she shyly peeped over the back of the sofa before she ventured into his company. She amused the young lovers with her childish antics and so she precociously performed all the more.

"Abigail Hawthorne," Meg scolded, "There is no need to be daft. Phil doesn't want to see how silly you can be."

"Sorry, Meggy," she whispered sheepishly and crept out of the room before she found herself doing something else Meg didn't like.

One afternoon whilst Phil was waiting for Meg to get changed, he picked up a *Woman's Own* magazine she had left on the settee. Abigail watched as casually he turned the page to reveal an advertisement for women's underwear and she was aghast. "Philip Wilkinson!" she remonstrated, "You shouldn't be looking at that!"

"Oh sorry," Phil said penitently, "I won't do it again, miss!" and he duly closed the magazine immediately. "How are you going on at school, Abi?" he asked in an effort to divert her attention from the fact that he had dared to look at a picture of a half-naked woman.

Abigail took the opportunity to tell him about her new class teacher, Mr Davies. "He's a man!" she announced, wide-eyed. "I've never had a man teacher before, but he's really good and he comes to school on a motor bike." The ice was broken and she felt she might tolerate his being around in future, even though there were times when she wished he had never appeared, especially when Meg talked to Patty about him when they were in bed at night.

"Will you two shut up?" she would say, "I'm trying to get to sleep and I don't want to know anything else about Philip flippin' Wilkinson." She was too young to savour the delights of young love.

Meg sighed and turned over in her single bed. "Goodnight," she said dreamily, "Goodnight, my loves!" The other two who were sharing a double bed would both sigh too, Patty in total agreement with Meg and Abi in sheer exasperation.

Meg and Phil's relationship survived their time apart whilst they both pursued their career training, Meg going to teacher training college and Philip at Birmingham University to study engineering. When they were both qualified, Phil proposed to her as soon as they had secured jobs. They had married at St Peter's on a rather dull day at the end of August 1956, but the weather did not detract from their happiness. It was a very proud day in the life of John Hawthorne. He had known from the start that Phil was right for Meg and he was happy to hand over his daughter to a man of integrity who would give her the love and security she deserved.

~ * ~

Meg woke up one Sunday morning and was sick. When she was sick again on Monday morning and again on Tuesday, she had already looked on the calendar to check her dates. Phil was eating breakfast as she desperately fought to hang on to hers. She gulped down some water and leaning against the kitchen sink, she whispered, "I'm pregnant."

"Pardon?" Phil thought he had heard correctly, but asked her to repeat what she had just said.

"I'm pre..." And she was whisked off her feet and spun around amongst shouts of jubilation and ecstatic exclamations of joy from her delighted husband. "Phil!" she gasped, "Put me down before I throw up all over you. I take it you're pleased?"

"Pleased? I'm over the moon! Me, a dad! I can't wait."

Meg, herself, was going through a whole plethora of emotions. She had secretly pondered over the possibility of being pregnant for days. *I desperately want this baby, Phil's baby, but day and night, but can't get my mother out of my thoughts. She's even dominating my dreams and it's making me afraid, very afraid and very confused. Oh how I wish I could talk to Mam about it; how I wish I might discuss the intricacies of childbirth with her. What was it really like? How bad are the pains? Only a mother could explain in everyday language what I have to expect during the next nine months and afterwards too. Phil's mum is lovely, but she isn't my mother and I so want my mother just now. She* sighed deeply. *Until the reality of my pregnancy hit home, I hadn't considered that I might react so dramatically to the situation. Even when Phil and I had talked about having children, it never entered my head that Mam had died in childbirth.* But now, with desperate concern etched upon her face and questioning tears in her eyes, she turned to Phil, who reached out to her and drew her in close, trying to rationalise her fears. "I'm scared, Phil. Look what happened to my mother," she said, her concern distorting all logical reasoning in her words.

"I can imagine how you must feel, love, and it's understandable, but you have to accept that it happened almost twenty years ago. Surely you must realise that they know how to monitor and deal with things these days."

Meg knew she hadn't really been thinking straight and she had allowed her evaluation of the situation to become emotionally distorted.

Phil continued in an effort to put her mind at ease, even though he knew he was stating the obvious. "The doctors will keep a close watch on you and I know they definitely wouldn't leave you in labour as long as they left your mum. Your dad and I had quite a long chat about it a few weeks ago..."

Meg looked at him wide-eyed.

"... I know, I know, he didn't really talk about it to you, but just that day, he must have needed to open up to someone and I happened to be there. I don't know whether or not he anticipated that you'd be pregnant one day. It does happen to married couples, you know!" Meg smiled at him, a knowing and appreciative smile and she knew at that moment that she'd cope with everything having Phil by her side.

And cope she did. After nine months of knitting bootees and matinee jackets, collecting baby towels and nappies, decorating the nursery and gradually becoming fatter and heavier, Nicholas John Wilkinson arrived safely one very sunny and significant Thursday morning, a healthy seven and a half pounds, much to the delight of the whole family. Her thoughts were happy and she was so, so proud. *Having now produced a child,* she pondered, *I think I have earned the right to consider myself an experienced woman.*

Ten

John's problems

It went without saying that John Hawthorne was extremely proud of his children. They had survived circumstances under which others would have crumbled. To bring up three girls without a mother had seemed a daunting task at the beginning, but with Nellie's help, they'd pulled through. He often thought of the times when he was at his wits end trying to fathom the workings of the female mind and now Meg was a mother herself, he couldn't help but hark back to the past.

"Meg?" he'd asked tentatively one day soon after her eleventh birthday when they unusually had the house to themselves for the afternoon.

"What, Dad? Have I done something wrong?" Meg looked at him quizzically, recognising the ominous, unfathomable expression on her dad's face. It was always the same when he was about to take her to task.

"No, you've not done anything wrong as far as I know, but..." he hesitated and fiddled with the buttons on his waistcoat. "I think we ought to have a chat."

"What about? Have Patty and Abi been doing something they shouldn't, because I try to keep an eye on them, but I can't be there all the time and anyway, Gran sees Abi more than me while I'm at school, so it's probably her you should be talking to, not me..."

"Just shut up, Meg and give me a chance," he urged feeling the sweat trickle down the back of his neck. "Oh heck, Meg, this is hard!"

"What is, Dad? For goodness sake, just say it, whatever it is. You're making me nervous."

"Well, I'll try. Er, well...er, well you know that now you are growing up, you'll soon be a teenager and the next step is being a woman..."

"I know all that, Dad. Girls grow into women and boys grow into men. I'm not stupid!"

"Well, things happen to girls..." *Maybe I should have called for Nellie's help as I'm not prepared for this at all,* but through their blushes, his and Meg's, he'd stumbled through his version of the birds and the bees. Meg had looked down at her shoes and straightened her dress with her hands until it looked like it had just been ironed, because she was too embarrassed to tell him they had already had a talk from the PE teacher at school. Several girls were unable to have a shower after the games lesson and the other girls were causing an argument about it not being fair that they were allowed to miss showers, especially when the water was freezing cold in the middle of winter. Miss Watson had grasped the opportunity and had talked to the girls freely and easily.

When Meg's periods started suddenly when she was almost twelve, she was already prepared for the event and it seemed reasonably uncomplicated when she announced quietly, "You know the talk we had, Dad, a few months ago? Well…" There was no need to explain further.

John always considered that he never had time to think about a new relationship. Apart from that, he'd grown used to being on his own and allowing another person into his life would feel like an intrusion. He often wondered if he should have thought more seriously about finding a lady to share everything and then he wouldn't have been faced with coping with girls and their adolescent problems. But oh, the embarrassment when Meg had asked him for some money to buy a bra!

"What do you want a bra for? You're only twelve."

"Dad!" Meg had said, exasperated with her naïve father, "I need a bra. All the girls have them at school and it's embarrassing when I have to get changed in front of them when we have PE." Since their discussion about periods, she had felt a bit more self-assured in approaching John in most matters feminine and he had to admit that he appreciated her confidence in him. "I did think of asking Gran first, but she's so old fashioned and it's pretty obvious that she never wears a bra even though she always covers herself up with that floral overall!" She could just imagine what her gran would say… *'You don't need a bra. You've got nothing to put in it!'* John decided to give her the money without much argument and had later confidently relied on her to sort out the other two when the time arrived for them to need a woman's guidance in such matters.

He remembered when Meg had taken up with that Mooney Street girl. He could laugh then at his own inadequacy in dealing with it. He almost lost his temper that night and he had had to chastise himself later so that he would remain in control of his emotions in future. Meg had thought her end was nigh, but she never gave him cause for concern after that. Now that she was a mother herself to little Nicholas John, that episode in her life would help her to deal with his rebellious actions as he grew up. And there would be moments when a firm hand would be required, of that he was absolutely certain.

Patty, the quietest of the three had blossomed since she went to university. John had worried about her being the middle daughter and felt that she sometimes became the buffer for the other two. Meg occasionally unwittingly used Patty's willing nature too much as they were growing up and Patty rarely complained. She had a way of quietly getting on with things without upsetting anyone, although there were occasions when she uncharacteristically stood up for herself with a show of shrewish expostulation. What was it she had said when Meg mistakenly blamed her for taking her lipstick? He thought carefully. *Oh yes... What would I want with your lipstick, Meg? There's only one person in this house who'd walk around with tutti-frutti lips and it's not me!* He smiled to himself. Meg had stormed off to her room as usual when she couldn't win an argument only to appear later with a half-baked apology. "Sorry," she had mumbled, "I found it under my bed." He also knew Abigail used Patty as a sounding board when Meg was away at college. Patty, born on a Sunday, generally personified all that the rhyme put into words and Mary would have been delighted. Now that she was working in London, he missed her, but she was happy in her chosen profession as an accountant and he couldn't ask for more than that. She had met Steve Ross and had made it clear she didn't want a big, lavish wedding. "Don't be planning the wedding of the year, Dad," she told him and he half expected her to turn up one weekend to say that she had married without a fuss. He'd have to deal with that if and when it happened.

Abigail was the apple of his eye; little Abi who was so determined in all that she did, the child for whom her mother made the final sacrifice. His eyes filled with tears as he remembered seeing her for the first time. How could he ever forget? He knew that there was a possibility of his blaming her for her mother's death, but once he looked at her beautiful face, he knew Mary would expect him to love her as much as he loved his other children. From the moment he held her, there was never any doubt in his mind that she would grow up to make him proud. Yes, John Hawthorne had much to thank the Lord for and he did so every day of his life.

John often found himself going over his life those days. "Must be a sign that I'm getting older," he considered "but there's life in the old dog yet!" He had worked at the Bleach Works since the end of the war and had become warehouse manager. He was a clever man, but had left school at fourteen without gaining any qualifications, a situation that irked him greatly. Grammar School places had to be paid for when he was growing up and his parents could not afford to send him to the school that would have given him the pieces of paper needed to gain what then would have been considered a decent job. He had always worked hard to feed and clothe his children without any real problems. His ambitions for his girls had been born from the fact that he felt he had missed out on schooling himself. "I've got to give them all the chance to make something of their lives," he told Nellie when Meg had appeared with the letter from school asking permission to enter her for the scholarship exam. "I never had the chance myself and by gum, Nellie, I'll make sure they do." Since 1944, when it had been made possible for all children to access grammar school places providing they showed they were academically capable, some of the happiest moments of his life had been when each of his girls had gone to Great Moor Grammar.

~ * ~

It was the day after Bonfire Night. The cold November air was heavy laden with smoke from the fires and the fireworks of the night before and people walked to work with scarves covering their mouths and noses to avoid breathing in the smog-filled air. It was typically dark, dull, damp and dismal for that time of year. Everybody seemed to have a demeanour that embodied the dreary weather outside. John was at work that afternoon when he needed to go to the office for an invoice. The short walk from the warehouse to the office took only a couple of minutes, but when he arrived at the desk, he couldn't remember why he was there. "Would you believe it? I've forgotten what I want. I'll have to go back and start again."

"Oh, I'm like that all the time at home," Mildred, the works secretary said, laughing with him in his dilemma, "I often go to the cupboard and stand there staring at it, because I don't know what I'm supposed to be getting. Mental lapses, I call them."

John retraced his steps and remembered the invoice when he saw the order on his desk. He took hold of the order form and kept it firmly in his hand until he arrived back at the office and asked for the required account. *I must be going daft,* he mused, and then dismissed the thought from his mind as he continued with his work.

As the months passed, the time came around to John's fiftieth birthday in June 1960. There was great excitement at Hillside Terrace when Meg announced that she would pay for the installation of a telephone for his birthday present. "What do I need a telephone for?" he asked, thinking he could always pop to the public phone box on the corner in an emergency.

"What happens if you can't get to the phone box, Dad?" Meg asked him, "You're not getting any younger and I want to know you can contact me at any time of day or night. You have to move into the modern world. Everybody has a home phone these days! With Abi going to uni soon, you'll be on your own and anyway, we'll all be able to phone you. Patty will call from London and Abi from Manchester. Keeping in touch regularly will make you feel that we're all still at home."

"I'll be glad of some peace and quiet when I'm on my own." He paused and smiled wistfully. "Yet it will be nice to know I can talk to one of you when I'm fed up of watching the goggle box in the evening. Thanks, Meg. You're still my little girl at heart."

"For goodness sake, Dad, I'm a big girl now," she retorted, "I'm not going to sneak off down Mooney Street when you're not looking. I might get more than I expect!" They both laughed at the memory of John marching up Belford Road with Meg in tow, her feet hardly touching the ground. "Well, that's settled then. I'll phone the post office about it tomorrow."

A few weeks later, the telephone proved paradoxically to be both a blessing and a curse. It kept John in touch with his family. That was Meg's initial reasoning in making sure he had his lifeline when Abigail left home to continue her studies. Strangely though, early in October, John had started to become agitated at work. The little episode with the invoice had repeated itself on several occasions. Everyday tasks were taking more than the time necessary to keep the warehouse running in the required efficient way. John had always run a tight ship and the usual methodical organisation seemed to be slipping. The routine was disrupted when John confused the in-tray with the out-tray. Orders were doubled, sometimes trebled. Other departments had been left with insufficient supplies to function adequately. "What the hell's going on, John?" Bob Holden asked him when, for the second time that week, the laboratory had been short of lime and the necessary chlorine to test the relevant proportions. The entire factory was dependent on the results produced by the lab and John was fast becoming unpopular with the industrial chemists.

"I'm sorry," was all that John could offer. He looked tired and often felt totally confused, but the feeling didn't last long and he was able to resume some semblance of normality in his work. Holden had worked with John for a long time and although he knew him well, he was, himself, feeling the strain of having to cover for John on a regular basis.

"Why don't you go and see t'doctor, John?" he asked after one particularly stressful day at work. "You 'aven't been well for a while."

"I'm okay," John snapped, his eyes wide, yet somehow unseeing. "Why don't you mind your own damned business? What would you know? Are you after my job or something?"

Bob was dumbfounded. He had never known John to raise his voice in temper and here, before him, was a man possessed. John began to wave his arms wildly and stamped around the warehouse, ranting and raving like a naughty child in the throes of a tantrum. "Don't you tell me what to do, Fred Holdsworth!" he shouted, unaware that the man before him was his close friend, Bob. His agitation grew and he continued with his onslaught. "When I get home, I'll... I'll... I..." and then the tears came. Leaning back against the wall, he slid slowly down until he was sitting on the floor, his knees bent and his arms wrapped round his legs as if he were clinging on for dear life.

Bob cautiously moved towards him and placed a friendly hand on his shoulder. "Come on, John," he said gently, "Let's get you home."

Meg came running at Bob's request. When she arrived at Hillside Terrace, she found the two men sitting in the kitchen. Her father looked pale and strained, but he managed a smile for her when she came through the door. "I'll be all right," he assured her, "I just had a funny turn and Bob brought me home. I'll go and see old Doctor McNeill in the morning. I probably just need a tonic. It's nothing that a bottle of Metatone won't put right."

Meg wasn't convinced. She looked at Bob Holden questioningly and he made his excuses to leave now that Meg had arrived. "The missis'll wonder where I've got to," he said and signalled to Meg to follow him to the door.

"I'll just see Bob out the front way, Dad. It'll save him walking all the way down the back street," Meg said as she led the way through the front parlour to the door. She took hold of Bob's arm and asked, "What's happened to him, Bob? I don't like the look of him at all."

Bob told her what had been happening at work over the past few weeks and explained that he hadn't thought it so serious until that afternoon. "I thowt it were just tiredness, or summat," he said, "But 'e 'as fot see t'doctor, Meg. 'e does need summat fot put 'im reet." Bob was one of the old school, one of the few true Boltonians who would never lose the local dialect, one proud of his roots and there weren't many of them around those days. "Sorry, Meg," he apologised awkwardly, "I should be trying to speak the Queen's English when I'm talkin' to a teacher, but I'd only be puttin' me aitches where there are none, so don't mind me."

Meg smiled affectionately at him as she thanked him for all his help. She wasn't concerned about Bob's pronunciation. It wouldn't be Bob if he wore his hat and not 'is 'at! She simply recognised his genuine concern for her dad.

On returning to the kitchen, her father spoke. "Put the world to rights, have you? Don't take any notice of Bob. He's an old fuss-pot. I do feel a bit tired though, Meggy." He hadn't called her that since she was a little girl. "I'll go to the doctor's tomorrow, I promise."

"Good," Meg replied, relieved that her dad had at least agreed he needed to talk to the doctor. "Shall I stay over tonight? Phil will be all right with Nicky for one night. I'll give him a ring, shall I?"

"No, I don't need you to stay. I'm okay now, honestly. I've got the phone if I need you."

"And thank God for that," Meg told him, "Who was it who said he didn't need a phone? The state you're in at the moment, you wouldn't have the strength to walk to the end of the street to use the public phone."

"Okay, okay. I promise I'll phone if I don't feel so good." John was adamant. *I'm not an invalid and I can manage on my own. In fact, I want to be alone. I don't want folk making a fuss and bossing me around, not even our Meg.*

~ * ~

He sat in the waiting room at Doctor McNeill's surgery and looked around him. It was a square room with chairs all round the four walls, which supported a few posters about immunisations and healthy diets. Nobody spoke. If anyone came in whom the others recognised, acknowledgement was a nod of the head, a shuffling of chairs to make room for the newcomer to sit and then silence prevailed again save for the sniffs and coughs and wheezing from red-nosed patients. John really didn't know what he was doing there. *I know I promised Meg I'd see the doctor, but I can't remember why.* He was tempted to get up and go home, but he was too tired to move. He leaned back and closed his eyes, thinking that the time might pass a bit more quickly if he nodded off for a while.

He woke with a start when the buzzer sounded loudly. He opened his eyes and everyone had gone except Mrs Roberts. She looked sympathetically at John, knowing that the other patients had just gone in before him and not bothered about him dozing in his seat. "It must be your turn, Mr Hawthorne. You were here when I came in. You go in now. I'll follow you when you've finished." She lived two doors away from him in Hillside Terrace, but they had never been on first name terms and the formality didn't seem out of place.

John didn't comment. He was confused and uncertain where he was, but when the woman pointed to the door marked 'Doctor,' he got up and padded across the waiting room. Once inside, he stood in front of the doctor's desk and waited. "Well, John, what can I do for you today?" Doctor McNeill asked, "It's not often I see you in here."

John just stood there. He didn't know why he was there and couldn't find the words to excuse himself. He was just about to turn and walk out of the surgery when the doctor came from behind his desk and said quietly, "Sit down, John. Let's have a little chat." He noted John's confusion. There was a vacant look in his eyes which had not been there previously and the fact that he had no idea why he was there, all added to the situation. "Do you know where you are, John?"

John shook his head.

"How did you get here? Did Meg bring you?" No response. "What year is it, John?"

"Ah!" John's face brightened. "It's 1960"

Doctor McNeill was delighted and said so.

"I knew that, because it says it there on your calendar," John stated, "Can I go now?"

Doctor McNeill was perturbed. "You can go shortly, John. I'll just give Meg a ring to come and collect you. I don't want you going home on your own."

The doctor informed Meg that he thought John had had a breakdown and that with the medication he had prescribed, he should be much calmer in twenty-four hours. "They're just sedatives, Meg, and they will help him to cope with life's stresses."

Meg was concerned. "I hadn't realised he had any stresses, Doctor McNeil," she whispered, stoically trying to fight back her tears. "How could I not have noticed?"

"These things creep up on us unannounced, Meg," Doctor McNeill reassured her, "He'll be all right when he's had a good rest and a bit of tender loving care."

"He'll certainly get that."

"I know, Meg. Don't worry. He'll be fine. He's a gutsy devil, your dad." The doctor smiled and Meg felt the warmth of his concern.

Meg was in a state. *How could my precious father be so ill and I hadn't noticed?* Here was the strong man who had always been there for all three of his daughters as they were growing up and now she had to be strong for him. She decided that whatever it took, she would take care of him. He deserved the best and come hell, or high water, he would get it.

~ * ~

During the next few weeks, John seemed to live normally and there was no sign of tension, or apprehension. Meg was able to relax a little and hoped against hope that the stress had been a storm in a teacup. Whilst she didn't hassle her father, she did keep an eye on him daily. He had taken time off work on Doctor McNeill's advice and the complete rest seemed to have worked. She had kept the specific details of John's illness from Patty and Abigail. Both were away from home and it was pointless to worry them too much. Meg could cope and for Abigail in particular, it was important that she settled into medical school without being anxious about what was happening at home.

Out of the blue, Meg received a telephone call at seven thirty one Monday morning. It set alarm bells ringing immediately. Nobody telephoned at that time in the morning. "I saw you," the voice said, "snooping in at my window."

"I'm sorry, but who is this?" Meg regretted asking the question almost as soon as the words were out of her mouth. She knew it was her dad. "What's the matter, Dad?" she asked, uncertain how to react to her father's accusation, but then she heard the click and he was gone.

"Who was that?" Philip called from the kitchen where he was having breakfast with Nicholas.

"It was Dad," she answered, puzzled. She was explaining what he had said about the snooping when the telephone rang again. "Gosh, it's like Piccadilly Station in here this morning," and then picking up the phone, "Hello?" she snapped in frustration.

"Will you bring my lawnmower back? I know you took it out of the garden shed. I saw you and I want it back… coming in my house in the middle of the night and helping yourself to whatever you fancy." John was sounding more and more agitated and the phone went down again before Meg was able to respond.

"Call him back," Philip advised, "Tell him he's mistaken. I know he's your dad and much as I get on with him, I think the man's going mad!"

"Oh, Phil, don't say that!" Meg was distraught. "He's obviously stressed about something. What am I supposed to do?"

When the telephone rang again for the umpteenth time in as many minutes, all revealing different outrageous accusations, Meg decided to call Doctor McNeill. He arranged to meet her at Hillside Terrace just as soon as he was able to arrange for his partner to cover his morning surgery.

John, meanwhile, had decided to have bacon and eggs for breakfast. He put a little fat in the frying pan and placed it on the gas ring. He put the kettle on the hob and thought he might just go and pick out a few weeds whilst he waited for the kettle to boil. Half an hour later, Meg and Doctor McNeill arrived. John waved to them from the garden and as if by some strange magnetic force, their eyes were drawn to the back door where smoke was billowing forth. For several seconds, they appeared to be rooted to the spot, but Meg was the first to react and she grabbed a towel from the washing line and dipped it into the watering can by the back door. Covering her face as best she could, she peered through the blue haze to see the frying pan ablaze. Instinctively, she threw the wet towel over the pan to smother the flames and edged forward to turn off the gas. The kitchen was a mess, a grey film having covered the walls and ceiling and there was an acrid smell of burnt fat and hot metal hanging around, making it difficult to breathe. She opened wide the door and windows, hoping that the fresh air would circulate and make the room a bit more accessible. She would have to wash down the walls and clean everything to make the kitchen functional again. "What a bloody mess!" she whispered and excused herself in the knowledge that her father would not approve of her using expletives.

Outside in the garden, Doctor McNeill and John were discussing plants and flowers. The good doctor needed to talk rationally with his patient and, keeping his mind occupied with something John enjoyed was the best way to give some reason and mental equilibrium to the situation. John appeared to be unaware of the problem in the kitchen which in itself was odd as the smoke was swirling around and leaving a pungent smell everywhere. Meg took a deep breath and tried to explain, hoping his mood swings wouldn't prevent her from telling the truth... "so you see, when you went into the garden, you forgot that you had left the frying pan on the hob," she said as gently as she was able without sounding too agitated herself. She couldn't help thinking that she was speaking to her father as though he were a child, but it seemed to do the trick.

"Oh my goodness!" John exclaimed, "Why on earth did I do that?"

Doctor McNeill took the opportunity to reason with the confused man in front of him. "John, you and I have known each other for a long time, wouldn't you say so?" he said.

"Oh yes, a long, long time."

"Well, I think I'd like you to have some tests done at the hospital to see what's causing these upsets." He hoped John would readily accept his judgment. "I'll make an appointment for you. Is that all right?" He recalled the morning weeks prior when John had visited the surgery. *The signs were all there and I prescribed tranquillisers to calm him down. Perhaps I ought to have been more acutely aware of his symptoms then, but it is difficult to assess anyone who shows signs of mental disorder.*

Now, I have to act as quickly as possible to help this man, not only to help John, but also to reassure myself that I truly acted responsibly under the circumstances.

Almost as if by telepathy, Meg took the doctor's hand. "Don't worry," she said. "Who could possibly have known what was going to happen?"

John didn't argue and Meg agreed to stay with him at Hillside Terrace until the appointment came through. The appointment was in fact arranged fairly quickly and within a few days, John was due at the hospital at nine o'clock in the morning. Meg made sure he was up and ready by eight-thirty.

The journey to the hospital on Chorley New Road was happily uneventful. Meg didn't force the conversation thinking that John would talk to her when he felt the need. She felt strange and strained, but had no wish to upset her dad and so kept quiet. He seemed to be a willing patient and hadn't objected at all to the request to see the consultant psychiatrist. She wasn't sure he realised whom he was going to see, but ignorance was bliss and as he hadn't made a fuss, it was a case of so far, so good.

Mr. Hartington, the consultant, asked Meg to wait outside whilst he did his initial examination. It seemed like hours sitting alone in the long, cold corridor. Her thoughts were confused and she really didn't know what to think. *Dad's not old and yet Doctor McNeill had mentioned dementia...surely not. It's perhaps a breakdown. Dad has had so much on his plate for a long time, since Mam died. Perhaps it's taken its toll; perhaps Abi, Patty and I have been too much for him; perhaps we ought to have noticed that he was getting tired. Oh God, what have we done?*

Her mind was tormented and she stared at the door of the consulting room, willing it to open. When it did, it startled her. "You can come in now, Mrs Wilkinson." The attending nurse smiled as Meg stood with a start. She walked to the door, uncertain of what to expect and she could see that her father was agitated.

Mr Hartington pointed to the chair next to John and she went to sit, taking hold of his hand to reassure him. That was mistake number one. John snatched his hand away and looked so angry that Meg was almost afraid.

"Don't you dare touch me!" he shouted, "You brought me here for this young upstart to tell me I can't live on my own, that I can't go back to my house... *my* house! Well, nobody tells me what I can, or cannot do... *NOBODY,* do you hear?" He stood up and stamped his feet like a naughty child. "I *shall* go home and neither you nor anybody else will stop me!"

Meg felt the tears burning her eyes. She couldn't speak. The man in front of her wasn't her father, the gentle man who had shared her joy when she did well at school, who had hugged her when she needed to be reassured, who had shown her that life was for living and for making it a success, that happiness was in sharing all the good things in life with people that you love, that the most important thing that mattered in one's life was one's family. Now, what she saw before her was someone raving like a lunatic and it frightened her. The nurse gently took John's hand. She led him to a side room and strangely, he followed like a little lamb to the slaughter.

Mr Hartington stood up then and went to put an encouraging arm around Meg's shoulders. "Your father is in the early stages of dementia," he told her, "You are going to have to be very patient with him, very patient and very brave."

"But he's only fifty years old," she implored, "Surely he's too young to be going senile." This whole situation had to be a bad dream and soon she would waken up to find the sun shining on her life again.

Mr Hartington sat on the chair where John had been sitting and he took hold of Meg's hand for reassurance. "Sometimes a younger person develops the symptoms and we call it pre-senile dementia. In such cases, the symptoms develop slowly over a number of years, but occasionally, a more rapid onset takes place. You may find that your father will have good days when there doesn't appear to be anything wrong. Other days, he will be totally confused and frustrated and that's when he will need constant attention."

Meg allowed the tears to flow. It was like she had lost her father and she was grieving for him. She determined at that moment to do whatever she had to do to make his life as happy as possible. That much she owed him.

She arranged to stay at Hillside Terrace for a couple of nights. Philip took Nicholas to stay with his mother and the little boy thought it was a great adventure to be staying at Nana and Grandpa's house. John appeared to be calm and went to bed early. Meg sat up late trying to come to terms with the situation and wondered how best to deal with it. She had to talk to John whilst he was still able to understand and she would have to bide her time and wait for a 'good day,' as Mr Hartington had put it.

"Dad? You know you haven't been feeling well just recently," she said to him when she felt he was calm enough to listen.

"I know, love," John agreed, "I feel that tired sometimes, even getting up in a morning is too much trouble."

"Well, that's what I want to talk to you about..."

"Not now, Meg. I'm going for a lie down. You wouldn't believe how much digging I've had to do to get the garden ready for my potato crop," he told her, even though his gardening tools hadn't seen the light of day for months.

"All right," Meg reassured him, "We'll talk another time."

"I said *NOT NOW*, Meg! Do as you're told. You're getting too cheeky for a ten year old. Now just get on with your homework and less of your lip!" And John stormed off upstairs, slamming the hallway door as he went through it.

The mood swings happened so quickly, up one minute, down the next. As predicted, there were days when John appeared to be coping normally and then he would do something totally out of character. The deciding factor came when he thought he would go into town to do some shopping. Bolton town centre was approximately five miles away from Belford and it was too far to walk. When he arrived at the bus stop, there was no one there. The road was deserted and rather than stand around waiting, he decided to set off walking. He could always flag the bus down if one came. Bus drivers were very obliging and would stop anywhere on the country lanes whenever and wherever they were needed. John walked for miles and there was no sign of a bus. He kept turning round to see if he could catch a glimpse of a vehicle in the distance, but there was absolutely nothing on the road and it was so quiet. He couldn't understand it. Where were the buses when you wanted one? When you didn't need one, three, or four would come together. At four o'clock in the morning, a patrolling police car spotted John at Bull Hill, almost in the town of Darwin. *Thank the Lord,* John thought, *a bus at last.*

"Well now, my good man, what are you doing out at this hour?" the kindly police constable asked, noting that the man in question was in his pyjamas and slippers and must be freezing to death.

"I'm going to my mother's in Preston. How come your bus is so late? She'll have my tea ready and it'll be stone cold by now." John was completely unaware that his behaviour was causing great concern to the driver of the vehicle that had stopped to give him a lift. Once in the car, the policeman drove straight to the hospital and endeavoured to ascertain where this disturbed gentleman had come from.

John had had to be sedated and had been admitted to the psychiatric ward before his records were found and Meg was informed. She had been exhausted that night after a difficult day.

Once her dad was asleep, she had retired to bed herself and was away as soon as her head touched the pillow. When the telephone rang at six-thirty in the morning, she was shocked to know he had been found wandering the streets. "You must be mistaken," she told the ward sister, "he's in bed here." Hurriedly, she put down the phone and went upstairs to check. She went cold, returning quickly to talk to the nurse. "I'm so sorry," she said. "How on earth did he get out without my knowing?"

"Don't worry," the nurse said, "He's not the first to do such a thing and he won't be the last. The main thing is that he was found before he got into trouble. We'll talk to you when you come to visit him. He's obviously in need of special care."

Meg was devastated. She felt that she had failed her dad and no amount of convincing from her husband that she was blameless would alleviate her guilt.

Eleven

Patty

Patty felt guilty that she didn't consciously admit to missing her mother until she was eighteen years old. She was too young to understand what was happening when her mammy had died and she had instinctively clung to Meg, her older sister. For the first few weeks, she had followed Meg around like a little lapdog, hanging onto her hand for comfort when she felt lost. Her daddy had been too consumed with grief to notice what was happening, even though he had tried from the outset to care for his children, perhaps overcompensating most of the time. By the time their lives had resumed some semblance of normality, he was happy to allow Meg to help with the little ones and Patty eventually achieved her independence following Meg's example.

When she was four years old, she followed in Meg's footsteps to Belford Primary School, but Meg had already moved on to Great Moor Grammar so she felt completely alone. Her gran had walked her to school as she held onto the handle of the big Silver Cross pram that contained the sleeping baby Abigail. She vividly remembered that. She also remembered forlornly looking around the big room full of tables and chairs and automatically reaching out for the nearest hand. It belonged to Rita. They stood silently, big eyes wide open and full of unshed tears, hanging on to each other for the security they had left at home.

"Will you be my friend?" Patty asked when they had been ushered onto little chairs by the nice lady with a big smile and a sing-song voice. Rita nodded enthusiastically, her red pigtails bobbing up and down as though they were attached to her head with wire and her green eyes sparkling with expectation.

"What's your name?" she asked. "Mine's Rita Teresa Morton."

"Patience Christine Hawthorne, but I'm really Patty. Meg, she's my big sister, says Patty suits me best. Have you got a sister? I've got two."

"No," Rita told her, "But I've got a big brother, Eddie. He's called Edward really and he hates it when I call him Teddy." They giggled. "Boys are stupid!" and they giggled again, nudging each other playfully, their initial fears forgotten.

Rita and Patty were inseparable from then on. 'Rita said her dad works down the pit," she told the family one afternoon as they were having tea.

"That must be a hard job," John said, showing interest. "It'll be very dark down the mine..."

"Pit," Patty informed him, "Not a mind."

"Okay, love." he agreed, trying to hide his amusement. "It must be very dark down the pit then."

"It is, Dad. Rita says his eyes are all red when he comes home from work and his hands and face are black. Rita says he chases her round the garden trying to daub her with his dirty hands. What's daub, Dad?"

John gave a relieved smile. Trying not to show amusement was too hard a task when your children unwittingly said hilarious things. "It means smear...you know, spread yucky stuff where you don't want it."

"Oh! Rita says that sometimes he rubs her cheeks with his dirty hands... that's not very nice, is it, Dad?" Patty's face was a picture of complete distaste.

"He's only playing, pet. I bet Rita squeals and giggles all the time she's running round the garden like you did when our Meg chased you with a worm. Do you remember?"

"I do! I do! And she dangled it right in front of my face! It was 'orrid!"

Meg came in with Abigail. She'd taken her to the lavatory for the third time since she'd arrived home from school. "I'll be glad when she's old enough to do a wee on her own," she said. "I think she just likes flushing the chain! What was 'orrid, Patty?"

"You and that worm! I'll get you back one day."

"You and whose army? Come back when you're older and uglier!" Meg knew she was winding up her sister, but did it anyway.

"Dad! Stop her. She always says things like that. She's awful to me. She never says things like that to our Abi."

"'Cos Abi's too young, ninny! Mind you, she wouldn't go off on one like you do," Meg continued, deliberately teasing her.

"Shut up, Meg," Patty shouted, 'I'm fed up of you and your big mouth. You say that again and I'll..."

"Stop it, the pair of you," John intervened. 'What happened to the two sisters who used to do everything together?"

Meg glared at Patty and mumbled sullenly under her breath, "They grew up."

"Meg!" John's raised voice was enough and a moody silence ensued. If Dad shouted, he must be annoyed. He, himself, knew that parenting didn't come with a manual and whilst he wanted to be all things nice to his little girls, he sometimes wondered if he should lay down the law more stringently. *I'll just have to muddle through and hope for the best,* he thought. *So long as they know right from wrong, they should be all right... please God.*

~ * ~

Patty discovered the library when she was eight years old. Mrs Tattersall had taken them on a visit from school and whilst she had always had a book for Christmas and birthdays for as long as she could remember, she was astounded at the number of books under one roof. She took to going to the library once a week at first and then more often when she learned to read more quickly. The first time she went on her own, she crept in quietly because the silence in the old building told her that she mustn't make any noise. An old man coughed and she spun round quickly at the sound of a loud "SH! SH!" from the librarian who was making more noise herself than the old man who had coughed. Patty stifled a giggle and composed herself before proudly handing in the form that her dad had signed so that she might become a member of the library. The lady gave her a ticket with her name on it. It was blue and had a little pocket on the front where the book ticket would go when she chose it.

She spent what seemed like hours wandering around the big, wooden shelves before the librarian crept up behind her and whispered that she should go to the children's section.

"You aren't allowed to borrow these books," she explained and led her to the lower shelves where the children's books were housed. "I don't think your mother would like it if you took these home." There was a moment of awkward silence, but Patty didn't think it necessary to tell the lady that she didn't have a mother. In fact, she had never told anybody that. The people who knew, never mentioned it and she felt comfortable with that so she didn't see the need to admit it to those who didn't know about her situation. The mere thought of actually saying that her mother had died left her cold and embarrassed. She couldn't explain why, she just preferred not to talk about it.

The children's section offered her everything she could possibly have wanted... *The Water Babies, The Treasure Seekers, Black Beauty* by Anna Sewell, *Little Women* by Louisa M Alcott and her favourite Enid Blyton books. Patty thought she was in Heaven and she read them all.

"Go to sleep, Patty," Meg demanded, "You'll be too tired for school in the morning. I can't be doing with you reading under the bedclothes every night. If Dad knew, he'd go mad."

"Aw Meg, don't tell! Please don't tell. Just let me read to the end of this chapter and then I'll go to sleep... promise."

"How many pages?"

"Two... well, two and a bit," Patty fibbed.

"Okay, but no more. I'm tired and I can't sleep with the torchlight shining through the sheet!" Meg really was tired and Patty was pushing her luck for the third night in a row. *I wish I could have my own room,* she thought wistfully, *then I could have one of those new portable radios and listen to Dick Barton every night followed by The Archers. That*

Philip Archer sounds lovely, almost as lovely as Dickie Valentine and Dennis Lotis.

"Come on now, Patty. Lights out... *NOW!*"

Patty and Rita had been best friends from the time they had clung to each other that first day in school. By the time they were eleven, they had learned to swim together at the swimming club, had learned to skip with a rope and to play two-balls, had made daisy chains on Rita's front lawn, had grown pinks and nasturtiums in Patty's little plot at Hillside Terrace, had made slides in the icy snow... in fact had done everything together except visit the library. Patty had tried to get Rita interested in reading, but she had failed.

"I'm not interested in books, Patty. I'd rather go on the swings in the park, or kick a ball around with Micky Finlay," she explained to her unbelieving friend.

"Micky Finlay? Oooh Rita Morton! Micky Finlay? Do you love 'im?" Patty shrieked, throwing her hands up in dismay.

Rita laughed. "Of course I don't love 'im! Only grown-ups love each other, but I like 'im a lot. He kissed me in the park the other night." She looked coyly at Patty who stood there speechless, her arms flapping up and down by her sides as though she were about to take flight.

When she resumed her composure, Patty asked earnestly, "Did he kiss you on the lips, because if he did, it means you're married. You might even have a baby. Flippin' 'eck, Rita, what have you done?"

"Don't be daft, Patty. I won't have a baby. You have to do other things to have a baby. My cousin who's a nurse told me."

"What other things?" Patty had no idea what Rita was talking about as she explained to the incredulous Patty the intricacies of the love act that makes babies.

"That's not true," she announced confidently. "I don't believe you or your cousin. My mam and dad wouldn't do that and they had three children. It's disgusting, so shut up, Rita, and go and play football with your precious Micky Finlay. I'm going home."

Patty recalled the conversation clearly and later surmised that was the day when she and Rita began to outgrow each other. When Patty went to Great Moor Grammar, Rita went to the secondary modern school and their friendship just drifted apart. There was no animosity; it just happened and neither of them felt the need to keep in touch after that.

When she was fifteen, Patty began to realise that boys could really be quite interesting. She had noticed a boy in the church choir who was so good looking and she had sat in the front pew making eyes at him, unbeknown to the rest of her family. She joined the youth club because he was always there and they began to talk as they listened to Frank Sinatra and Perry Como. Eventually he asked if he might walk her home and Patty was delighted. When he kissed her goodnight, she just melted and realised that Rita Morton had obviously experienced this at the tender age of eleven. "The fast cat!" she said to herself as she lay in bed that night and hugged herself tight, dreaming of the next time Colin Harrop would enfold her in his arms again and kiss her on the lips. This time she knew that she wouldn't get pregnant.

Her time at Great Moor was totally gratifying. Her school life was comparatively uneventful, but her social life through church activities was booming. She had joined the Girls Friendly Society and the Girl Guides and, whilst she would rather curl up with a book than be involved in sporting activities, she enjoyed the camping and the craftwork that these clubs encouraged. After she had taken her O levels, she made an announcement over dinner, much to the surprise of her family. "I'm going to do maths, further maths and economics at Advanced level," she told them.

"My goodness, Patty," John said, "Those are subjects that will take you into a man's world, aren't they?"

"Dad! Why would you say that? A woman is just as capable as a man in studying mathematics and economics."

"Dad expects you to do Domestic Science and Needlework and become a teacher like me," Meg broke in, still occasionally light-heartedly prepared to make jibes at her sister.

"No, I don't." John was quick to make amends. "It's just that it's all a bit alien to my world for a girl to become a mathematician, or a scientist. My, my how the world's changed! What would you want to do afterwards with those subjects, Patty, if you don't want to teach? Teaching is such a good job for a woman."

"Accountancy, or maybe I could become an actuary and work in the City," Patty reasoned with them. "I'm going to apply to the London School of Economics, but as it's so difficult to get in, I'll apply to Nottingham and Exeter as well."

"You've got it all worked out, I see," her dad said, "so I'm not going to stand in your way. I've always impressed upon you that life is what you make it, so go for it. I can't deny I'll miss you if you go so far away. I always thought, of the three of you, you'd be the one who would stay close to home and that's a fact. My little Patty is flying the coop."

"Oh Dad, stop it!" Patty knew they would all be surprised at her choices. "It's something I have to do, Dad. I've always been the middle child, I always will be, I can't change that, but I don't want to have to follow in Meg's footsteps all my life. In a way, I want to show Abi that she can make her own choices too when it's her turn. We have both been too influenced by our Meg, you know."

"Is that such a bad thing?" John enquired incredulously.

"No, but Meg's a teacher and I don't want to do that. I want to do things in my own way. Does that seem selfish?"

"Of course it doesn't, love. You wouldn't be a Hawthorne if you weren't determined to make your own way," John continued and then in a lighter mood, "What will Colin Harrop do when you go away?"

Patty gasped, but grinned mischievously, "He'll do what he's been doing for the past few months... walk Jeannie Ashcroft home from the youth club." She stood up with her head held high and said, "Anyway, he could only talk about motor bikes and how he was going to win the Isle of Man TT races when he gets his 500cc Triumph, so good luck to him." As a parting gesture, she screwed up her nose and said, "And he always had engine grease down his fingernails." Then very haughtily, "There's absolutely no way I could put up with that!"

Patty worked her socks off to gain a place at LSE, but was disappointed when she didn't make the recalls. Undeterred, she gave good account of herself at Nottingham and at Exeter. She was offered places at both and chose to go to Nottingham for no other reason than she felt comfortable in the place.

~ * ~

She lay on her bed in the hall of residence in Woollaton. Her new roommate perched on the end of her own bed at the opposite side of the room. "Why did you choose Nottingham, Rosie?" Patty asked.

"Because it's not far from Birmingham and I can go home when I want to, I suppose. My mum didn't want me to go too far away. Pathetic, or what?" Rosie said, "How about you?"

"When I applied, I wanted to go as far away as possible. My dad didn't think I would because I've always been the quiet home bird. I think I was making a stand. I thought I had a chance at LSE, but guess what…"

"Second best then, but what did your mum think?" Rosie was curious, knowing that her own mother had mollycoddled her through life thus far.

Patty stared up at the ceiling. She didn't answer immediately. "My dad's a widower," she said quietly, "and you're the first person I have ever told. My mother died when I was two."

"Oh I'm sorry," Rosie said, "I wasn't prying. I just thought that girls usually stay close to their mums… Sorry, Patty."

"Don't be," Patty reassured her. "I feel better now that I've said it. Thanks."

There was pensive silence in the room for a moment or two and then Rosie decided that they should go to the common room to meet the other freshers. "Good idea," Patty agreed and thus began her life as an undergraduate.

At the end of the first semester, she had established herself as a leader in her group and she threw herself into university life with gusto. "Where's the timid little Patty we all know and love?" Meg asked when the confident Patty arrived home for the summer break.

"All right, Meg. I had to break free of your apron strings sometime. I love you dearly, but it was a bit of a pain having to walk in your shadow. You were a bit cocky too sometimes, you know."

"Moi? Surely not!" Meg admonished her. "But I love the new Patty and I can see that Nottingham is good for you. Any boys on the scene?"

"Oh truckloads of them, but not in my bed!"

"Hold on… It's a good job Abi isn't around to hear stuff like that." Meg could hardly believe that Patty had changed so much.

"Our Abigail is wiser than you give her credit for. She's sixteen going on sixty and a Hawthorne through and through. Dad dotes on her much more than he did on us. She gets away with much more than we ever did. I know he always does his best for us all, but when it comes to Abi... well, you know as well as I do. I don't have to spell it out."

"Yes I do know, but she'll be okay. She has a stubborn streak in her that would put a donkey to shame!" Meg felt responsible for her sisters even then and Patty knew more than anybody that she would always feel the same, however old they were.

"Meg?"

"What?"

"Do you ever tell strangers that you have no mother?" Patty eyed her older sister carefully.

"What are you asking, Patty? I do have a mother, so do you. She hasn't been around for a long time, but she's still my mam. I won't ever forget her." Meg couldn't talk about it without becoming emotional.

"I feel terrible, Meg," Patty stumbled over her words. "I have never been able to tell anybody that my mam died until I told Rosie at the beginning of term. When I was younger, I felt different to other children who had a mam *and* a dad at home. It embarrassed me to admit that mam had died and I just wanted to be like all the rest."

"But you *were* like all the rest, Patty. You were loved and you didn't miss out on much," Meg told her.

"I know, but I was in denial, Meg. I denied Mam the right of being my mam for all those years. I didn't talk about her, not even to you, or Dad and certainly not to Abigail. I didn't admit to missing her until my first day at uni, not even to myself and the strangest sensation happened to me."

"Oh heck, Patty, what can I say? I suppose we all had to cut her out of our lives physically, but I never went one day, still don't, when I didn't think about her. We all cope with a death in the family as best we can. Don't feel guilty about it. Mam would understand. I truly believe that."

"Well, it's hard for me to say this, but I definitely felt her presence when I arrived at the door of Woollaton House. It was a funny sensation, not frightening, more reassuring. I was thinking that was my home for the next few years and I shivered at the thought of leaving Hillside Terrace and all that was familiar to me. But then I felt a warm surge of love run through my whole body and my confidence grew. It wasn't a life-changing experience, but something I felt inside and only I could understand. Does that make sense to you, Meg?"

"I understand, love. Mam is never far away from everything we do. I often dream about her and I think that's her way of taking care of us. Oh Patty, let's not be maudlin about it. Let's just accept that from now on we'll never be alone in our hour of need and you know I'm always here for you." Meg hung on to her memories and learned by them.

"Don't tell Dad, though," Patty pleaded. "I wouldn't want to upset him."

Twelve

Stephen Ross was thirty years old when he met Patty Hawthorne. She was twenty-two. She had breezed through her interview and impressed the panel with her confidence and yet there was a delicacy about her that made Steve think she might not be up to the job. He had observed her at a distance as she waited in the office after her initial appraisal and noted that in quiet moments, she was deep in thought and had a vulnerable quality about her. "Hello, Miss Hawthorne," he said as he approached her, "How are you feeling after that gruelling experience?"

"Not too bad," Patty declared, "but I wouldn't like to do it every day." She grinned at Mr Ross and admitted, "There were some pretty stern people on that panel."

"All there in their own right, I'm afraid. Accountancy is a cut-throat business, you know. You have to realise what you're letting yourself in for. Whoever takes up the position will be at the cutting edge of the business world." He shrewdly regarded Patty for any sign of nervousness.

"I know that," she told him. "I wouldn't be here if I thought it would be easy. If you knew my dad, you'd understand that no Hawthorne would ever shy away from a challenge." And Steve's earlier concerns were instantly allayed.

Patty found her niche in the big accountancy world and Steve was her first boss. She still had a penchant for getting on with the job quietly, but often viewed a serious situation with a light-hearted acceptance that what had to be done had to be done, whilst others around her moaned and groaned when the going got tough. Early in her career, Steve had asked her to investigate the financial situation of a big electrical company. Shareholders were becoming concerned that their annual commission hadn't been paid. It was a daunting task, not least because Steve, himself, was a shareholder and although at that point, they had hardly made eye contact, she needed to create a good impression to prove she was up to the job. Night after night, she pored over the accounts as she did the yearly audit, and eventually, she found where the deficit lay. She went into Steve's office the following morning.

"Wyvern Electrics," she announced, "I've seen the light!"

Steve looked over his half-spectacles, grinned broadly and then fell about laughing. Patty regarded him curiously and then grinned too as she realised what she had said. "What a cracker!" he said, appreciating Patty's shared sense of humour, "You'll have to switch on to investigation procedures on a regular basis, or was it just a flash in the pan? I hope it wasn't a short in the circuit!"

"Well, I was fused with enthusiasm!" she added, flirting with the new found humorous side of her boss.

"Electrifying!" Steve declared, acknowledging that he had found his match in the deceivingly delicate form of Patty Hawthorne. From then on, they worked closely together on various projects and when he eventually asked her out to dinner, the seeds of a beautiful relationship had been sown.

As they stood outside the door of Patty's flat after a wonderful evening in the West End, Steve held Patty close and nuzzled her hair. She was comfortable with him and they had recently let it be known at the office that they were an item.

"Listen, PCH," he said quietly.

"I'm listening. I always listen to you, oh wise one!" she teased, "But why are you being so serious? You only call me PCH when you're being very serious, or when you are telling me off!"

"I never tell you off," he told her, "I wouldn't dare!" and he laughed at his little joke.

"What about that time when I shredded your notes?"

"Oh well, we can forget about that. I never told you that I'd kept another copy...sorry," Steve admitted sheepishly.

"You bugger! And there was I expecting the *hasta la vista, baby*!" Patty was about to hit him.

"Marry me," he said and he got down on one knee on the doorstep. Taking her hand, he asked, "Will you marry me, Patty?"

Never had Patty felt so overcome with emotion. Tears ran down her cheeks as she found the only word necessary. "Yes, I will Mr Ross... but I'm not floating down the aisle in a frilly white frock!"

When Patty and Steve married, it was in St Peter's Church, Belford and true to her word Patty wore a simple gown of pale turquoise silk. Steve's family had travelled north and were the only guests other than the Hawthorne family. Never wanting the limelight, Patty was happy that her marriage to Steve was romantically personal. John had walked down the aisle to give his daughter away, but nobody could be sure that he knew what was happening. He was quiet, and helped by Meg and Abigail, he managed to get through the day without too much hassle.

Thirteen

Abigail in the big, wide world

At the end of September 1960, Abigail packed her belongings into Philip's car, ready to begin the journey of a lifetime. Her brother-in-law had agreed to drive her to Manchester so that Meg might stay with her father. The pretext was that Philip knew the ropes, having been a university student himself. John's symptoms had not been so apparent at that stage and although Abigail had seen how tired he was on occasions, she had not equated it with the onset of an illness. Abigail, his youngest child, was leaving home. She had clung to him as she said goodbye and he had placed his hands on her shoulders, looking into her bright eyes, glistening with tears. "You go and do yourself proud, love. Remember that you get nothing in this world without hard work. You'll reap the rewards, I know you will. Don't forget that I'm always here for you. We are family and family matters," and with that she had been driven off along the road to her future.

That had been before Meg had disclosed that her dad wasn't well. When she offered to go back to live at home, Meg wouldn't hear of it. "You'll do no such thing, Abs. He just needs a rest and he'll be fine. I'll keep you informed and perhaps it might be best not to phone too often. I'll tell him that you'll phone when he's feeling better. If you just do as he advised and work hard, that's all the medicine he'll need to make him well again."

Abigail wasn't convinced that her father was merely under the weather as Meg was suggesting, but she knew that she had to concentrate on her studies and after all, university life needed to be lived to the full. Her arrival in Manchester heralded a wealth of new experiences just waiting to materialise.

Manchester's Faculty of Medicine was one of the best and most respected establishments in the country. Situated in the heart of the city, it was renowned throughout the world for its teaching methods and its first class training of members of the medical profession. Abigail was certain she had made the right choice even though her sixth form tutor had tried to persuade her to apply to Cambridge. She had steadfastly stuck to her decision to submit her forms to Manchester and when she was offered a place, she delighted in the fact that this was the first big step she had taken on her own and she had made it. *I am looking forward to the next five years of study. To some people,* she thought, *five years seems like a lifetime, but not to me. This is the only way to realise my dream.*

She had opted to live out of Halls and the university administration department had allocated her to a students' house in neighbouring Salford. There were four people sharing the house and whilst the facilities were rather basic, they were adequate. Abi hadn't met her housemates until Philip had dropped her off. He had helped her in with her luggage and made sure she was all right before he left. "I'll be off now, Abi. The sooner you get settled in, the better," he told her. "Good luck, little sis."

"Thanks, Phil, I really appreciate your help, but I'm glad you've decided not to hang around for the others to arrive," she admitted as he left. "I need to feel that I'm standing on my own two feet,"

Philip smiled and gave her a hug. "I had picked up the vibes anyway, so I won't stay a moment longer than necessary."

"You're the best, Phil,' she told him. "What would I do without you?"

The house was a big, Georgian, terraced property which had been refurbished to accommodate students. There was a spacious entrance hall with a gigantic dresser and a hallstand. Opposite the front door, a regal staircase wound its way up to the four bedrooms and a large bathroom with a shower. The comfortable lounge was through a door on the right of the entrance hall and at the back of the house was an enormous kitchen with a dining table and six chairs and the most glorious kitchen range that reminded Abigail of home. The Belfast sink was obviously new and gleaming white and there was a functional cream and green metal kitchenette. Abi smiled to herself. *I hope we have enough food to put in it,* she contemplated. *At least Meg has set me up with a big box of groceries. Meg has lived the student life and knows all about empty larders and lack of cash.*

Each girl was to have her own room. The furniture was old, but well-maintained and each room housed a single bed, a wardrobe and chest of drawers as well as a very functional desk and chair. The walls were washed in pastel shades and there was a gigantic notice board above the desk upon which a note was pinned— 'Students are requested not to use Sellotape on the notice board or walls. All posters and notices must be pinned to the board and not stuck on the walls. Thank you.' For convenience, each bedroom was numbered and each girl's allocated room was written on her key fob. Abigail was in room two, a first floor front room which got the morning sun, making it warm during the day and cool at night. Perfect.

The other girls arrived as Abi was finding her way around the kitchen. First Jenny came in, loaded with cases and boxes, and the other two seemed to arrive together. Jenny was from Caerleon, South Wales; Ruth had travelled south from Northumberland and Anne was from the Midlands. They were all from very different backgrounds, but with introductions over, they were chatting and giggling as though they had known each other forever. That was indeed a stroke of luck. So far, so good.

Jenny was a small, plump girl, her dark hair pulled severely over her head and secured in a matronly bun at the back of her neck. She was going to study history and archaeology and waxed lyrical in typically Welsh strains about her interest in the past... how Wales was full of fascinating historical intrigue and without appearing arrogant, she made it very clear that patriotism featured prominently in her choice of subject. "I was also inspired by the discovery that Piltdown Man had been a forgery."

"How can you be inspired by something so negative?" Ruth had asked, puzzled by Jenny's obvious fascination.

"It's easy, *cariad*," Jenny had assured her, the lovely lilt in her voice confirming her passion for her subject, "It made me determined to show that we can find our roots, however many fly-by-nights try to cheat the world out of its heritage." It was a simplistic way of looking at it, but Jenny's enthusiasm by far outweighed any sceptical views of Ruth, or any other person for that matter.

Ruth was an English and American Literature scholar. She was more concerned with Shakespeare and F Scott Fitzgerald than with any old relics dug up after of thousands of years, although when she thought about it, she conceded that she was dealing with the world's heritage too, in delving into the minds of powerful writers, past and present. She was a Geordie, strong-willed and opinionated, but with the endearing quality of self-acceptance. "What you see is what you get!" she told them. Her sense of fun was infectious and there were very few serious moments when Ruth was around. When she slipped into her broad Tyneside accent, it took a very keen ear to understand what she was saying. The others collapsed into fits of laughter just trying to pick out the odd word here and there.

Anne was the quiet one and she reminded Abigail of Patty. She didn't say much, but when she did speak, it was usually pearls of wisdom and full of common sense. She was a shrewd judge of character with a keen wit and was a most agreeable house companion. The other girls loved her for her sincere friendship right from the start. She was studying Modern Languages with geography as an additional subject. She wanted to work with an airline, but felt that she could just as well be employed as an interpreter. "I don't need to decide yet," she said, "I'll wait to see which way the world is going when I do my finals." That, to the others, seemed reasonably sound judgment and typical of Anne's attitude to life in general.

The first few days were mad. There were literally hundreds of people milling around looking for lecture rooms, searching for tutors, signing up for activities and joining clubs, registering with the Students' Union and making sure that text books and stationery were available before lectures began. It was not a situation for the faint-hearted and even the usually confident and competent Abigail felt that she was swimming against the tide on occasions. However, after the first week, everything seemed to fall into place.

Abi's tutor group consisted of eight medical students, five of whom were young men. The other two females were mature students, one in her early thirties who was making a career change after several years in the RAF and the other had trained as a nurse, but had decided to take the more ambitious route into the medical professions. Both had children and didn't appear eager, Abigail noted, to involve themselves in university life like the younger students. The small groups attended seminars with their tutors, but the main lectures were attended by all medical students and these were held in the large lecture theatres. All students were expected to take responsibility for their own learning and any prolonged lapse in application to one's studies would be dealt with severely by the university authorities.

The lecture theatre was full on the first day of the term. It was Abigail's nineteenth birthday and she couldn't think of a better way to spend it. Everyone was nervous. It showed in their faces, but there was no mistaking the anticipation and eagerness in all of the young men and women as they waited for the Professor of Medicine to appear. There was a general buzz of expectation about the place, which was replaced by sudden silence when a bespectacled, black-gowned, diminutive, yet imposing figure appeared at the lectern at the front of the theatre. There was a shuffling of papers and of feet as the students stood to show respect for the man who was to be their tutor, mentor and mediator for the next few years. He waved a nonchalant hand to signal them to be seated and there began the first lesson.

Two hours passed reasonably quickly, but there were audible sighs of relief at the end of the session. Abigail had sat engrossed throughout, taking copious notes and had not noticed the admiring glances from the student several places to her left. As people started to move from their seats, he waited at the end of the row until she moved towards him. "Hello," he said with an almost arrogant air of admiration, "Allow me to introduce myself..."

Abigail was taken aback. Of all the people around her, this boy was surely the most handsome person she had ever set eyes on. He was tall and blond with dark brown eyes, unusual in one so fair. His manner exuded confidence and breeding. "I'm James... and you are?"

"Abigail. Abigail Hawthorne. Hello to you too."

"Will you join me for coffee?" James invited, "We don't have to be back here until two-thirty, so it gives us time to get to know each other."

Quickly assessing the situation and deciding it could do no harm, Abigail accepted the invitation. She had not spoken at length to anyone in her group thus far and it would be good not to be left feeling awkward and alone amongst new company, so she followed James to the refectory where he ordered two coffees and guided her to the end of a long table near the window which looked down on to busy Oxford Road.

"And if I may make so bold to ask, where is home for you, Abigail?" James enquired, appearing to be genuinely interested and not simply making polite conversation.

"I'm from a little place called Belford, just outside Bolton," she told him. "And please call me Abi; everyone does. Abigail is so formal."

Conversation was easy, not strained and James revealed himself as James Sylvester-Jones, son and heir of Lord Lionel Sylvester-Jones, Seventh Earl of Trethowen. Abi thought she ought to feel in awe of this young man, but his charm and wit had made her feel comfortable in his presence and after all, he was a medical student just as she was.

The first few weeks flew by and the four girls in the Salford house settled quickly into their routine. They were all thoroughly enjoying their new-found independence and although they contacted their respective homes each weekend, they were in no hurry to rush back to the bosom of their families. Abigail had been assured by Meg that all was well at home and so she felt that she ought to throw herself into university life and soak up the atmosphere of the monumental place of learning.

James Sylvester-Jones had made himself Abi's constant companion, although she really had not encouraged him to be more than a friend. When the time came around for the Freshers' Ball, he was eager that she would go as his date. "Please say yes, Abi," he pleaded, "I would love to take you and it will be such a splendid occasion."

"Oh all right then," Abi conceded, "But don't get any ideas! We go just as friends."

"Oh, jolly good show!" James enthused, his plum-in-the mouth accent making Abi grin at her exuberant suitor. "What are you grinning at?"

"You!" She was always honest, sometimes to a fault. Honesty was the best policy. That way others would always know that she meant what she said and would accept her word. That was a lesson learned the hard way when she was growing up and she remembered as if it were yesterday such had been its impact...

...I was nine years old and had desperately wanted a bicycle for my birthday, but Dad told me he couldn't afford to buy one and as Meg and Patty had managed without having a bike, I would have to have something else as my birthday present. I was devastated, especially since I had told all my classmates that I was having a bike and I didn't want to be the odd one out. They all had bikes and some even rode their bikes to school. Totally disillusioned, I continued the pretence and insisted that I did have a bicycle, but wasn't allowed to ride it on the roads. All was well until one Friday after school. I was walking along the high street with Gran when we bumped into Christine Greenhalgh. Christine wasn't a special friend, but she had heard me talking about my new bicycle and she called out to me as she passed, "Hiya Abi, are you coming out on your bike? A few of us are going to look at the horses at Highfield Farm."

I was furious, more with myself than with Christine Greenhalgh. "What's she talking about, Abigail?" Gran asked. I didn't know what to say and I felt very uncomfortable. "She hasn't got a bike," Gran told the confused girl, "so she won't be coming to Highfield Farm, or anywhere else."

"I was only kidding," I said, trying to make a very feeble joke out of the situation, but all the time knowing that I had been well and truly caught telling lies. Gran didn't shout at me, but quietly reprimanded me and said that she wouldn't tell Dad providing I promised never to lie again whatever the circumstances. I was so embarrassed and hoped against hope that Christine Greenhalgh wouldn't pass on the word of my deceit to Betty West. I recall feeling hot tears of shame trickling down my face and I resolved always to speak the truth in the future...

... "A penny for your thoughts," James said, interrupting her reverie.

"Oh I was just remembering one of those childhood indiscretions," she admitted and then, "You make me laugh with your upper class accent sometimes! I find it quite endearing in a way. Where I come from, we'd say, Great! or Brilliant! not Jolly good show!"

"Does that mean you will accompany me to the ball, Cinderella?" James continued and that made her laugh again as she recalled the last time she had been called Cinderella, but she had no intention of telling James the story of Tony Simpson and that first kiss, which still lingered in the secret depths of her soul.

James Sylvester-Jones was quite obsessed with Abigail Marie Hawthorne. She presented him with a challenge. *She is so deliciously naïve and virginal. Girls in my circle of friends are usually far too jolly-hockey-sticks types, or so horsy. I wouldn't touch them with a barge pole. Abi is different.*

The days before Freshers' Ball were hectic. The girls were buying, borrowing, or making ball gowns and the boys were hiring their dinner suits and polishing their shoes until they could see their faces in them. James looked on in amazement. Black tie was commonplace to him and Anne noticed his arrogance one evening when he dropped Abi off at the house after lectures. "What a prat he is at times," she commented to Ruth, "There's something about him that really gets up my nose. I hope Abi knows what she's getting into."

Ruth grinned. *Dear Anne. Her shrewd sense of assessment is never far off the mark.* "I don't think much of the supercilious James either, but at least he's acted the perfect gentleman with us all and so I don't think there's any need to worry."

The Ball went off with a bang. The Students' Union bars were full of noisy, excited, young people, all dressed up to the nines and having a wonderful time. With the traditional dance band in the upper hall, couples were waltzing the night away and there was a traditional jazz band in the basement adding to the liveliness of the occasion. "Just look at this," she said to her partner for the evening. "Everything is so beautiful...the girls in evening dresses, the colours, the music, the men in evening suits twirling their partners round. It's like something out of a Fred Astaire film. I love it."

"Whatever you say, Abi, whatever you say." James was just glad that Abi was with him and not on some other student's arm.

Abi and James spent most of the time dancing close together in the upper hall. It brought back memories of the party at St George's Youth Club, but for Abi, the wonderful, tingling sensation she had experienced with Tony Simpson was not there. She did enjoy the dancing and James was excellent company on such an occasion. She smiled her way through the entire evening as James had been the perfect partner and a good friend, not his usual pompous self for once and for that she was grateful.

James called a black cab to take Abi back to the house in Salford. They climbed into the spacious vehicle and having told the driver where they were going, James closed the window that separated the driver from the passengers. It was very dark and the dim street lights offered no illumination whatsoever inside the cab. James put his arm around Abi and, since she had been dancing with him all evening, she felt comfortable with it. "This has been one of the best nights ever," she told him. "I have loved every minute of it."

"Good," James said. "I have enjoyed it too." He leaned over to kiss her.

Abigail felt her muscles tense, but then thought that a kiss could do no harm, so she tilted her head to allow his lips to meet hers. James held her close and savoured the smell of her perfume. With his left arm around her back, his right arm moved across her waist, feeling the silk of her gown, soft and delicate. She pulled away. She sensed his intensions and decided that one kiss was enough to keep him at arm's length. As the taxi drew up to her door, she said, "Thank you for a lovely evening, James," pecked him on the cheek and got out of the taxi before he could say anything. "You might as well stay in the cab and go home. That makes sense. Goodnight and thanks again."

The driver turned round and smiled knowingly. "Where to, mate?"

James was totally nonplussed. "Balmoral Road, thanks."

Abi smiled to herself and went quietly into the house.

Fourteen

The first year, though demanding, proved rewarding for each of the girls in the house. With first year finals out of the way, they packed up their belongings and went their separate ways for the summer recess. Ruth had managed to find a holiday job in her home town of Blythe and was working in a local hotel as a waitress. Anne and Jenny had decided to go across to the Isle of Man to find seasonal jobs and Abigail was spending some time with her father and working her holidays in the nursing home in Belford.

"*Adios amigos!*" Anne called as she left. "*A bientot! Auf Wiedersehen!*"

"See you later," they called to her as they lugged their heavy suitcases to find the right platform. It seemed that the whole of Manchester University was on Piccadilly Station all at the same time.

For Abi, the shifts in the home were long and tiring. Old people were demanding and whilst most of them were very placid and endearing, others were cantankerous and difficult. Abigail decided there and then that geriatrics would not be her priority when she was later required to select her specialty. Living at home with her father again was a bittersweet experience. She saw the deterioration in his condition at first hand. "I understand why you haven't kept me informed, Meg," she complained, "But don't keep me in the dark in future. I want to know what's going on."

"Okay, Abi. I just thought you had enough on your plate settling in at uni, that's all."

She did understand Meg's reasoning in not burdening her with her father's problems, but Abi felt that she owed it to her dad to be there for him as he had given all his support to her as she was growing up.

"Poor dad. He doesn't know what's happening to him," she said and both she and Meg knew that had he been able to see himself, he would have been devastated that he was so incapable of looking after himself. During that summer, the Hawthorne girls decided they would have to arrange residential care for John. They needed to know he had round-the-clock care, and none of them was able to provide it for him at home. Hillside Terrace would have to be sold to finance his stay in the nursing home and it broke their hearts to think that their childhood home would belong to someone else.

"It's only bricks and mortar," Patty said, "No-one can take away our memories. They go with us wherever we choose to live. We don't have to plaster over all our childhood recollections, do we?" Patty had crossed the great divide between north and south. She had even picked up a southern accent, much to the amusement of her sisters.

"My goodness, Patty, have you forgotten where your roots are?" Meg asked her. "I have never heard anybody born and bred in Bolton say *plarster.*" And they giggled very childishly at Patty's transformation. She had come out of her shell as she had grown older and Abi in particular had noticed the difference in her. *My sister Patty is no longer just the middle child and I admire her in her new guise as a confident, independent, young woman,* she thought as Patty returned to London.

Meg, as the next of kin, took on the responsibility of arranging everything. She would have to obtain power of attorney over her father's estate and so would have to see a solicitor. She resolved to leave all that until the other two had returned to their respective situations.

Abigail returned to Manchester in the middle of September. It meant that she would have a few days to settle in the house again before the other girls returned. She needed to write up her report of her holiday job, making her observations of the care of the elderly. It would be an integral piece of her folio when she submitted it later in the year. She knew that without distractions, she would be able to complete it before the beginning of term. She thrived on the peace and quiet that allowed her to work undisturbed at her task.

Two days into her self-enforced labours, she met with unexpected company. Whether it was by co-incidence or design, she never really understood, but James just happened to turn up at her door at midday. "What are you doing here?" she asked him. "How did you know I came back early?"

"I have my sources," he said lightheartedly. "Didn't you know about my telepathic powers?"

Abi sighed loudly and turned to walk away.

"I thought you might like some company," he continued. "I've brought a bottle of Chablis and some cold chicken. We could have a feast!" and he laughed at his little joke, but Abi wasn't impressed. She really did not want James to be there at that moment.

"I have work to do, James, even if you don't. Some of us take our work seriously, but I guess that thought never entered your head."

"You work too hard, my angel," he said as he pushed past her and made his way to the kitchen.

She had not kept in touch with him during the recess. She hadn't wanted to encourage him too much, since she hadn't liked the fervour in his attachment to her before the end of last term. Her thoughts were running riot in her head. Her resolve to keep the relationship on a platonic basis had not changed. James's tactile approach had unnerved her. He was constantly taking hold of her hand, creeping up behind her and putting his arms around her, making sure his hands brushed across her beasts as he did so, touching her leg when they sat together in lectures, all obviously making it clear that he felt they were more than just friends. Misguidedly, she had allowed him to kiss her occasionally, nothing heavy nor intimate, but when his kisses became too forceful and urgent, she immediately put a stop to any show of affection. She didn't want it, wasn't ready for it and certainly not with James. She had decided to give him a wide berth during second year, not only because of his unhealthy interest in her as a woman, but also because he had missed lectures, had not handed in work on time and had generally become the pompous, supercilious, arrogant prat that her flatmate, Anne, had perceived him to be from the start. How he had managed to pass his first year finals was a mystery to everyone. Rumour had it that Lord Lionel had had more than a little to do with James being allowed to return to continue the course.

"James! I need to work. You can please yourself what you do, but please don't do it here!" Abi was becoming exasperated, "Are you listening to me?"

"Yes, I'm listening and even workers need to eat, so take a break and then I promise I'll go and leave you to it," he replied, but somehow his words of assurance did not ring true. There was a hint of insincerity in his voice and Abi didn't like the glazed look in his eyes, almost as if he'd been drinking already.

Reluctantly, she agreed to eat whatever food he had brought, only because he had gone to the trouble of preparing it and she reasoned that she would have to stop to eat anyway. "But I mean it, James," she scolded, "As soon as we've eaten, I'm throwing you out!"

The food was delicious and Abi complimented James on his culinary skills as he poured her a second glass of wine. She felt more relaxed and she lay back on the sofa smiling contentedly. James went to sit beside her and handed her the glass.

"Thank you, James," she purred, "You have added a little bit of interest to an otherwise tedious day."

"That's why I'm here, my dearest Abigail, to brighten up your life."

She took a sip of her wine and grimaced. "Ugh! This wine tastes a bit funny to me..."

"Oh? It's probably because the lemon chicken was so sweet," James interrupted. "Have another drink. It'll taste fine then... promise. You know that I worship you, you gorgeous little pussy cat," James whispered as he inched closer to the absolutely beautiful creature whose eyes were closed in total relaxation.

She felt gloriously at ease and she smiled at James, who sat and drank in the beauty of this woman... *pure, fresh, virginal...* the mere thought of the word aroused him. He placed his arm around her and she wasn't aware that he was so close. He smelt of cologne, a heady, musk smell that added to her sense of euphoria. James lowered his face to hers, feeling her warm breath on his cheek. His lips found hers and she responded by parting her lips to suggest that she quite liked his kisses after all. Abigail was in another world, but she was oddly aware that she was being transported to where she didn't want to go and yet she had no strength to deal with it. James was moving too fast. "Come on, my darling," he groaned repulsively, offensively. "You want it, don't you?" His ardour was taking over and he delighted in taking complete control.

As if by some divine intervention, Abigail was stirred out of her hypnotic state by the vulgar ramblings of the animal who by this time was on top of her. "James!" she screamed, "What are you doing? Get off me! No! No! NO!" Hot tears of terror coursed down her face and she struggled to push him away, but he held on to her tightly.

"You want it, you know you do! You were crying out for it! I'm going to have you, Abigail Hawthorne, so lie back and enjoy it!"

"NO!" Abi screamed again, "Don't hurt me, James! I never asked for this. Stop it! Stop it! STOP IT!" and she lifted her knees with all the strength that she could muster to force James's body upwards. With one almighty kick, she sent him flying backwards, over the end of the sofa and unceremoniously sprawling on the floor. She was working on auto-pilot and she ran from the room towards the front door, adjusting her clothes as she did so, fearing that he was in close pursuit. She fumbled with the latch, her hands seemingly in her panic not receiving the right messages from her brain. Suddenly, the door opened and there was Ruth. Abi fell heavily into her arms and clung to her as if for dear life.

"What the hell is going on?" Ruth was shocked to see Abi, her face tear-stained and her clothes in disarray. Abi sobbed, struggling to tell her what had happened.

"It's James...in there," and pointing towards the lounge, "He..." She couldn't say it...

Ruth sat Abi on the bottom step of the stairs. "I've got the message. Wait there," she said, "You're safe now," and she marched into the lounge where the dishonourable James Sylvester-Jones, son and heir of Lord Lionel Sylvester-Jones, Earl of Trethowen, was sitting on the floor in a semi-state of undress.

"You!" she barked at him, "Cover yourself up, you despicable specimen of masculine filth! You'll not get away with this. Daddy won't be able to help you this time." She quickly checked on Abi and immediately called the police.

Strangely, James did not try to run. He knew it was no use. He was a marked man and it didn't take a super brain to accept that he had nowhere to hide, but he did try to hide the evidence he had in his pocket. He went to the bathroom and flushed the pethidine tablets down the lavatory. He smirked at the thought that it had almost worked. He had nearly had Abigail Hawthorne, but cursed under his breath because he had failed to take her virginity.

When the police arrived, he went quietly and looked directly at Abi as he left. The frenzy had disappeared from his eyes and had been replaced by hatred, not particularly for Abi, but for the failure of chalking up another conquest. She watched him go. *I'll not allow you to ruin my future, you arrogant upper-class twit.* In spite of the state of shock which had momentarily overpowered her, her thoughts were lucid and somewhat aggressive. *I am more than determined not to be weakened by this socially unacceptable and grossly obscene situation, so think about that, James Sylvester-Jones.*

As for the spurious James, he disappeared without trace. He was charged with the possession of stolen prescription drugs. Abigail's glass of wine had been analysed and there had been traces of the pethidine in James's pocket. There was no evidence against Abi, but as the victim, she had the right to press charges for the attempted rape. She declined. She did not wish James any harm. He had violated her prerogative to say no, but he had not hurt her. Her career was too important to her to allow James Sylvester-Jones to shatter her dream. He was just a temporary blot on the horizon, no more than that. Rightly or wrongly, she just wanted to get on with her life and she would handle it in the only way she knew how.

"I know the police will inform the university authorities," she told the girls on their return, "But I don't want it to go any further.

Nobody else need know. Promise me you'll not say anything to anyone...*promise.*"

The three girls agreed and understood Abi's reasoning. In turn, she trusted her friends to keep her secret.

Weeks later when the dust had settled and Abigail had shut out the memories of that afternoon in September, Ruth spotted a tiny article in a corner of *The Times*. Only the dean of the university and Abi's personal tutor knew what had happened and apart from Ruth, Jenny and Anne, no other students were aware that anything out of the ordinary had gone on. It was in Abi's interest not to publicise the facts.

"Listen to this," Ruth announced. Folding the newspaper to make it easier to see, she read out loud, *"The Honourable James Sylvester-Jones, elder son of Lord Lionel Sylvester-Jones, Seventh Earl of Trethowen, was today found guilty of possessing stolen prescription drugs. He was fined £2000 and placed on probation for two years. Neither Lord Lionel nor his son was available for comment. It is believed that the young man will not continue his studies at university."*

"That's the end of that then," Abi stated calmly and she really meant it. Her three housemates did not need to respond. They knew that Abigail Hawthorne had the strength of character to forget.

Fifteen

Responsibilities

Meg moved in with John when Patty and Abigail returned to London and Manchester after the summer break. She had taken little Nicky with her and it meant that, to all intents and purposes, she was not living with her husband, putting a terrible strain on their marriage. Philip stayed in their new house in Bromley Cross and as he was working in Blackburn, a few miles north of Bolton, he was unable to see her and Nicky during the week. Weekends were always so busy and Meg refused to leave her father for fear of his wandering off again. Philip tried to understand, but he felt that he was being neglected and he told her so. "I'm your husband, damn it!" he complained, "Your place is with me. You've got to do something about it, Meg, before it ruins us!"

"What do you mean, ruins us?" Meg cried, thinking only of her father at that moment, "This is my father, Philip, the man who has been everything to me as I was growing up. He was always there for me. I will not desert him now when he needs me to take care of him." She was shouting and giving vent to her own frustrations. "You are meant to be supportive, Phil, not obstructive."

Philip sighed. His view was that Meg was so bound up in her father's illness she couldn't see what it was doing to their marriage. She expected him to stand by and watch whilst she was slowly being devoured by her fierce sense of loyalty. "Look," he said gently, "You arranged with Patty and Abi to sell Hillside Terrace and you haven't done anything about that yet. You are going to have to do it eventually and John isn't aware of what's going on around him, so it won't hurt him, if that's what's worrying you. He is not the person we know and love, Meg. He really doesn't know who we are, or where he is anymore."

Meg went to put her arms around her husband and the tears ran down her cheeks as she sobbed uncontrollably into his chest. She couldn't speak, but he understood her feelings without putting them into words.

"I'll stay here with you this weekend and we'll sort everything out. We'll ask Mrs Roberts to sit with your dad whilst we go to the estate agent's and then we'll make an appointment to see Doctor McNeill to find out about suitable nursing homes. We have to do it, sweetheart, not only for your dad, but for us too."

Meg knew he was right, but she found it so difficult to let go. She had done her best during the past few weeks and there were times when she thought John was responding to her, but there were also occasions, lots of them, when he was obstinate, cantankerous, obstreperous and downright abusive. The hardest part was the fact that he wasn't, indeed, the dad she knew and loved. He was making her life so difficult and she knew deep in her heart that he needed specialist care, but to institutionalise him seemed abhorrent to her. Much as it hurt her to do it, she agreed with Philip to start the ball rolling.

Doctor McNeill advised them to try to find a nursing home close to Belford so as not to uproot John totally. The Birches was situated in Edgworth and it would be easy to visit from Bromley Cross. "When Patty and Abi come home…" she paused… "Patty and Abi will have no home," she said, speaking her thoughts to her cup of coffee as she tried to wade through the mound of paperwork needed to sell the house and apply to Social Services for their support in relocating the unfortunate man who had become old before his years. She felt the tears well up in her eyes again and she brushed them away, stoically making an effort to be calm and focused. *It has to be done and Patty and Abi will stay at my house, correction, mine and Philip's house, when they need to be in Bolton. Patty has bought a flat in Crawley, so she is able commute to the City each day. She really doesn't need a home in Bolton anymore, just a place to rest her head when she comes to visit.*

Abigail is different. She is still a student and needs somewhere to live during her holidays. She could live with Philip and me in Bromley Cross. We have the room and we can make her a bedsit so she can maintain her independence. That's settled then. She scolded herself for looking for obstacles when really there were none. *I'll just have to be more positive in my approach to becoming the honorary head of the family. The mere thought of it makes me feel sick.*

~ * ~

One Monday morning, she asked Mrs Roberts to sit with John, took Nicky to playgroup and went into Bolton to arrange the services of a solicitor. She realised that she couldn't sell the house without gaining power of attorney to manage her father's estate. She knew it would be difficult as he was only occasionally aware of others around him. She arrived at the offices of Marcus Cohen and Company feeling tense, but reasonably in control of her emotions. She was asked to wait until Mr Cohen was free and she sat, rigidly upright, clutching her briefcase, hoping she had brought all the necessary documentation. *It is important that I make everything as easy as possible, not only for Dad, but for myself. I need to keep Patty and Abi informed. They have a right to know what is happening and I've promised them I'll inform them at every stage of the proceedings. Abigail has been strangely quiet since she returned to Manchester for her second year, but I guess when she went back a few days early, she would throw herself into her work as is her wont. I think she is too serious about everything at times, but that's our Abi and she'll get in touch if she needs to. I won't bother her with details of the house sale just yet.*

The secretary interrupted Meg's reverie. "Mr Cohen will see you now, Mrs Wilkinson. Please come this way." She showed Meg into the office on the right and she was a little surprised when she saw the young man behind the desk.

"Do come in, Mrs Wilkinson. How can I help you?" he said. He was a very young man and Meg was taken aback. "I'm David Cohen..."

"Oh," Meg's expression must have made it clear what she was thinking.

"Is there a problem, Mrs Wilkinson?" Cohen asked, "Would you prefer someone else to deal with your legal business?"

"Oh no...thank you, Mr Cohen," Meg replied feeling more than a little stupid. "I was expecting an older man. I'm sorry. I don't mean to be rude."

"No problem. I'm Marcus Cohen's son. My father usually deals with property and legal aid cases, but I'm sure he would be pleased to attend to your needs if you prefer." Cohen seemed to be at ease in offering his father's services. He was particularly forthright, almost to the point of appearing overconfident and very blunt.

"Not at all. I'm embarrassed that I have made you feel that I don't want you to act for me." Meg was blushing. "I am quite happy for you to deal with my problems, truly."

"Right then, let's get down to business."

Meg outlined the situation and explained that as the eldest of three daughter she would have to take responsibility. She briefly told him about Patty and Abigail, "Patty is an accountant in London and Abi is a medical student in Manchester. They have both agreed to allow me to manage things."

"Good. That's an encouraging start at least. However, I shall have to insist on meeting all three of you together at some stage in the not-too-distant future so that I might clarify exactly what you and your family are taking on board," the young solicitor explained. "Now, for the first steps to be taken, I shall have to visit your father to gain his permission for you to take over his affairs."

Meg paled at the thought. She was anxious and it showed. *How will Dad cope with the interrogation? If David Cohen catches him on one of his obstreperous days, we'll have a riot on our hands.* The solicitor sensed her unease and reassured her by saying he would telephone first before he made his journey to Belford.

As it turned out, John was quite amenable for the meeting and with very little coaxing, he signed his name when instructed to do so, nodding his head to Cohen to indicate that he knew what he was doing. Then just as the young man was about to leave... "I know your game," John declared angrily. Meg was horrified.

"Oh, do you now?" Mr Cohen asked, forcing himself to smile at the prematurely old man sitting by the fire in the cosy little kitchen of Hillside Terrace.

"I know you fancy our Meg, don't you?" John continued unabashed. "Well, she's too young for boyfriends and she's got to finish her...her..." His voice trailed off as if he had lost interest in what he was saying.

"All right, Mr Hawthorne," Cohen said. He really didn't appreciate this foolishness, but he took the tension out of the situation and pointedly joked with his unwitting client, "I won't elope with her today then!"

"Go on, bugger off!" John called and then leaned back in his chair and closed his eyes.

"Dad!" Meg admonished her father. She was mortified at his outburst.

"Don't worry, Meg...you don't mind my calling you by your first name? We'll need to get to know each other better, then things will run smoothly," the solicitor said as he turned to shake her hand.

"I don't mind at all and thank you so much," she said hastily, feeling extremely awkward with the premature over-familiarity in his remarks. She rapidly dismissed the thought. "Let us know when you need to see us again." She was so relieved that the meeting had gone comparatively smoothly. The next task was to get John settled in The Birches where he would receive the appropriate care and attention. She sighed deeply. *Life is very cruel at times.*

~ * ~

The meeting with the three sisters and the young Mr Cohen took place during the Easter break. With John in The Birches and Hillside Terrace under offer, they met at the Wilkinson house in Bromley Cross. Meg made tea and scones in an effort to create an appropriate, yet informal atmosphere for the occasion. She needed to be relaxed, but for some unfathomable reason, it was also important to her self-esteem to prove to this young man that her social standing was equal to his own. It irked her slightly that she should find herself feeling beholden to the young solicitor whose demeanour she could not always comprehend. Momentarily chastising herself, she put her feelings of social inferiority down to the stress of the past few months.

Patty deliberately kept quiet, not trusting herself to be so diplomatic should she contradict the patronising, self-righteous, legal pedant sitting opposite her. She dutifully acknowledged what he said with polite responses.

Over tea, Cohen explained to the Hawthorne girls that John no longer had to deal with his affairs and that Meg would be legally responsible in all eventualities arising from John's finances and the management of his estate. She would be able to sign everything on his behalf. If they had any concerns, the solicitor would be available at any time to answer their queries.

"Where on earth did you find *him*, Meg? What a supercilious prick!" Patty protested as he drove off.

"Enough, Patty," Meg insisted, "And watch your language. He's been very helpful and at least he's given me the confidence to get on with this awful business."

Abigail hadn't joined them to say goodbye to the solicitor. She just needed to get back to Manchester and settle back into her studies.

Cohen's thoughts were not really on the job in hand. His mind had been distracted by the vision of loveliness before him in the shape of Abigail Hawthorne. He felt he had been successful in charming two of the three young women. *When have I ever been unsuccessful on that score?* he mused. However, it concerned him a little that Abigail was too quiet, perhaps more than a little distant. There had been no eye contact and she had allowed her sister to speak for her, only nodding her agreement when necessary. Driving back to the office, he wondered, albeit aimlessly, if she were always like that. *Something of a mystery,* he contemplated, smiling at the thought of what the future might bring.

Sixteen

At the beginning of her third year, Abigail decided to rent a flat in the suburbs. The big red-bricked house with steps leading to the impressive, carved double doors at the front was situated on Warrington Road. The busy road was on the main Manchester/Stockport bus route, so commuting each day was not a problem. Ruth, Jenny and Anne had also found alternative accommodation and whilst she would miss their company, Abi felt that she needed the space to do her own thing without the constant babble from housemates and the hassle of not being able to use the bathroom on mornings when all four girls had to be in lectures by nine o'clock. The fact that they were all following different courses often made life difficult. After the episode with James Sylvester-Jones, she had lately become more focused than ever on her work. She preferred it that way.

She had made friends in her tutor group and they occasionally got together for supper and for evenings at the cinema, but she had not become particularly close to any of them. Most times, there was a distinct lack of female company for Abigail. Medicine apparently attracted more males than females. Leaving Ruth, Jenny and Anne behind had been a necessary wrench and although she missed them, she assured herself that she had done the right thing. Several student colleagues had invited her out on dates, but she always declined. *I have no need of a relationship and after the last fiasco, I have no intention of being alone with any over-sexed student ever again,* she mused. *If I'm in danger of becoming a bore, so be it. I couldn't care less.* She usually smiled at would-be suitors and gave them the brush-off. Amongst them she was gaining the reputation of being the proverbial ice maiden, the elusive and evasive Abigail Hawthorne. She did, however, in spite of all this, have male colleagues and they appeared to respect her stance even though most of them secretly thought she was being unnecessarily standoffish.

When Peter Fitzgerald, friendly Fritz to the tutor group, formed a working partnership with her, Abigail responded favourably to his companionship. He was studious and keen to do well. His shock of red hair and his horn-rimmed glasses made him the typical student and he was very popular with his colleagues. He was not, however, your typical lady's man and had never been seen with a girl around the college. In fact, he came over as being rather shy with girls, but he had clear green eyes that sparkled when he had something interesting to share with the group. For Abigail, that was his most endearing quality. At first, their working together was during the day in seminars, in the library, in the tutor room. They bounced ideas off each other and had heated discussions as to the treatment of various medical conditions, until they reluctantly decided that they needed a textbook to confirm their final conclusions. Once they had qualified, it would all fall into place, but in the meantime, it was good for both of them to explore the knowledge they had acquired so far. Occasionally, Abi invited him to her flat where they could study without interruption.

During one of their meetings, Abigail noticed that Fritz was preoccupied.

"What's wrong?" she asked.

"I have a problem, Doctor," he said, half joking, half serious.

"Oh dear. You'd better tell me your symptoms and then I'll make the diagnosis," Abi said, going along with his little scenario.

"Well...I might have a heart murmur..." he said, his face showing the strain of imparting the news to his dear friend. His cheeks were flushed and he was beginning to perspire.

"Are you serious, Fritz? I thought you were joking. How do you feel? Have you checked the symptoms?"

"Well," Fritz continued bravely, "I'm finding it increasingly difficult to breathe when I'm around you," he said, his face breaking into a boyish smile.

"Oh Fritz! You devil! You had me going there for a minute. Don't be stupid," and she lunged at him, intending to push him playfully in the chest. Fritz grabbed her to stop her falling and for the first time in a long time, Abigail felt herself physically close to a young man. It didn't un-nerve her; on the contrary, she felt quite at ease. She looked him in the eye and he was smiling down at her. "Oh heck, Fritz," she said, "This is not what we intended, but we can deal with it, can't we, providing it doesn't interfere with our studies."

"Ever the practical, objective one," he said with a hint of disappointment in his tone, but then, "It won't, I promise. We do have a sort of chemistry, though, don't we?" and he kissed her gently. She tasted good and he floated on air as she responded affectionately.

Their relationship became the talk of the medics. *'Peter Fitzgerald and Abi Hawthorne?' 'Are you sure?' 'What's he got that I haven't?'* and so on. For a while, Fritz and Abi were inseparable and she, at least, was happy that he hadn't expected a full-on, heavy relationship. Their time together was generally spent working as before and usually was rounded off with just a goodnight kiss and the occasional cuddle as they watched a movie on television. The crunch came when Fritz boldly fondled her breast one evening as he kissed her goodnight.

Abi froze. "Don't," she said.

"Why not? We have been a couple for ages and most other people would have slept together by now. We know each other well enough, don't we?"

"Fritz, I'm not most other people. I thought you realised that. I'm happy with the way things are, aren't you?"

"Do you want the truth?"

"Of course I want the truth. What would be the point of lying?"

"Well, no, I'm not really happy. I thought you cared about me and caring means making love. I have held off for so long hoping that eventually you might care enough to make love to me. I was obviously mistaken." Fritz couldn't hide his feelings any longer.

"You promised me that it wouldn't interfere with our studies. Sleeping with you would be asking me to forsake all my principles and I'm not prepared to do that. My work is the most important thing in my life right now." She couldn't believe that she had to spell it out to him. "I like your company and we certainly have the same aims in life, but I won't jeopardise my studies by jumping into bed with you. I know you men. Your brains are in your pants, because that's what your hormones do to you. Sex rules your lives. I can't be a part of it, Fritz and yes, I believe that it would definitely take precedence over our studies, for you anyway. I'm sorry and I hope you understand."

Fritz eyed her carefully and waited for his opportunity to respond. Abi expected him to agree with her whole-heartedly and was taken aback when he said, "That's a pity, Abi. We could have made beautiful music together. And I do understand, truly, but perhaps we should cool it for a while. I really don't think I could be close to you now without wanting you and yes, you're right. It would interfere with our studies, mine much more than yours." He kissed her swiftly on the cheek and left.

She stood at the window and watched as Fritz walked purposefully out of her life. He didn't look back. Abigail's first thoughts were full of disappointment that he had succumbed to his animal instincts, but she knew that she couldn't blame him for simply being a man. Her time now would be strictly her own and her social life was the least of her concerns.

Her grit and determination to succeed were her driving force almost to the point of obsession and she worked with a passion at every aspect of her course. Her tutors were amazed at her application and resolve. They observed her with admiration and respect without realising the real reasons behind her tremendous efforts. For Abigail, her self-enforced labours were both cathartic and purposeful. With her father completely unaware of everything around him, she dedicated all her work to him. Half way into that academic year, medical students were required to consider various special study modules and since she had had firsthand experience of caring for the elderly, Abigail decided to go to the other end of the human time scale and look at paediatrics.

"...and finally, Miss Hawthorne, how would you alleviate the fears of parents whose child is admitted with breathing difficulties?" This was the final question in the *viva voce* at the end of third year.

"With a calm approach at all times. Parents need to know that the doctor is confident and competent. To remove the fear with immediate effect is difficult when emotions are running high, but reassurance that the required help and medical expertise is at hand gives the necessary initial support." Abigail felt that she needed reassurance that she had chosen the correct approach this time. *They hadn't asked for diagnosis, nor treatment, so I think the general, social response to the question was adequate.*

"Thank you, Miss Hawthorne. You may go now," the examiner said irritatingly and peering over his frameless half-spectacles without a hint of pass or failure, he dismissed her without ceremony.

"Thank you, sir. Good morning," and Abigail made a controlled exit despite feeling the need to run from the room where for the past half hour, she had felt like a caged animal. *Exams are the pits!* In those situations, the proverbial ice maiden felt sure that she had revealed cracks in her surface and everyone knew what happened when the ice broke.

Although it was only days before the results came through, it seemed like a lifetime. On the designated day, hordes of anxious students hovered around the faculty notice boards waiting for the lists that would seal their futures. The constant drone was intermittently interrupted by a nervous shriek, but generally the atmosphere was tense and there were periods of expectant silence which all added to the seriousness of the occasion. Abigail met Ruth and Jenny in the reception hall and Anne waved as she chatted to Colin, her latest boyfriend.

At precisely ten thirty in the morning, the administrative officer walked sombrely out of the office to loud cheers that made his solemn expression change into a smile. He was trying to maintain a sense of decorum, but he laughed as he fumbled in his pocket for drawing pins, rather like the best man at a wedding searching for the ring.

"Come on! Get on with it!" one over-eager student called out and everyone joined in good-naturedly to coax the young clerk into posting up the results more quickly. Once the last pin was in place, the security men removed the rope barriers and there was a surge forward, eager eyes searching feverishly for a D, M, or P after one's name and dreading the ominous R which meant repeat the examination in most cases, but occasionally repeat the whole year. Fritz had qualified with a Merit and was ready to move into Year Four with renewed enthusiasm for his studies and without the distraction of the untouchable Abigail Hawthorne.

Ruth and Jenny had just scraped through, but were happy with their results. They could pursue their planned careers, both in teaching after completing their Post-Graduate Certificate of Education. Anne had gained a Merit and had already been successful in securing a post with the Diplomatic Service when she had completed her final year. It would mean frequent travelling to Europe, but with British politicians talking about joining the European Community in the future, the world was her oyster.

"We'll see you later, Abs," the girls called as they went to call home. "We'll all celebrate together... like old times, eh?"

As was her usual ice-cool approach, Abigail waited until the crowds had dispersed before she ventured forward to look for her name. There was something very personal about this procedure for her, an unexplained, poignant moment when she felt the spiritual presence of her family. This time she was in a state of incomprehensible limbo and she didn't like it. She had a sense of foreboding about these results. The first two years had gone well and she had managed a distinction and a merit. The merit had irked her as she set herself such high standards. Somehow, this time she felt that she had tripped up somewhere along the way. She searched the lists for her name. It wasn't there. She began at the top and worked her way through every name on every list to see if her name had been placed on the wrong one. No, it simply wasn't there. Panic hit her; her heart started to beat faster in her chest. Tears welled up in her eyes. The ice maiden was starting to melt. Hot tears trickled down her cheeks as she turned and leaned against the board that had delivered the earth-shattering blow. She had worked so hard and all for nothing. Everyone else in her tutor group had passed and she couldn't understand where she had gone wrong. Failure was a bitter pill to swallow. Now she would have to repeat the whole year if indeed they would allow her to. *Oh, Dad,* she thought miserably, *I've let you down.*

The office door opened and the admin officer appeared again with another piece of paper, this time looking more sombre than the first time he made his entrance. He said nothing to Abigail, in fact, he didn't even look at her and dutifully pinned the sheet to the right of the other lists on the board. Abigail walked sadly away, wishing with all her heart that the floor would open and swallow her whole.

When she arrived back at Warrington Road, she could hear the telephone ringing in the hallway. She hoped that someone else would answer it. She didn't want to speak to anyone at that moment in time. She would have to tell Meg and Patty of her failure when she had come to terms with it herself. Her whole world had fallen apart and her dream had become a nightmare. Failure had not been in her vocabulary until then.

She wandered up to her flat and sat on the edge of the bed, her heart heavy and her head aching. She couldn't think straight. She thought of Janet, her school friend then at Oxford. This was how she must have felt when she thought she was pregnant; her dreams shattered into a thousand little pieces. "Oh God," she prayed, "What do I do now?"

The telephone started to ring again and Abigail called out, "Will somebody answer that dratted phone?" but it kept on ringing relentlessly. With heavy heart and matching footsteps, she trundled down the stairs to take the offending telephone off the hook. She grabbed it viciously from its cradle and was just about to place it on the table so that it wouldn't ring again when she heard her name...

"Abi? Is that you? Abigail, speak to me!" It was Anne. "If I didn't know you better, I'd say you were refusing to speak to mere mortals such as we!"

"Don't Anne, please," Abi managed to whisper into the mouth-piece, "I need time on my own to mull over what has happened."

"What?" Anne sounded surprised, shocked almost.

"I can't cope with the disappointment of not finding my name on the list," and the tears came again. "What shall I do, Anne? I feel so ashamed of myself..."

"You mean you haven't seen the board?" Anne asked in dismay. "Get yourself down here *now* and I won't take no for an answer. If you're not here in half an hour, we'll come and drag you by your hair! Now, do as you are told and hurry up, Miss Hawthorne!"

Abigail didn't want to go back to Oxford Road, but Anne had been so insistent. *Perhaps she has seen that my name wasn't there and just wanted to see my tutor with her...moral support... typical Anne, a friend to the last. Better to deal with it immediately than to wallow in self-pity,* so she quickly splashed her face with cold water and went out to catch the bus.

Anne and Colin were at the top of the steps waiting animatedly as she arrived at the university. When Abi climbed the steps to meet them, without a word Anne took her by the arm and frog-marched her to the notice board where less than two hours ago, she had frantically searched for her results. "Look," Anne pointed towards the gold-edged sheet that had been pinned up just before Abigail had left. "Colin left his rucksack in the cloakroom and had to come back for it. We didn't see the honours board before."

"What are you talking about? I failed...I can't bear to think about it. They didn't even put my name on the list!" Abi was beginning to cry again.

"You idiot! You didn't fail!" Anne was laughing and literally forcing Abigail's head towards the board to look at the special list by the side of the rest. "Abigail, my friend, your naïveté astonishes me at times."

Through her tears, Abigail read the bold, golden, Roman lettering at the top of the elaborate sheet. UNIVERSITY OF MANCHESTER—

DEAN'S RECOMMENDED GOLD AWARD WINNERS—there were five names on the list, all with a large gold D after them.

AINSLEY Gordon Charles

BECKETT Oliver George Christopher

DELVARD David Walker

HAWTHORNE Abigail Marie

TRENBATH Jeremy Stephen Buxton

Abigail continued to cry. In the last couple of hours, she had gone from eager anticipation through the depths of utter despair and finally had emerged in the golden glory of success. Anne hugged her dear friend and whispered in her ear, "Good girl! And take note—you are a fine example for the Women's Rights Movement. Go show those male scholars what you can do!"

Abigail smiled. Her political views were limited, but her ability to work hard was an innate characteristic, not born of the recognition of women's rights. She was her mother's Saturday's child and she intended to keep that in mind as she entered into the realms of the noblest of professions. She owed everything to one very special John James Hawthorne.

Seventeen

The life of the academic suited Abigail. She thrived on educational challenges and her increasing knowledge and skills acquired in previous years were materialising into clinical competence. By the end of year four, she felt that she was becoming proficient in all aspects of medicine; her dream, whilst still not yet fulfilled, was visible on the horizon and more than ever was she focused on the pursuit of her ambition. Her resolve never wavered, yet she was grateful when Rag Week gave her a well-earned break.

Rag Week was a time when Manchester city centre was taken over by carefree exuberant, over-enthusiastic, sometimes mildly offensive students in the name of charity. Rag Mag sellers were on every corner, touting their wares, magazines that were both entertaining and downright vulgar. Students were allowed to exploit vulgarity for this week only and the Manchester population looked forward to taking a peek into the realms of student artlessness and sharing in the crude sense of humour without feeling awkward or guilty.

This was the Sixties, the age of flower power and self-expression. All the major cities in Britain were lively, bustling and vibrant. The Swinging Sixties had the population optimistic and enthusiastic. Life was simple. With employment high, most could enjoy a comfortable income and there was a notable increase in consumerism. Leisure time could be enjoyed by shopping, going to the cinema, watching television and wonder of wonders, travelling overseas. More young people were learning to drive and every family wanted to own a car. With the introduction of the contraceptive pill, promiscuity was given some notoriety, although certainly not acknowledged as socially acceptable. Those born in the Victorian age looked down their stiff, turned-up noses and failed to see the benefits of the freedom the younger generation were afforded at this time. England really did *'swing as the pendulum do.'* Youth culture took the lead in music and fashion with girls showing more than a glimpse of stocking in their mini-skirts and Vidal Sassoon cutting hair in styles that were radical and often outrageous. Boys grew their hair much longer than the usual short back and sides and Arran sweaters and fish tail parkas were the gear.

University Rag Week fit in perfectly with the times. Deansgate was awash with posters and leaflets; Piccadilly Gardens the same. Youngsters in fancy dress, some traditional, others more risqué, thronged the streets, and shoppers were waylaid in an effort to glean donations to each worthy cause adopted for that week. Manchester was alive, well and truly alive with all manner of activity. The climax at the end of the week was a huge parade through the city and every university faculty participated with its own brand of exhibition.

The Med School tableau was a doctor's surgery with every conceivable messy injury and medical condition on display. Stage make-up made wonderful messy, pus-filled abscesses and tomato ketchup-stained bandages were extremely effective on accident victims. There were bedpans and vomit, urine bottles and blood, all precariously balanced on the edge of the lorry which transported the tableau around Manchester city centre.

Abigail was the patient in the brass bedstead which was pushed and pulled by drag queen nurses and which carried several collection boxes for the generous donations from the public. She certainly attracted many admiring looks and the money rolled in. *Rag Week has made me realise that there really is life after work,* she silently reasoned, *and I'm thoroughly enjoying my part in it. I love the camaraderie and if I'm being totally honest with myself, I have missed the girls who shared the house in Salford. But having said all that, I have to admit my self-imposed solitary confinement has reaped the academic benefits. I do hope, however, that I haven't become the proverbial bore as a few of my student colleagues have suggested. My life has been ruled by driving ambition. I've risked the possibility of isolating myself from everybody and I really didn't want to do that.* She had had to bear the brunt of one or two cruel remarks from her group members recently regarding her refusal to socialise with them. "What's the matter with you, Abigail? Aren't we good enough for you? We're sick of asking you to join in the fun. All work and no play..." She'd heard that before. At the time, she had merely shrugged and lamely said something about needing to work, but Rag Week had put her life into perspective and she decided to try to relax more and make a point of having a night out occasionally.

Lying on the rickety bed was not the most comfortable of situations and she soon found it increasingly difficult to remain in one position, especially when the castors on the bedposts were not capable of absorbing every bump and crack in the tarmac of Market Street. As they were passing by Lewis's, she stood up in her pink baby doll pyjamas and grabbed a bucket which had been dangling under the bedstead as a makeshift chamber pot. Shouting to the crowd, she encouraged the onlookers and well-wishers to try to throw their money into the bucket and she bounced up and down on the mattress in an effort to catch the coins as they rained on to the bed. "Come on, folks! Throw your loose change and if you've no loose change, rolled up pound notes will do!" This was Abigail at her sociable and beautiful best and the crowds loved it. Suddenly, she spotted Meg, Philip and little Nicky in the crowd and they were waving madly at her and running alongside the parade, laughing and calling out to her. "Good old, Abi!" "Well done, Sis!" "Fab, Auntie Abigail!"

Abigail giggled playfully at them and called back, "Hi, Meg. Thanks, Phil! Hey, Nicky, come on up here. You can help me rake in the cash!" Nicholas didn't need asking twice. He was up like a shot and bouncing on the bed as though it were a trampoline. The day just got better and better.

Once the parade was over and all the proceeds handed in to the bursar, tired but happy students wended their weary way home to reflect on the day and on the week as a whole. Later, back at Abi's flat, Meg was helping with the dishes whilst Philip and Nicky played a game of chess.

"Do you remember bouncing on your bed like that when you were little?" she asked Abi. They always seemed to reminisce when they got together and apart from Meg's brief report that John's condition was still the same, they did not discuss the gravity of his illness at that time.

"Yes, I do remember," Abi replied with a glint in her eye, "And do *you* remember Gran coming in and catching you and me trying to touch the ceiling? Only you could manage it! I was too small and Patty just sat on the bed reading a book and bouncing up and down as we jumped!"

Meg giggled. It made her feel young again when she was with her little sister. "I think it was the first and last time I ever heard

Gran use strong language. She said, *'Stop it, yer silly little beggars. Yer makin' more bloomin' fluff on that floor than there is int' weaving shed and I've just flippin' done this bedroom!'* We all started laughing at her language and she told us off again. Poor Gran. We must have driven her to distraction at times."

"I know," Abi agreed, "but she loved us and I know she covered up for you when you sneaked out down Belford Road!"

"How did you know that?" Meg asked aghast at the very idea of Abigail knowing her long-kept secret, "I never told you, nor our Patty about that!"

Abigail laughed. "Gran told us when you were away at college, but she swore us to secrecy! Do you think she's looking down on me now and saying..." (she mimicked Nellie's voice),

"You little beggar! You couldn't keep a bloomin' secret after all, could you?"

Philip appeared at the kitchen door. "Time we were heading back to the sticks, Meg love. Our son has beaten me again. I'm sure he'll be a Grand Master before he's much older. Thanks for tea, Abi. We've had a lovely day." He handed Abigail an envelope saying, "Don't open this until we've gone."

After she had waved them off, Abi looked down curiously at the brown foolscap envelope in her hand. "What has Philip done now?" He was always sending her little snippets of information he found in newspapers and magazines, sometimes cartoons and caricatures of eminent physicians, but mostly articles about research into cancer and senility. He was so thoughtful and she couldn't have wished for a more considerate brother-in-law. Carefully, she opened the envelope and pulled out five crisp ten pound notes. She gasped. He and Meg had often helped her financially to subsidise her student grant...a pound here, ten shillings there, but they couldn't afford all that. Fifty pounds was a fortune. What on earth was Philip thinking? With the money was a note... *'Dear Abi, Don't be shocked. We have had a bit of luck which we want to share with you. Bolton Wanderers' draw with Stoke City last Saturday brought us a first dividend on the coupon. Tony Simpson scored the equaliser in the dying seconds of the game. Spend it wisely. We know you will. Don't throw any wild parties and above all, don't spend it all at once! Love, Meg, Phil and Nicky.'*

Abigail smiled to herself. "Gosh, Tony Simpson! Now there's a name to conjure with!" She recalled that he had become a professional footballer after he had left Great Moor Grammar. *I wonder how many girls have succumbed to his kisses during the past few years,* she mused. "Gosh, Tony Simpson!" She would telephone Meg in a little while to thank her and Phil for the more than generous gift. She had almost forgotten that she had work to do, but she would allow herself a couple of hours to be self-indulgent, to listen to a few records and have a couple of glasses of wine. The thought of drinking alone didn't worry her. She settled down to have a blissfully quiet evening to re-charge the batteries before fourth year finals.

Abi's record collection was limited, but she had usually tried to budget herself so that she could afford to buy the latest Cliff Richard hit and she had accumulated quite a few of his records. *When I was at school, I was secretly madly in love with Cliff and thought that one day I would marry him and live happily ever after.* She smiled to herself. *Janet used to say the same. Janet? And Robin? I haven't heard anything of either of them for ages.* Her mind wandered back to the time when Janet thought she was pregnant. *I wonder how I would deal with that situation now,* she thought. *I would probably look at the possibility of termination. It's odd how time and a little bit of experience changes one's views. It's a funny old world.*

The Dansette record player she had had for her nineteenth birthday quietly provided the background music that lent an almost serene atmosphere to the moment. Abi sat back listening to her teen idol and allowed the words of the love song to wash over her ... *Love? What is love?* she pondered, *Tony Simpson and that first kiss? Nah! James Sylvester-Jones? Definitely not! Fritz? Maybe not. Dear Fritz has just not been able to handle the rejection and has hardly spoken to me recently.*

Despite her resolve to steer clear of boyfriends, she had recently been introduced to Mick Delaney, a veterinary student who had invited her to the cinema and was very gentlemanly whilst they watched the film, simply holding her hand and squeezing it gently occasionally to confirm that he was enjoying her company. When they had arrived back at her flat, he had expected to be invited in, but Abi instinctively knew that he had ulterior motives and she wasn't ready for his amorous advances. This was their first date, after all, and when he moved in to kiss her, she held him off. She felt he didn't need to know why she was being so wary of his touch and he threw his hands in the air in exasperation. "If I were a medical dictionary, I'd have more chance of getting into your bed," he said scathingly as he turned and left with a curt, "Okay. Goodnight."

Abi had actually thought it might have been the start of an acceptable friendship. Mick had been such a pleasant companion at first, but he hadn't invited her out again after that night. *Love has eluded me, so what? I have no time for love at the moment and I'm certainly don't intend to go looking for it. I have more pressing and necessary things to do before I'll be in a position to give my time and commitment to a relationship.*

~ * ~

Year four had presented a number of objectives aimed at moulding the complete doctor. Communication skills and examination procedures, psychiatric history and prescribing appropriate drugs, investigation and management of diseases both in hospital and community settings gave the student doctors the opportunity for hands-on experience. Abigail flourished in those situations. She found herself constantly absorbing new information and kept a very comprehensive diary of everything that happened during the day-to-day routine. She watched and listened, responded and acted at the appropriate times. She observed how consultants dealt with patients, how they handled nursing staff and communicated the necessary information to colleagues. She felt the pressure of diagnosis and prognosis, but showed that she was prepared to ask relevant questions and request guidance when she deemed it pertinent to the circumstances. She saw how some consultants humiliated unprepared students and prayed that she would never be on the receiving end of such a tirade.

During the final year, it became clear that it was down to the survival of the fittest. It came as quite a shock to Abigail that two of her group had dropped out and were pursuing careers with pharmaceutical companies. She had thought that all her group would go all the way to the finishing line and that they would all qualify together, but she understood that the pressures of succeeding in medicine were far greater than anything she had ever experienced. The demands on one's time and energy were unbelievable and no other job necessitated total concentration, even when the head was aching through tiredness and the eyes were half-closed through lack of sleep. Yes, only the truly dedicated and the most committed of persons would succeed. She often wondered if all medical students were born on a Saturday. It would certainly explain all the hard work they put in and she was under no illusions about that.

It was during one of her placements at Westerton Hospital that Abigail's armour was almost dented. She had been on duty for fourteen hours when a serious road accident victim was brought into Casualty. She ought to have gone off duty hours before, but chose to stay; firstly, because she thought she would be able to help and secondly, because she felt that she would gain valuable experience in dealing with an emergency. It was two thirty in the morning, the witching hour, Staff Nurse Green had called it. Casualty had been comparatively quiet for a Friday night until the ambulance siren broke the silence and as the automatic doors flew open, the department sprang into action. Nurses manned their posts, the duty doctor rushed to meet the incoming patient transported on a trolley supporting saline drips, oxygen cylinders and bright red blankets to keep the victim warm and prevent him losing too much body heat through trauma. The victim was a notorious local vagrant... "Oh no, not again!" ...who was frequently admitted to Casualty on a Friday night after hours of over-imbibing on anything that would blot out his miserable existence, but it made not the slightest difference to his treatment. He was noted for being a complete nuisance, but this didn't affect the dedication of the staff on duty and it was immediately clear that he was in a bad way. Abigail joined the ranks and assisted with the initial examination, not a task for the faint-hearted.

"Male Caucasian...I think," the ambulance man told them as they wheeled him in. "Unconscious; has not communicated with us at all; left leg fracture and multiple cuts to his face and arms. Police were at the scene."

"Thanks, Harry," the Casualty doctor said in response to the brief assessment. "We'll take over from here," then to his staff, "On my count of three...one, two, three" ...and the unconscious victim was transferred from the trolley to the examination table.

Apart from the obvious injuries he had sustained, Abigail was quite overcome by the stench of this unkempt, unwashed, pathetic individual who lay unconscious on the trolley in a sanitary cubicle, surrounded by green clad medical staff whose masks did little to alleviate the rancid odour emanating from beneath the red blanket. Ignoring their plight, they got to work in removing his clothing, merely rags which were drenched in urine and blood and which would have to be incinerated at the earliest opportunity. Abi's stomach retched, but her sheer grit and determination forced her to carry on, regardless of her own discomfort. As filthy garment after filthy garment was removed, it revealed the truly deplorable and distressing existence of the poor creature whose broken body lay limply at the mercy of those who were trying desperately to help him. Abi felt the colour drain from her cheeks and she was close to losing her grip on the situation, but a voice in the distance shocked her to her senses and she pulled herself up abruptly.

"I'm fine, damn you!" shouted the young man, "I don't need a doctor. There's nothing wrong with me. Where's the bloody idiot who couldn't look where he was going? My MG is a wreck! I'll sue him from here to kingdom come!"

"Will you please try to calm down, sir?" Sister Blackwood was saying as Abi slowly appeared from behind the curtains that scantily hid the patient from prying eyes. The arrogance of the ranting man came through with all guns blazing.

"Don't you speak to me as though I were one of your hospital lackeys! My father will hear about this ..." And Abigail knew immediately whose voice was bellowing around Casualty and who was hell bent on creating as much havoc as possible to get his own way. She wished she hadn't recognised him, but she had. He appeared to be drunk and he still felt that daddy dearest would have the political clout to save his skin. What on earth was he doing in Westerton at this time of night? What was he doing in the north of England at all? Keeping her head down, she walked quickly away before he realised she was there. Suddenly she felt a heavy hand on her shoulder and she spun round.

"Now just look who we have here. The noble virgin herself. Well, well, well! How are you, Abigail?" James asked, leering at her in his own inimitable way.

Abi froze. She had no desire to get involved with this despicable character ever again and she desperately hoped he had not revealed a flaw in her otherwise hardened exterior. Steeling herself, she dared to look into his cold, unfeeling eyes.

"By the look of things, I'm faring better than you are, James," she replied with forced confidence, wrenching herself free from his grip. "Sister, he's all yours. Treat him and then send him on his way. I'm sure these police officers will see he is taken to where he belongs."

"Bitch!" he hissed as he was forcefully guided into the examination room by another competent, young intern, this time under the careful watch of the local constabulary.

As she made her way back to the residential block, Abigail shivered and pulled her white coat around her as if to protect herself from any intruding forces, the main one at this time being the bad memories of the upper-class twit who had previously invaded her privacy. *I will not allow him to interfere in my life ever again.*

~ * ~

The intensive study and four placements during the final year prepared students for the following year's internship. Being academically qualified was the first part; putting those skills into practice without supervision, sometimes in life-threatening situations, was the greatest challenge in a young doctor's life. Abigail thrived on the challenge and she had developed a confident manner as her knowledge and competence increased. Throughout her five years at Medical College, her innate sense of application had steered her to success. Her sheer strength of character had sometimes been stretched to the limit and lesser mortals would have crumbled under the strain, but Abigail Marie Hawthorne had triumphed over adversity. She knew her beloved dad would be proud, and he deserved to be.

Almost as if he had waited until Abigail had earned the right to be called 'Doctor,' John James Hawthorne passed away peacefully in his sleep a few days after being told of his youngest daughter's success. At the age of fifty-five, he ought to have been enjoying his middle years, but the Hawthorne girls comforted themselves in their belief that with his job completed, he was now able to join his Mary at peace. He had been a wonderful father, a tower of strength when many men might have given up. John Hawthorne's epitaph would read: My strength came from my children; in them I found my joy.

Eighteen

Doctor A M Hawthorne

The hospital in Bolton stood in all its Victorian splendour on the edge of the industrial town. The blackened stone edifice was a legacy of the times when filthy smoke belched from cotton factory chimneys and coal fires in cosy parlours, adding to the unhealthy air that hung around all town centre buildings. Almost in spite of this, no matter what the time of day, there was always a vibrant atmosphere and powerful energy about the old place. Cars filled the sloping car park outside the main entrance and it was usually impossible to find a convenient spot even at official visiting times. Parking on Chorley Street or Spa Road meant that there was an uphill walk to the hospital and visitors were often in need of the WVS cuppa before venturing along the corridor to the wards. Those little old ladies serving tea and biscuits were green-clad angels in disguise, many of whom had undertaken their voluntary work during the war and were only too willing to carry on in peacetime. They were a very important part of hospital life. It seemed that the whole place would fall apart without them.

At all times during the day there was a constant stream of walking wounded, stretcher cases and accident and emergency victims. The out-patients' department was always crowded and waiting times varied from a few minutes to a few hours. Nobody seemed to mind. This was the norm and people waited patiently with noses in magazines and books, the stillness occasionally interrupted by nurses calling out the name of the next patient who was to enter the realms of consultant gynaecologist, the orthopaedic surgeon, or the orthodontist. As soon as a nurse appeared, all eyes looked expectantly in her direction, eyes that hoped, *Please let it be me next,* but when it wasn't, each returned to his previous occupation with the patience of Job.

Everywhere else was a hive of activity. Amidst the smell of disinfectant and the constant clamour of urgent voices, white-coated doctors with the obligatory stethoscope dangling around necks and from out of pockets, moved purposely from ward to ward, usually accompanied by several attendant nurses. Green-attired theatre orderlies pushed recumbent patients back to the recovery wards and blue uniformed physiotherapists put unwilling victims through grueling, excruciating exercises, unconvincing in their explanations that it was necessary to be cruel to be kind. Hospital life never stopped; hospital staff never gave up in their endeavours to heal the sick and also tend to the wounded.

After her internship, Abigail chose to work in her hometown for personal reasons. She felt that she would like to give a little back to the town where she had grown up. She knew that she could identify with many of the people in the town. They were her kind of people; strong, open-minded folk, full of northern determination and basic honest graft. Her inbred knowledge of her townsfolk would help in prioritising their needs.

"And I can spend my off duty time with you, Meg!" she told her sister. "I'm hoping to catch up with Janet too. I haven't seen her since we left school." Being in Bolton would give her the opportunity to relax amongst the people she knew and loved. All this, of course, was assuming that she would have the time and the energy to spend on her social life, which had been sadly lacking of late.

True to form, she threw herself into her work and the first couple of months she spent in the various departments, familiarising herself with routine procedures and getting to know her colleagues. This was the usual practice and Abi felt that the time was invaluable for learning, observing, caring and treating. Some days the hours were long and demanding; other days, she actually found time to take a coffee break in the staffroom, though those occasions were rare. She learned the value of comfortable shoes and she acknowledged the necessity of being able to switch off during those moments of peace and quiet.

"We have an unwritten rule," her colleagues told her. "Patients and cases are not discussed over coffee. Once the drinks are finished, you do what you have to do, but as you can see, we have the biggest cups we could find to make the breaks longer!" Abigail had to laugh. The mugs reminded her of her father's white pint pot. Every man in Lancashire had a pint pot. It was his status symbol in his home, clearly not very elegant, but necessarily functional.

After the initial induction period, she was assigned to paediatrics. Working with children was what she intended to do and this was another exciting period of her life. Treating anyone who was sick gave her the ultimate satisfaction. Treating children added extra depth to her vocation. Sick children brought out a special sense of duty and care, and the rewards of seeing a child's health improve were wonderful motivation. Of course, the other side of the coin presented situations where treatment failed, or efforts to resuscitate were hopeless. Abigail hated that, but knew that every member of the medical profession would fight with all his might to save a life, but a child's life always brought out an inner strength of will to succeed.

The eminent Sir Percival Sinclair was Consultant Paediatrician at the hospital. He was an expert in his field and had been rewarded for his research into children's diseases. He was tall and distinguished and his hair, greying at the temples, gave him an almost regal appearance. He must have been a very handsome young man in his prime. His strict regime in the operating theatre was counteracted by a fatherly attitude on the ward. Children loved him, nurses were in awe of him and his colleagues had the greatest respect for him. His very presence in a room gave everyone a sense of well-being and that was a wonderful medicine for sick children as well as being a tonic for worried parents.

Abigail shadowed PG on his rounds and assisted in theatre for the first few weeks. PG was his moniker, as he put it, and insisted that everyone referred to him as PG (Percival Gerald) from the youngest patient to the oldest ward orderly. Most of the cases involved the removal of tonsils and recovering from accidents. Children were generally rapid healers and there was a regular turnover of patients on the two paediatric wards. PG's natural manner with the little ones certainly provided the necessary tonic and encouragement. Tears quickly turned to smiles, pale faces soon became rosy and haunted looks changed to contented expressions as children warmed to the gentleman doctor who had time for everyone, regardless of how trivial the situation might be.

The young Doctor Hawthorne rapidly became a favourite with the children. They loved her gentle touch, her quiet manner and the efficient way in which she dispelled their fears when they were afraid of the unknown. Abigail often stood at the entrance of the ward, hidden by a strategically placed screen and just watched all the activity going on in front of her. "Wow!" she said quietly, marvelling at the patience and competence of the nurses, some of whom were only just out of school and beginning their training. *They look so young and yet they attend to their duties with an enthusiasm that could only come from complete dedication*, she thought. She also recognised herself in some of those young nurses and hoped that she too would remain enthusiastic and dedicated as she progressed in her chosen career.

It wasn't long before her skills were put to the test and when a little girl was admitted with cuts and bruises after a fall in the park, the child was distraught and would not leave hold of her mother who, herself, was becoming distressed. The child, Barbara Barton, had bumped her head and it was imperative that she stayed in hospital overnight to monitor her condition. Fear of concussion or compression demanded that a close watch should be kept, but Barbara, wide-eyed and confused, clung desperately to her mother's arm. There were four boys at home, all under the age of five and Mrs Barton was unable to stay with her little six year old girl, but Barbara clung to her as she prepared to leave. Doctor Hawthorne took hold of Barbara's hand and gently coaxed her to let go of her mother. "Hello, Barbara," she said, "I'm Abigail and I'm a doctor. I'm going to make you feel better. Is that all right with you?"

Barbara looked disdainfully at the young woman who was sitting on her bed. "You're not a doctor," she declared, "Doctors are old and wrinkly! You're too pretty to be a doctor." The child was distracted and she released her grip on her mother's arm.

Abigail continued, "You know the bump on your head? Well, if you stay here with me tonight, I'll magic it away whilst you're asleep. I have some magic sweets which make little girls better..."

"I'm a big girl!" Barbara remonstrated.

"Whoops! Sorry, but my magic sweets work on big girls too." Abigail was quick to make amends. "Please tell me you'll stay, please Barbara," she pleaded.

Barbara looked at her mother, who by this time had moved towards the door in the hope that she might slip out unnoticed. "Mum?" she called, still a bit uncertain of what she should do, "Doctor Abigail is giving me some magic sweets to make me better and says she wants me to stay with her here. Can I, Mum? Please?" a complete reversal of emotional blackmail! "You will come back for me in the morning, won't you?"

"Of course I will, love," her relieved mother replied, "I know the kind doctor will look after you. Now be a good girl and do as you're told. I'll come back first thing in the morning. 'Night, night, sweetheart. Sleep tight."

"Mind the bugs don't bite! 'Night, night, Mum," and the child lay down, still holding on to Abigail's hand and her favourite teddy until she went to sleep. The young doctor determined that she would be there when the child awoke.

After a long and tiring shift, Abigail wended her way back to the residential block feeling quite desperate to rest her weary head on her pillow and close her eyes, shutting out the trials and tribulations of her busy day. The living quarters were situated a little way from the main building and necessitated a walk round the back of the geriatric block. She quickened her pace and as she approached the alleyway between the kitchens and the physiotherapy department, she thought she heard footsteps behind her. Looking back in the direction from where she had come, she peered into the darkness warily, but could see nothing and it was very quiet, almost eerily quiet. Perhaps she had imagined it. She was tired, very tired and the sooner she was back in her room, the better. She started to run towards the light at the end of the alley and as she turned the corner, someone grabbed her from behind. She screamed, albeit a half-hearted scream as two powerful arms enfolded her. A sickly smell of pipe tobacco mixed with the pungent whiff of strong liquor hit her nose and she struggled to get away from the obnoxious stench. "Well, well, well, Abigail. What are you doing out at this time of night and all alone, too?"

"Oh, Sir Percival!" she exclaimed, relieved that it wasn't a prowler, "I thought my end had come!" She laughed nervously. "I've just finished my shift and I'm going back to my quarters to get some sleep. I'll see you in the morning. Good night!" Her voice was shrill. She didn't feel at ease with this eminent physician and trying not to be rude, she excused herself in an effort to be free of an awkward situation.

"Let me walk you back to your quarters," PG offered. "I wouldn't like anything to happen to you between here and there." He put a big, heavy arm across her shoulders and almost forcibly guided her across the car park to the main entrance of the residential block.

Abigail wasn't comfortable. She didn't know why, but reasoned that she was just tired and PG was merely being protective of his junior paediatrician. "Thanks, PG," she said and punched in the security code to open the door. "Goodnight."

PG pulled on her arm as she was going in. As she turned, she was once again sickened by the awful stench on his breath. "Abigail," he said softly, repulsively.

"Yes?" She realised that she had snapped and felt guilty.

PG's grip tightened. "Abigail," he whispered, breathing out deeply and causing her to hold her breath in order not to be overcome by the stale fumes exuding from his mouth. "I'll see you tomorrow." Still keeping hold of her arm, he lowered his head and kissed her on the cheek. "Goodnight."

It was only a fatherly kiss, but it sickened Abi. She made a hasty retreat to her room, the security door closing firmly on the world outside. Sir Percival Sinclair strode out manfully into the darkness, a self-satisfied smile appearing across his middle-aged face.

Abigail lay on her bed and stared through the semi-darkness towards the window. The curtains were thin and the outside light shone through, making the place eerie and yet safe. She liked the semi-darkness. As a child she had preferred to go to sleep with the landing light left on at Hillside Terrace. She admitted to herself that she must have been afraid of the dark, perhaps afraid of not being able to see what might be lurking in the blackness that blotted out her comfortable world. Her sleep was disrupted by disturbing dreams. She began to run, her heart beating fast. Her legs were heavy and the hill was too steep to climb. Before her was a long corridor, but to reach it she needed to climb big, stone steps and her leaden limbs hindered her progress. Once at the beginning of the corridor, she was able to see what lay ahead, but there was no end. There were windows with no views, only emptiness. Settees were strategically placed along the never-ending passageway, but she dared not rest. Her mission was to find the exit, but still her legs would not move and she appeared to be rooted to the spot. Heavy rain poured down and covered her in black ink that she tried desperately to wash away. Suddenly, she heard a familiar voice. "Damn you, Abigail Hawthorne! I shall be behind you wherever you go." It was a girl's voice, Betty West's voice and yet the manifestation of the bodily form was not Betty West at all, but James Sylvester-Jones. He beckoned with a wizened finger and shouted loudly, "I don't need a doctor! Don't talk to me as though I were one of your lackeys," and Betty West joined in, taunting and grinning evilly as she always did. "What are you going to do now Miss Know-it-all Hawthorne? What now? What now? What ...?"

~ * ~

Abigail woke sweating and shaking. Nightmares paradoxically gave a sense of relief and comfort in the realisation that there was no substance to what had happened. She turned over and tried to recover a feeling of well-being, but disconcertingly, it was a feeling which eluded her and she spent the rest of the night tossing and turning until the alarm clock told her that it was time to start the day all over again.

When she arrived on the ward, the night staff were just going off duty and the day staff were already bustling around clearing up after breakfast and carrying out ablutions. Her first port of call was Barbara, to ask her if her magic sweets had done the trick. The little girl was already dressed, sitting on the edge of her bed and still hanging on to the teddy bear.

"Well, my friend, how are you this morning?" she asked the child, even though she could see that she was much better.

"Okay...thank you," Barbara replied, "My mum's coming in a minute. I'm going home."

"Oh I see. Good," and Abi wondered who had given the all clear, seeing that she had only just arrived on duty and had been the admissions doctor the night before. She ought to have examined the child before she was cleared to leave the hospital. She was just about to go to find the ward sister when PG appeared and greeted her in the same over-familiar way as the previous night in the hospital grounds.

"Abigail, my dear," he gushed, holding her by the shoulders and bending low so that his face was only an inch away from hers. She stiffened and recoiled from the sickly smell that emanated from this over-bearing man, a mixture of toothpaste and aftershave which might have been quite pleasant in different circumstances. "I checked your patient for you," PG continued, "You don't mind, do you, darling? She's well enough to go home. I've signed her out."

Abigail was irritated. She wondered who would be responsible if Barbara should have a relapse and be forced to return to the hospital. Would PG accept the responsibility for her then, or would he pass the buck and make her take the blame for his mistake? Abigail was embarrassed. Not only had PG made her look incompetent, he had attracted stares from the nursing staff who were surprised by his familiarity with her. His unwelcome attention unnerved her and she felt herself blushing as she freed herself from his grasp. "Thank you, PG," she managed to say, trying not to show her irritation in her voice, "Shall we start our rounds?" and she walked to the first patient, intent upon putting that little episode behind her.

PG completed his rounds in record time, almost as if he had a pressing appointment. When he left the wards, he instructed Abigail to take over and then barked, "In my office please at eleven thirty before lunch, Doctor Hawthorne." Then he was gone.

Abigail looked at the ward sister and shrugged. "I wasn't late on duty, was I?"

"I don't think so, but I have never seen him in that mood. Have you done something to upset him?" Sister Bennett asked. She thought that if the young Doctor Hawthorne had said something out of turn to PG, it would be a first. All the nursing staff hung on his every word and it was unheard of to contradict, or question his wisdom. The sister looked at Abigail with disdain. The very thought of upsetting PG appalled her.

At eleven thirty precisely, Abigail knocked tentatively on PG's door. "Come," boomed the voice from within and she opened the door to find PG ensconced in a very large armchair near the bay window that looked out over the well-tended hospital gardens. "Ah, Abigail, I've been waiting for you. Do take a seat."

He motioned her towards the smaller chair opposite his and she went to sit down, hoping to get this over as quickly as possible. There was an awkward silence, an uncomfortable, intimidating atmosphere between them. Abigail was the first to speak. "Have I done something wrong?" she asked, aware that if she had offended the mighty PG, she would have to apologise and get on with her job. There was no place for antagonism in the hospital environment and she would like to have this sorted without any fuss.

"Wrong? Why, of course not, sweet Abigail. You could never do any wrong in my book. I just wanted to spend some time alone with you, to find out more about you, to get to know you better."

He smiled revealing crooked, creamy teeth and it crossed Abigail's mind that he ought to have worn braces when he was younger, but this was no time for dental assessment and she needed to, wanted to, get back to her work. What was she doing here anyway? Alarm bells were clanging inside her head, but she silently rebuked herself for being so suspicious. This man was her boss and he had the right to get to know her. They had to work together, to trust each other's judgement, to know how each would react in given situations, but there was still something about PG's attitude that felt like an intrusion into her privacy.

"What would you like to know?" she asked, hoping that her discomfort didn't show. She told him about her childhood and how her father had replaced her mother who had died at her birth. She told him about Meg and Patty and briefly about her ambition to be a good doctor.

"No, no, no," he interrupted, sounding more than a little irritated, "I don't want your family history. I want to know about *you*! What makes you tick? What turns you on?"

"Excuse me?" Abigail said, "Am I missing something here, PG?"

"You are a very beautiful young woman, you know," PG stated and moved to kneel at her feet. "I would like to get to know you better, really get to know you, in the biblical sense if you understand," and he gently took her hand in his, stroking it as he gazed up at her bewildered face.

"I'm sorry, Sir Percival," she said calmly, "This isn't what I want and if you'll pardon my boldness, it's not what you need neither. Now, if you'll excuse me, I have work to do." Without another word, she unceremoniously removed her hand from his and left the office, her dignity still intact.

PG sat in silence. *What a spirited woman*, he thought, spurred on in his quest. He smiled to himself and thought of all the glorious days he would have in the company of Doctor Abigail Hawthorne. Job satisfaction? Oh yes, he would have that.

The next few days were hectic. Theatre lists were full and it seemed that every child in Bolton needed to have his tonsils removed. The extra work suited Abigail, since it adhered to her philosophy in life that problems were solved by throwing oneself into one's work. The fact that PG was constantly breathing down her neck didn't help at all, but he had not done, or said anything more which offended her sensibilities, so she felt that perhaps he had realised his mistake and decided to forget the office incident. She began to relax again and her job became more and more demanding, more and more interesting, more and more satisfying. Hospital life suited her and she blossomed in her contentment with life in general.

She was scrubbing up for an appendectomy when PG walked in. She had seen him through the mirror, but kept her head down so that she wouldn't have to make polite conversation before pre-op consultation. Her relationship with him was strictly business and he seemed to have accepted that, at least that's what she had thought.

"Hello, my favourite Junior Paediatrician," he crooned and slid his hand down her back, pausing briefly to squeeze her bottom. Abigail froze momentarily, but chose to ignore it until he said, "Come to dinner with me." He leaned towards her and she could feel his breath on the back of her neck.

"Thank you, but no thank you," she replied, realising that she had to keep a cool head and not allow this nasty, obnoxious, middle-aged, smarmy individual to take advantage of his position. "I would prefer to keep this as a working relationship. You are a married man and an eminent physician. Please don't do anything to tarnish your reputation, PG."

PG's expression changed from condescension to anger. "I am your superior and I could demand more respect than that,

Doctor," he spat through clenched teeth, "But seeing that you wish to play hard to get, I'll bide my time and then you might see what is on offer if you play by my rules."

Abigail was astounded by his audacity and turned to face the ... she couldn't give him a name ... just a contemptible creature who appeared to be propositioning her. "Are you making improper suggestions?" she hissed at him, "If so, your motives are less than honourable and you leave me no alternative but to report you to the authorities." She was desperately trying to keep her voice low so as not to be heard by the bevy of PG's attendant nurses all twittering around at his beck and call.

"Go ahead. They'd never believe you. As you say, my reputation goes before me." There was something objectionable in his tone and Abigail was temporarily silenced when she noticed that the theatre staff stood watching as the conversation had progressed. They were standing far enough away not to have heard clearly, but their faces showed expressions of confusion and morbid interest. Body language had made it obvious that the exchange had not been friendly and for the second time in a couple of weeks, she had to work under the added pressure of being harassed. Perhaps it was just a hiccup and she hoped it would cure itself very soon. No such luck. The situation didn't change and PG frequently made a nuisance of himself in order to gain the attentions of his Junior Paediatrician, so much so that it was becoming noticeable to others, faceless individuals who chose to hide behind their jobs rather than to admit to any wrongdoing on the part of their errant superior.

Abigail kept the problem of PG to herself, yet when she visited Meg, she confided with her that PG was becoming over-bearing, but it was nothing she couldn't handle. Meg, ever astute, knew it irked and upset Abigail, otherwise she wouldn't have mentioned it. "Look, Abs, you can tell me to mind my own business if you like, but if there is a problem, it has to be reported. Don't let protocol stand in the way if indiscretions are taking place."

"Meg, leave it!" Abi said. Meg was commenting on something she knew nothing about. "You can't possibly understand, because you haven't been there. I'll handle it. I don't need you to tell me what to do. I only told you to get it off my chest."

"Okay, okay, Doctor. Don't bite my head off! I know when I'm being told off."

"It's such a delicate situation, Meg and I'm sure it's a clear case of male menopause. It may not be a recognised condition, but I think some men feel the need to prove that they are still desirable and attractive to women. He comes across as a very polite and honourable man most of the time. Unfortunately, when he opts to display his more objectionable side, PG has chosen to lavish me with his unwanted attention."

"You don't have to put up with it," Meg argued, "Talk to someone, please, Abi."

"Okay, I'll see about it after the weekend," she agreed, "but I don't want to be the instigator of an enquiry. It might get messy, not to mention the embarrassment it will cause. In the meantime, this is my weekend off and I don't want PG to ruin that too!"

The hospital was buzzing with rumours when Abigail returned after her weekend off. A couple of trainee nurses had been openly talking about PG and his 'wandering hands.' Abigail overheard and went to verify what they were saying.

"Are you sure?" she asked the nurses, "This is a very serious allegation, you know," yet in her heart she knew that what they were saying was absolutely true, every word of it.

The bolder of the two was quick to reply. "Look, Doctor, we might be young and inexperienced, but we know when we're being touched up. He doesn't exactly grab our boobs; more like brushing his hands across our chests accidentally on purpose as he looks at our name tag, or straightens our apron and always with that lecherous glint in his eye."

"He's pinched my bum more than once," rejoined the other, quieter nurse, "and told me he'd like to examine me." She blushed. "In private," she continued, "He even asked, 'your place, or mine?'"

"Right!" Abigail made her decision there and then. As their senior medical officer, she could see that it was her duty to make a stand and she resolved to approach the chairman of the hospital committee with a formal complaint. She hadn't intended to instigate the enquiry, but it was obvious that PG was making a bigger nuisance of himself than she had at first realised.

The hospital authorities had no choice but to take the allegations very seriously indeed and everyone whose work involved contact with PG would have to be interviewed. Statements would have to be made and it was quite obvious that they wouldn't make pleasant reading. Apparently, whilst Abigail had thought that she was the only one attracting the attentions of her randy superior, he had frequently been seen outside the nurses' quarters and had pestered for favours of a sexual nature. Until then, nobody had had the courage to speak out. It just wasn't the done thing to make complaints about one's superiors, but someone had to make a stand for the little man. As for PG, he must have been mad. After so many years of respect in his profession, his uncharacteristic and unpredictable behaviour had caused great embarrassment to the authorities. Keeping all knowledge of it within the hospital was their chief priority and all staff were warned of legal action should any information be leaked to the press. The biggest concern was to preserve the fine reputation of this excellent establishment at all costs. Sir Percival had to be relieved of all his duties until the situation was resolved.

Abigail gave a very full and thorough report of what had taken place between Sir Percival and herself. "Why didn't you report the misconduct earlier, Doctor Hawthorne?" the chief administrator asked, looking over his glasses at Abigail who was seated opposite a long table of erect, stern-faced adjudicators.

"At first I thought Sir Percival was just being kind. The night I bumped into him as I was going off duty, his attitude was fatherly. When he began to be more persistent, I was worried that his word would be accepted before mine and he intimated as much." It was a great relief for her to give her version of events and, knowing that she was not alone gave her the motivation to continue.

"Doctor Hawthorne," the leader of the stern faces enquired, "Did you ever give Sir Percival any encouragement to...to...er..."

"No, I did not!" There was no need to elaborate.

"Are you able to say that unequivocally?" another of the stone-faced jurors asked.

"Yes! Unquestionably, absolutely and totally," Abigail answered, irritated that her own reputation was under scrutiny, but she didn't wish to antagonise the panel of judges. She took a deep breath and tried to relax. "I really would prefer not to be here," she said, "It would have been much easier not to give evidence, but since I'm honour bound to speak the truth, I am here as a victim, not as a woman scorned. I respected an eminent paediatrician who chose to abuse his position. I am not here to instigate his downfall. He did that for himself. I have spoken the truth and trust that you will assess that in your own way."

"Thank you, Doctor Hawthorne, you may go now," the chief administrator said, his tone and manner giving no hint of how Abigail's evidence had been received. She sighed as she closed the door behind her. *Now I have work to do.*

The weeks that followed were busy and yet there seemed to be a cloud hovering over the department. Decisions had not been made and, although a locum paediatrician had been engaged, much of the responsibility fell on Abi's shoulders. She relished the hard work and she thrived on the sense of duty, but felt that they wouldn't be able to enjoy their work again until they all knew what was going to happen as a result of the enquiry.

Nobody in the hospital saw PG again. Six weeks after the official complaint had been lodged, they were informed that, on the recommendation of the Board, he would take early retirement from his post. Since he had expressed deep regret for having caused such stress and embarrassment and had admitted responsibility for all misdemeanours, it was unnecessary to hold an industrial tribunal. Sir Percival Sinclair would not return from suspension and a new consultant paediatrician would be appointed. It was rather an anti-climax. No one had wanted to see PG sacked, but nor did they wish to be placed in compromising positions and they would never be able to trust him again. It was a very sad end to a distinguished career and Abigail couldn't help wondering if she would ever find the vocational fulfilment she craved. *If I am to progress along the road to my dream, I need to do it without the likes of Sir Percival Sinclair as my example. Of that I am certain. A highly respected physician has been universally admired in his field, but has run out of respect through his own stupid behaviour. What a fool he's been!*

Nineteen

After the episode with Sir Percival Sinclair, Abi decided it was time to apply for a post in a different hospital. With her fierce ambition still ruling her decisions, she knew that she needed wider and more varied experience with children to achieve her goal. She moved back to Manchester and was able to continue her studies whilst working at the inner city hospital. Her work with children was all she had expected it to be: demanding, stimulating, satisfying and rewarding. With each week, each month and another year providing her with more valuable experience, her professional status was being regarded with great esteem. It would not be too long before she could be called Consultant Paediatrician in her own right, her dream becoming reality.

Out of the blue, she received a telephone call from Meg. "Come for dinner on Saturday," she insisted, "Phil and I are having a dinner party with a few friends and the change will do you good."

She hadn't been out to dinner for ages and she enjoyed the company of Meg's friends. "Okay, you've twisted my arm! I'll be there. Have my bed aired and ready. I don't think I'll drive back to Manchester after dinner. I'll be able to have a glass of wine, or two, or three!" she laughed.

When Saturday came, Abigail dressed casually in tailored trousers and silk shirt. Her hair still framed her face with little wispy curls and she was a picture of rosy contentment. At twenty-seven years old, her appearance was still youthful in spite of the toll taken by her demanding job. There were to be eight guests, including Abigail, and seating was arranged so that everyone would be able to join in over dinner conversation. There was nothing worse than feeling isolated at the end of the table. It surprised Abi that she was sitting next to David Cohen, the solicitor. She hadn't known that Meg and Philip had invited him, but she realised that they must have done so as a thank you gesture. Meg had once said he had been very helpful when she had obtained power of attorney to manage their father's estate and afterwards.

"How good to see you again, Abigail. It must be three or four years now," he said as he took his place on her right, with Philip on her left. "I hear that you are fast becoming an authority in children's medicine." She recalled the last time they had met. She knew she had been very preoccupied with all sorts of temporary stress and she felt now that she might have previously misjudged this man in thinking him supercilious and prying. He smiled and she noticed for the first time that he was extremely handsome and had the most engaging gaze, rather unnerving in that he seemed to command her attention with a mere look and yet she didn't feel awkward in his presence.

"Oh, I wouldn't say I'm an authority just yet. I'm merely doing my job," she offered. "I feel blessed that I'm doing what I love and getting paid for the privilege."

"The last time we met, we had very little time to talk," David continued, carefully measuring his words. "You were a little remote then, if I might say so, but I realised that your studies and your father's condition were obviously dominating your thoughts. Perhaps now that we aren't wearing our working hats, we can get to know each other better."

"Perhaps," Abi replied. *Is David Cohen flirting with me? What audacity,* but she had to admit to herself that she was warming to the person behind the smile. He appeared to be interesting, attentive and very polite. She hadn't seen those qualities in a man for a long time and her heart surprisingly skipped a beat.

Dinner was a huge success and Meg had noticed her little sister was getting along famously with the dashing solicitor. "Wow!" she enthused when the guests had left and, endeavouring to show sisterly interest, she continued, "Talk about chemistry! We could see the electricity flowing between you two! Come on now, little sis. What gives?"

"Meg! Don't be so nosey! But since you ask, we have agreed to meet for lunch next week and before you start match-making, it's just lunch!"

"Okay, Abs, but..."

"But what?" Abi tutted loudly. "Meg, I'm a big girl now. I can make up my own mind, you know!"

"I know. I'm just playing the role of big sister, that's all,"

"Well don't. I'll lead my own life, if you don't mind." It was a very bold statement for one so inexperienced with men, but Meg took the hint and said nothing more about it.

~ * ~

David Cohen's practice had recently moved to Manchester and his offices were on Deansgate. They had arranged to meet at the Midland Hotel when Abi had a couple of hours to spare and he was able to take an extended lunch break. When she arrived, he was already there and greeted her with a kiss on the cheek. Abigail was taken aback, not because he had kissed her, but because of the sensation that overwhelmed her. She hadn't experienced that since...well, since Tony Simpson had kissed her at the school party. She couldn't believe how she felt, but she maintained her composure and told herself that her hormones were playing havoc with her sensitivities. Try as she might though, she could not hide from the fact that this man had awakened her soul again. A little kiss on the cheek had excited her. Her eyes sparkled and he was aware of the radiant glow about her.

"You look wonderful, Doctor Hawthorne, or should I say Miss Hawthorne now that you are aiming to be a consultant?"

"Abi will do," she said, and she thrilled at his touch when he took her hand to lead her to their table. Lunch passed quickly and they both had to return to work. Abigail thought it was such a pity that they weren't able to prolong their time together, but didn't wish to show her eagerness to her companion for fear of his thinking her too forward. They did, however, plan to arrange a proper date, a night out...dinner, a show, whatever. *Whatever?* she wondered, but quickly banished the thought as soon as it popped into her head. *What is this man doing to me? He has appeared out of the blue and is very quickly and inexplicably getting under my skin.* They had met only a couple of times and she felt she was in a very sensitive situation, but she couldn't deny she liked it!

Because of punishing schedules, the promised date with David Cohen didn't materialise for a couple of weeks. For her part, Abigail didn't have time to dwell on the matter, but in quieter moments, she wondered if she would ever hear from him again. Then to her surprise, she found an invitation on the doormat when she arrived home after a particularly busy day. Coincidentally, she had a long weekend free for the first time in weeks. *I'll pick you up at 8.00 pm. Wear something special. Love, David x*

She made a special effort and wore her little black dress which hugged her figure and which was the fashionable mini length without being too revealing. With black suede court shoes and matching handbag, she looked every inch a model, her blonde hair and perfect skin tone displaying a beauty beyond any man's wildest dreams. David collected her on the dot of eight o'clock. "You look divine," he said and guided her gently into the waiting Rolls.

"Chauffeur driven?" she exclaimed, "Where are we going in such splendour?"

"This is my father's limo and this is Morgan, his chauffeur. Morgan, may I introduce Doctor Abigail Hawthorne? You are still just doctor, aren't you, Abi?"

She acknowledged the driver with a friendly smile. "I am for a while longer yet. I have a lot of work to do before I can progress up the ladder. I take up my new post at the Children's Hospital next week. I'm really excited about it!"

"Does that mean I'll have to make another appointment before I may see you?" David laughed ominously.

"Not at all. By then I shall be able to organise my time sensibly, but one can never account for the unexpected and children don't fall ill to order. It always seems to be in the early hours of the morning, or just as I'm sitting down to dinner."

"Let's hope that doesn't happen tonight," David declared. "Mother wouldn't wish you to miss her *paté de foie gras!*"

"Your mother?" Abigail asked realising that she must have sounded like a frightened schoolgirl who had been summoned to see the headmistress.

"Fear not, fair maiden," David teased, "My parents are looking forward to meeting you and they have arranged this dinner party in your honour. It isn't every day that I bring home the girl of my dreams!"

"Now you're being facetious," Abigail scolded. "I just wish you had told me in advance that I was to meet your parents. I hope I'm up to it."

"You, my darling, will be a sensation," he said, kissing her lightly on the cheek as the car drove through impressive wrought iron gates just off Stand Park Road. Morgan drew right up to the front of the house. He dutifully opened the door of the limo and David climbed out first. He duly took Abigail's hand as she slid her long, elegant legs out of the limousine and gracefully stepped on to the paved driveway that led to the beautiful, stately house. Walking up to the door, she smiled to herself as she thought fondly of Hillside Terrace. *My childhood home would have fit into one corner of this palatial residence, but to me, it was the very foundations of my future and I owe everything to those humble beginnings.*

~ * ~

Marcus and Magda Cohen were gentle, quietly spoken people who had come to England in 1932, just before Adolf Hitler became chancellor of the country in which they had been born. They had been young then and found life in England difficult, but Marcus had studied law in Germany and quickly gained a place at university where he gained his degree, thus setting up his law firm with a compatriot, Isaac Zatman. Cohen & Zatman, Solicitors, very soon became established at the forefront of the Jewish community in Manchester and with the increase in the numbers of exiles seeking refuge in Britain, their services were needed more than ever. The company thrived and Marcus Cohen would remain eternally grateful for the opportunities given to him in this fair land.

Magda took longer to settle and felt isolated in a country where she could barely speak the language. When she was alone on dark winter evenings, she was left at home in a two-bed terraced house with no bathroom, an outside lavatory at the bottom of a flagged yard surrounded by high brick walls and closed off from the cobbled back street by a padlocked gate for fear of intruders. At first she thought she might as well have stayed in the ghetto in Munich, but if they had stayed there, they would have had to wear the Star of David on their sleeves and the authorities would have taken all their belongings and eventually their pride, if not their lives. Here she felt she was safe and so were her children. With her two little girls, she spent the days at home cooking and experimenting with her own recipes. She made friends at *schul* and eventually she was able to feel more confident about her new life. When Golda Liebewitz discovered her talents in the kitchen, she used her own business acumen and Magda's skills to set up a delicatessen in Cheetham Hill. Once the children were in school, Magda was able to dedicate herself to running the business and, within a very short time, the deli was a thriving concern. With Marcus becoming established in his office and Magda happy in her shop, the Cohens soon became respected members of their community and settled well into their adopted country.

David was delivered in 1939, the son they had prayed for after the two girls had been born. Magda had worked right up to the day of the birth and had taken the sleeping baby to the deli almost as soon as he had made his appearance into the world. When war broke out, Marcus had joined the RAF. He had survived many sorties and by the end of the war, was able to settle in Whitefield and rejoin Isaac in his law practice, with some pride in the fact that he had made a stand, however small, against the tyrant who had forced him to leave the country of his birth. David had been growing up whilst he had been away, but now this father had the time to prepare his only son for manhood. God was good.

~ * ~

The Cohens were in the drawing room when David introduced Abigail. "Ve are so pleased to meet you, Abigail," Marcus Cohen said, the slightest trace of an accent making him sound rather appealing. "David has told us so much about you."

"Oh goodness, that sounds ominous," Abigail answered, "I'm delighted to meet you both, Mr and Mrs Cohen."

"Please," Magda Cohen entreated in her tiny, unassuming voice, "I'm Magda and this is Marcus. Mr and Mrs Cohen is far too formal. Would you like an aperitif, Abigail? Martini? Sherry?"

"Martini Rosso would be lovely, thank you," Abigail replied and David took her hand as they went to sit on the sofa in front of an enormous marble fireplace, where pine logs burned brightly to give the room a cosy, homely feel. The whole atmosphere was relaxed and Abi wished that the butterflies in her stomach would stop fluttering. She told herself there really was no need to be nervous, and slowly, as she sipped her martini, she began to feel more at ease.

David's sisters and their husbands arrived just before dinner was served and apologised for being late. "Sorry, Mama," Rachael said quietly as they arrived. "Businesses and children don't really make the ideal combinations for arriving early for dinner appointments." However, they soon relaxed as they sat round an exquisitely laid table and with the help of good wine, the conversation was genial, light-hearted and occasionally enhanced by family humour and Cohen witticisms. The dinner was perfect— Magda's own *pate de foie gras* delicious. Abigail thought she was exactly where she wanted to be and felt an instant rapport with the Cohen family. David particularly noticed how his family had taken to Abigail and glowed with inner pleasure.

It seemed like a spur of the moment thing. Surely it could not have been planned. David decided that the time was just right. He tapped his coffee spoon gently on his saucer in order to gain everyone's attention. "Mother," he said looking to the end of the table where Magda appeared every inch the matriarch in spite of her diminutive stature. "Thank you for providing a most delicious meal. Father, the wine was perfect. Rachael, Naomi…"

"Come on, David. No speeches," Rachael's husband, Nathan chided, "This is a family get-together, not a law court!"

"Ah well," David continued, "Humour me. Just give me a moment. This is important." He took hold of Abi's hand. "Now you have all met Doctor Hawthorne…"

"Of course we have and about time too. You've been raving on about her for long enough!" Peter said. Peter was Naomi's husband, an engineering factory owner and he always called a spade a spade without fear of being offensive.

"We've heard all about you, Abigail," Naomi informed her. 'Didn't David meet you at your sister's dinner party?"

"He did, although we had met very briefly before that when I was a student."

"Well, he's quite besotted with you, I can tell you…"

David coughed deliberately and continued unabashed, "Well…I have something to say." The atmosphere was most electrifying and looks of anticipation passed from one to the other in pregnant silence. He smiled at Abigail, her face flushed as a result of the claret. As he knelt on one knee by her side, still holding her hand and looking lovingly into her shining eyes, he asked, "Abigail, will you marry me?"

Abigail gasped and the others cried out in joy, tears trickling down Magda's cheeks and pride swelling in the heart of Marcus, the head of the Cohen family. Abi wasn't shocked, more surprised that this devastatingly handsome young man was proposing to her in front of his adoring family and so soon after they'd met. Here was an eminent Jewish family welcoming a Gentile woman into its home and the son and heir was proposing marriage. She thought she had fallen in love with him at Meg's dinner party. Since that kiss on the cheek when they went out to lunch, she had gone to sleep each night with him on her mind and had wakened with him in her thoughts every morning. She decided there and then that she definitely did love him, of that there was no doubt. She knew that she was allowing her heart to rule her head. How could she possibly behave in this way? She was Abigail Marie Hawthorne, sensible, level-headed, practical, realistic Abigail Hawthorne. Looking up into his dark eyes, she quietly answered.

"This is totally outrageous," she whispered and then more audibly, "I think I need somebody to pinch me to convince me that I'm not dreaming, but..." she paused and looking round at the expectant faces, she blushed slightly, not because she was embarrassed, but because her mind was spinning with confusion... "You have certainly swept me off my feet, but in answer to your question...Yes!"

Whoops of delight followed and champagne corks popped, heralding the emergence of a new era in the lives of two very different families. For their part, the Cohens approved of David's choice. They were ready to accept this Gentile woman into their fold. This was 1968 and attitudes were changing. Religion would not be an obstacle for them. If there were children, they would be Jews as their father and his father. The matter would not come up for discussion. In the meantime, Abigail was blissfully unaware of how hasty had been her decision and went happily into the preparations for the big day. She was following her heart and her head was uncharacteristically in the clouds.

Meg and Patty were happy for Abigail and were able to see for themselves that she was totally consumed with admiration for this man. She had at last found someone to love. At twenty-seven, she should be wise enough to make her own choices. They accepted David and his family had made them all welcome. Meg, in particular, was pleased that she might relinquish responsibility for Abi's well-being, even though it had all happened so quickly. Patty married and living contentedly with her stock-broker husband, considered that Abi wouldn't have married so hastily had she not been sure of her man.

"You're not pregnant, are you?" Meg asked her when she broke the news.

"No, I'm not, Meg, and I'm not going to dignify that question with an explanation." She didn't feel the need to tell Meg that she had guarded her virtue against all the odds. There were some things she would not disclose, not even to her big sister.

Meg and Patty had each wondered about her urgency to marry even though they couldn't explain their feelings and chose not to discuss the matter. Interference would only create bad feeling and that was the last thing they wanted. They threw themselves into the preparations and soon became enveloped in the happiness of the occasion—Abigail's happiness—and so their negative thoughts were locked away in the back of their minds.

The Cohen/Hawthorne wedding was the local event of the year. The civil ceremony took place at Arley Hall and the wedding breakfast at the Midland Hotel, where Abi had first felt the thrill of David's touch when he kissed her cheek. Since then, she had felt the rapture each time they kissed, but they hadn't consummated that love. David had respected her wishes, difficult though it had been, not to make love to her until their wedding night. As a doctor, she appreciated his dealing with the frustration wrought by her steadfastness regarding her maiden state and she frequently reminded him that she loved him all the more for waiting. He told himself that he was only human and a man had to do what a man had to do, but the thought of taking a virgin to his bed on his wedding night was almost unheard of in 1969 and well worth waiting for. Man landing on the moon in July of that year paled into insignificance by comparison, as far as David was concerned.

David and Abigail spent their first night together at the Midland Hotel before flying to Sorrento for their honeymoon. The bridal suite was wonderfully romantic and the four-poster bed was draped with the most delicate of ivory lace. The whole room was exquisitely decorated in ivory and gold and there was a warm glow emanating from the two people who were locked in each other's arms between the satin sheets. He had taken her into his arms as soon as they had closed the door on the world outside. He had kissed her, gently at first and then with a mounting passion. His kisses made her dizzy with expectation. He held her face in his hands and playfully kissed the tip of her nose. She held on to him, feeling his well-toned body and sensing his eagerness to take her to the realms of ecstasy. She pulled away slightly, feeling extremely innocent and hoping her inexperience wouldn't disappoint him.

"Don't move, darling," he whispered and began to unfasten the tiny pearl buttons down the back of her dress until it fell to the floor in a pool of silk around her feet. He removed his jacket and his tie, never taking his eyes off the vision of loveliness, his wife, standing before him and smiling a little self-consciously at the handsome man who was her husband. "You are very beautiful, Mrs Cohen. I adore you," he continued. For months he had imagined this moment and he wasn't disappointed. She closed her eyes and followed her instincts. Her senses were on fire and she had an overwhelming desire to please her husband as Nature intended. David was totally absorbed by the loveliness of the woman in front of him; a woman who had kept herself pure just for him. He was the man who was her lover. He was the first. He was the one.

Abigail too, had waited for this moment. Her sexual awareness had been awakened in her youth, but she had guarded her purity until she had found the man whom she could trust with her life. David was that man. He was everything she ever dreamed of and she was ready to open up to him. This was what she had waited so patiently for. It was surely the most wonderful feeling in the world. Their energies spent, they melted in each other's arms and slept until dawn when they made love again and again before breakfast was served to them in bed. Abigail thought she would never be happier and David felt a sense of masculine pride that he had been her first encounter with sexual desire.

Returning to work after the honeymoon was a wrench. Abigail was on cloud nine and every delicious moment of their love-making was etched in her mind, a mental record of the value of her long awaited fulfilment. She often found herself smiling and had to take a deep intake of breath in order to keep hold of her emotions. In quiet moments, she tried to work out for herself, what constitutes a good marriage. *David is my soul mate; he seems to know how I feel without having to say anything. Maybe eventually, I will learn to sense David's innermost thoughts too, but sometimes I find it difficult to anticipate his reactions. This deep relationship situation is a totally new experience for me and I am well aware that two people have to grow together to achieve perfection. The seeds have been sown and now it is time for our life together to mature.*

Once they were home again, reality set in. They both had to adhere to a new routine and at first, being apart for most of the day was difficult, for Abigail at least. Work dominated much of both their lives and she was only just becoming used to the situation when their first anniversary came around, seemingly very quickly.

Twenty

To Abigail, the life of the solicitor and a young doctor was the perfect blend of two people whose careers were completely different and yet in some ways the same. Whilst Abigail healed the sick with her medical expertise, David tended to others whose problems needed his legal judgment. She had tried to show an interest in his work, to find some links between his legal background and her own career, but David rarely, if ever, discussed his work with her and he didn't appear to be very interested in her days at the hospital.

"Please leave your work at work, Abigail. This is our time, not the National Health Service's." Abi was taken aback by the implication of his retort, but consoled herself with the idealistic thought that he didn't wish their blissful existence to be marred with work schedules and their time together should not be spoiled with discussions of their respective days at the office.

In the comparatively short time they had been living together, Abigail had been fully aware of the changes she had to make in sharing her life with another person. She had felt the complete transformation in her daily routine, but she wasn't totally convinced that David had made much effort to adapt to such changes in his life. He warmed to the times when Abigail was on duty during the day as she was generally home before he was by the time he had finished at the office. On those occasions, he was able to take full advantage of having a loving wife there to enhance his conjugal state.

"This is what married life is about," he told her when he arrived home from work and she was standing at the hob stirring the red wine sauce for their steak. "I want to come home to this every day. Coming into an empty house after a hard day at the office is not my ideal situation."

Abigail listened and smiled. "I understand what you are saying, David, and I do enjoy being able to make dinner for you every night, but my job..."

He interrupted the explanation that he'd heard on numerous occasions recently. "Let's have dinner and then you can make this man very happy."

"Oh you..." she sighed, trying to smile good-naturedly. "Don't you ever think of anything else?" Sometimes she would prefer to sit back and relax without the sex, but it was very clear that David's needs were far greater than hers.

Settling into an easy routine was difficult with Abigail's work schedules, but she felt they somehow worked around the odd times when they were able to be together. *Maybe this is what marriage is all about,* she thought, *even in this day and age. I don't think I'd go as far as burning my bra like those women in the news, but I certainly don't intend to become a slave to drudgery. Whatever David says, I will not give up...* She smiled to herself. *I do accept the need for equality and independence, but I also need to feel that my man will treat me like a lady, giving me the love, affection and respect I desire as a woman. I want the best of both worlds—women's liberation and loving acceptance from my man. Surely that isn't impossible.*

It did, however, begin to irk when she realised how David perceived her role in life differently. Since she insisted on going out to work, she would have to find the time somehow to do the necessary housework, but unless she could find a spare minute or two for necessary mundane chores like cooking, washing and cleaning, those things were left undone.

David appeared to be totally oblivious of the effort she made in juggling her time between work and home as she tried to be the perfect wife. "Do you think you might prepare the vegetables before I arrive home, David?" she asked him one morning as she gathered up her patient files to load into her car. It was only a simple question.

"That's women's work, Abi. A man doesn't cook, not this man anyway. His wife does that. Mother always does it for my father. I don't recall ever seeing him slaving over a hot stove," he replied indignantly.

"You're incredible, do you know that?" she told him, smiling amicably. "This is nineteen seventy and women go out to work these days. Making a home is a shared responsibility."

"You don't have to work, Abi. That's your choice. We could always hire a housekeeper if you can't cope. You know what to do if your work is interfering with what you have to do here."

"Allowing someone else to do my housework is totally alien to me, David, and I would feel extremely uncertain about having somebody going through my things in my absence."

"What is it with women these days? Mother's the same. Doesn't want a daily whilst she is still capable of doing the housework herself. It's feminine pride gone mad!" David scoffed.

"I can't believe you're saying that, David, but I hope you don't mind waiting for dinner then, because I'll be late tonight. We have a group meeting at seven o'clock," she explained.

"I'll eat out at the Club. But don't let it happen too often, Abigail. It's bad enough when you're on the night shift. Off you go then. I don't want to make my wife late as well as expecting her to cook dinner for me," he said with pointed sarcasm. He kissed her on the cheek and ushered her through the door. Abi decided to leave without further response. She had ward rounds at nine o'clock.

It didn't come as a complete surprise to her when David said, "I would like you to stop working, Abi. I want a wife who is at home for me and who isn't distracted with outside influences."

Abigail didn't like what she was hearing.

"I thought that once we were married," he continued candidly, 'you would see that it isn't necessary for both of us to be going out to work."

"What exactly are you saying, David?" Abigail asked, her voice unable to hide her dismay.

"I think it's very clear what I'm saying. I don't like you going out to work. I want you at home where you belong and I think I have the right as your husband to demand your compliance with my wishes." His out-of-place legal tone was very high-handed.

Abigail was dumbfounded. "You have to be joking, David. You cannot possibly have thought this through. Asking me to give up my life-long ambition in order to become a stay-at-home wife is excessive to say the least. What's the matter with you? I won't do it. No discussion; end of argument."

"I demand more respect than that, Abigail. I am your husband."

"And I am your wife and I shall do everything I can to make you happy, everything, that is, except giving up my job. You cannot ask me to do that."

David was angry. He hated not being in control of the situation. His male attitude told him that women obey their husbands and he would make sure that Abigail came round to his way of thinking eventually.

There was uneasy silence in the house for a while. For a few days afterwards, the row had made Abigail uncomfortable, but gradually, she thought that David softened and appeared ready to accept the situation. However, each time Abigail was on evening, or night duty, he started to go to the Club on a regular basis.

"It's preferable to coming home to an empty house," he told her and she accepted that with good grace.

"That's good," she replied. "At least I'll know that you'll have a decent meal provided for you. Thank you for being so amenable to alternative arrangements. I really appreciate it."

~ * ~

Weeknights at the Club were generally very quiet and after he had had dinner, he usually sat alone savouring his malt whisky and reflecting on life in general.

"Hello," she said, "Mind if I join you?"

He politely stood and shook her hand. "Please do," he replied. "I could do with a bit of company. I'm Dave."

"Linda."

"What's a nice girl like you doing in a place like this?" he asked, in an effort to be sociable.

"Nice? That's what you think, is it? Flattery will get you everywhere," she joked. "Actually I don't know what brought me in here. Maybe it was your magnetic personality." She was flirting with him and he liked it.

"Do I know you?" Dave asked her. "Your face is familiar."

"I don't think so, but I have been in here before. You may have seen me at the bar."

Dave laughed. "That makes you either a ballet dancer, or a lawyer." A moment of concern made him sit up and look at her more closely. "You're not a lawyer, are you?"

Now it was her turn to laugh. "A lawyer? Never in a month of Sundays, but I did learn to dance when I was younger. I didn't get further than grade one, though. I never knew the difference between third and fifth positions!" She laughed again, thinking of the significance of her remark.

Dave laughed with her. "What do you do then?"

"You first," she urged, "What do you do?"

"I'm an architect—in the city. I designed all those big office blocks that are going up," he told her. "Your turn."

Linda thought for a moment. She wasn't sure he had told her the truth, because he answered too quickly, but there was something about him that she liked and his eyes told her that he was interested in her. *He has a certain charm about him that oozes breeding,* she thought, *but such breeding usually comes with a beautiful wife at home. Men like him aren't left on the shelf.* "I'm a model," she lied.

Linda was a tall, leggy brunette, not at all like the girls he had been attracted to in his youth. Through the alcoholic haze, she looked about thirty-five and carried herself well. "Yes, I thought you were. You have both the looks and the graceful movements. Can I buy you a drink?"

"Thanks. I'll have a gin and tonic."

Dave the architect didn't have a wife. "You surprise me," she told him. "A man drinking alone in here usually has a wife who doesn't understand him."

David the solicitor had a wife, a wife who was wilful and too independent for her own good, but he silently reiterated, *Dave doesn't have a wife.* Linda didn't need to have access to David at all. Tonight he was Dave and Dave wanted to have some fun. Linda was a welcome and willing part of his little game.

Several drinks later, they were touching hands across the table and making eye contact that told them that they would be in bed within the hour. Dave leaned over and whispered in her ear. She smiled at his suggestion and stood up. Taking his hand, she guided him towards the door.

"Just a minute," he said, "I need the little boys' room." He hastily felt in his pocket for loose change, hoping the machine wouldn't be empty. "Better to be safe than sorry," he said waving the packet at her.

"Sensible man," she said, smiling invitingly, "Come on. I know just the place."

David hadn't planned it. It was just a set of circumstances that brought Dave and Linda together and Linda asked no questions when he left. She liked him and he paid up without argument. He called her his contact and he knew that he would see her again and again and again, whenever he chose. His actions had been scurrilously improper, but it excited him and it was a part of his life that *he* was able to control. He began to lead his double life without anyone knowing his whereabouts. He visited his family as he always had and when he felt like an evening with his contact, he made sure his tracks were covered. He discovered that he needed her and it suited him very well.

Abigail's job was more demanding than most in respect of time spent in the hospital. Whilst her schedules showed regular hours, her actual working time was sometimes, in fact, half as much again, occasionally doubled. Her dedication never wavered even after David's declaration that he wanted her to give up her career. Two years into her marriage, incredibly, she became very aware of the cracks that had appeared in the relationship, but determined that she could smooth them over. "We'll work at it," she told herself. "It seems that all marriages aren't made in heaven." *That is something with which I shall simply have to come to terms.*

David thought he had some control over his life, but he was still rankled by Abigail going out to work and her undivided devotion to her patients. He started to feel neglected in spite of the fact that he regularly found solace elsewhere. Whilst his casual sexual activities were very gratifying for him, he made sure of his wife's regular attention too to satisfy his needs and to make her think she was all he desired. She was so sexually naïve that she would think his libido was still in its honeymoon prime. It irked him greatly that she wasn't always there for him and at those times he often took refuge in his Johnnie Walker. A few drinks usually eased him into a state of complete relaxation and his Abigail irritations disappeared for a while. When she arrived home from a late duty, she often found him asleep in an armchair, the scanty remains of the whisky bottle by his side. At first she woke him to tell him she was home, but that annoyed him greatly and after several weeks, he was so bad tempered when he was disturbed, she began to leave him to sleep it off. Very often, he didn't bother to go to bed at all.

"Are you drinking so that you'll sleep better?" she asked one morning when David woke with the mother of all headaches. "Here, take these. You can't go into work like that."

He took the tablets from her and grimaced as he swallowed them. "In answer to your patronising question," he growled, "I *am* able to sleep without a drink. I drink because I enjoy it."

"Is it necessary for you to drink every night?" she dared to ask.

"What do you mean?" David's expression was becoming hostile.

"I mean is the alcohol a necessity, perhaps a problem?" Abigail was trying to show her concern without provoking what was an already inflammatory situation.

"No, it is not a problem. Can't a man have a drink in the comfort of his own home without the third degree? Give it a rest, Abi." His head hurt, but he needed to go to the office if only to escape the antagonism of his condescending little wife.

Abigail sighed wearily as David left for work, her confused mind trying to make sense of what was happening. He always chose to walk out when she needed answers.

After a month of night duty, Abi had a week off. She decided that she would try to make it up to David and lavish him with all her love and attention hoping that they might rekindle the spark that seemed to have been eluding them recently. David didn't respond. He was displaying a side of his character she certainly hadn't encountered before they were married. She longed for his tender touch, for the love he had shown her in the early days of their marriage, but he wasn't playing. "Oh, you have time for *me* now, have you, Doctor?" he asked with venom in his voice, "Are there no little patients who are demanding your undivided attention? God forbid that *we* should ever have children, Abigail. I would never get a look in."

"That's not fair, David, and you know it," she cried, hurt that he was apparently jealous of her career. "You were aware of the demands my job makes on my time when we met. Please don't make a major issue again of my going out to work." She went to put her arms around him to show him that she loved him, even though he was being most objectionable at that moment. David grabbed her roughly and kissed her hard and urgently. He appeared agitated, disturbed almost and his eyes glared at her with an intensity she didn't understand. She wasn't sure that she could handle him like this. His animal passion was taking over and she suddenly understood that she had neglected that side of their marriage whilst she had been on night duty. Perhaps the easiest way was to allow him to satiate himself even though she was apprehensive about it, but he disregarded her feelings and urgently devoured her, releasing all the pent up anger which had built up whilst she had been at work. Right there on the hearthrug, they made love if one might call it that, for it was more like cold, calculated sex than gentle, romantic fulfilment of their feelings for each other. The tenderness and gentleness had gone and he was going at her like a man possessed.

For a short while after that night, they had been a little more accommodating with each other, although that special feeling of togetherness seemed to have disappeared. They went to work, they came home, they had dinner and were polite to each other. They occasionally made love as a matter of routine, but the atmosphere was often tense and in spite of aborted attempts to talk it through, Abi was at a loss as to how to deal with it. Emotions were strained and making it difficult to communicate logically. She couldn't believe that only two years into the marriage of her dreams, she was struggling to keep it together. She had stayed away from David's parents and from Meg. That way she didn't have to make excuses and they would assume that she was working odd shifts when she hadn't been to see them. David hadn't visited his parents either and his moods had gone from bad to worse, especially when she had to work nights again. She had done her best to avoid night duties and her colleagues had covered for her on several occasions, but she couldn't expect them to do it on a regular basis. When Dave couldn't be bothered to see Linda, David was drinking heavily and he was often in a drunken stupor when Abigail arrived home. Abi noted too that he was going into the office late and much the worse for wear. She needed him to be sober. His words of a few weeks ago still echoed in her brain. *God forbid that we should ever have children!*

The opportunity for them to talk didn't arise for days. Their work schedules meant that they were like ships that passed in the night and that in itself didn't make for a stable relationship. During that time, there came the awful realisation for Abi that she had rushed too hastily into the marriage. She had been so very much in love with David and her heart had dictated her actions. She had failed to question her decision, because she had been so totally consumed with love for this man. Now, she knew that she had to make the best of a bad lot. *Perhaps the baby will bring us closer together, especially if I delay my consultancy until the child is at school. David would be happy if I were at home all the time, wouldn't he?* she reasoned silently.

That weekend, Abigail didn't have to work and it provided the long-awaited opportune moment to break the happy news. She prepared a special Saturday meal and David was surprised when he arrived home after a round of golf to find soft lights and sweet music and a table fit for a king. "What's all this?" he asked and for the first time in days, he smiled at his wife who was, he observed, looking absolutely radiant. She had a healthy glow about her that was extremely becoming.

"I thought it was time we spent some quality time together," Abi told him as she offered him a martini and patting the sofa, invited him to sit down next to her. "I have something to tell you. I'm going to delay my consultancy for a while..." David was ready to interrupt. "...No, don't say anything yet. I won't be able to work when our baby is born." She said it gently in the hope that her quiet approach would invoke a calm response and she looked appealingly at David.

He didn't reply at once. He rose and walked over to the fireplace where he stood, feet apart, arms behind his back and rocking slowly backward and forward with measured deliberation, almost like a headmaster about to reprimand a miscreant. He smiled again and Abigail was heartened by it. He breathed in deeply before he spoke. "Get rid of it," he said coldly and walked out of the room.

Abigail was stunned, but after a few moments, she chased after him and found him in the drawing room looking for his Glenfiddich. As he poured himself a large one, she pleaded with him to be reasonable.

"Reasonable?" he yelled, "That's what you call it, is it? It isn't reasonable when children take up all your time at work. It won't be reasonable when a child intrudes in our home!"

"That's not fair, David. You are never fair when you have to resort to that stuff in your hand in order to speak to me. You knew what my job entailed..." She had said all this on numerous occasions and she halted abruptly. How she hated confrontations. He took a large gulp of the malt and put down his glass. Menacingly, he moved towards Abigail, who was determined to stay her ground. This was their child and she had thought it had been conceived of their love. Now, she wasn't even sure that there was any love between them at all. The situation saddened her greatly. She turned to walk away, but as she did so, David swung with his fist and caught her on the side of her head. "I said *GET RID OF IT*!" he shouted and hit out again, this time with a flat hand across her face. Abigail fell to her knees and shielded herself from further blows, but David stormed off, out of the house.

There was no need for Abigail to wait for his return. She had no intentions of trying to salvage the already doomed relationship. She tended her bruised cheek before hastily packing as many of her belongings as she could carry and going Meg's. She hated to burden Meg with her problems, but she knew her room was always kept ready and Meg would understand her need to isolate herself from David. She admitted to herself that she had seen this coming for weeks, but she had chosen to ignore the signs hoping that the rough waters would subside and life would become normal again. Normal? She was beginning to think that normal was completely eluding her. She realised only too well that she had married in haste and now she must repent at leisure.

Twenty-one

Abigail reflected on the incidents of recent weeks. Her confidence in the male species had been shattered yet again. Having been set the example by her father, she realised she had been searching for a perfection that in her view was unique. She was in despair. The men who had touched her life so far had come nowhere near the ideal she remembered in the gentle man who was her hero and her mentor, her guiding light and her dearest, dearest friend. Perhaps she was seeking the impossible, chasing a dream. In David Cohen, she had thought she had found a close second to her beloved dad. She thought she could have trusted him with her life. *How wrong could I have been? How could I have been so naïve? I gave myself to him willingly and totally and expected the same in return. I realised too late that he wasn't the deeply caring person I had thought him to be. He seemed to metamorphose into another character and I have to wonder if his family saw that side of him too. Somehow, I doubt it. He was clever, as sly and as devious as a fox. He hoodwinked me into believing I was all that he had dreamed of in a wife, but he had not been satisfied with me.* She thought of the nasty, vindictive note he wrote after she had left, the contents of which showed how gutless he had become when he gloated that he found satisfaction elsewhere when she had *'neglected her wifely duties in preferring to heal sick children.'* Abigail knew in her heart that she could never be the person he wanted her to be, a sad little creature of a subservient wife whose only duty in life was to tend to her husband's needs. She was stronger than that, independent and ambitious. David had known that when he had swept her off her feet and eventually into his bed. Her emotions were in shreds and under no circumstances would she entertain becoming close to a man again. She wondered if all men were so self-centred that they were incapable of contributing to a loving and caring relationship. But then she thought of Meg's Philip and of Patty's husband, Steve, and realised that somewhere in the world, there were men who genuinely cared.

Her prime concern at this point was for her unborn child. She simply had to work and she went about it in the only way she knew how, with true grit and focused attention to detail. There were no half measures for her. All through her life, she had solved her problems through sheer guts, determination and dedication to the job in hand. This situation was no exception. *A baby needs to be clothed and fed. At least my work will secure a comfortable life for him...*she instinctively felt it was a boy.

After a short stay with Meg and Phil, Abigail moved into the residential quarters at the hospital for convenience more than anything. She had had no contact with David and when she filed for divorce, it was not contested. All communications were done through her solicitor, which seemed ironic really. However, divorcing David was comparatively easy once she had made the first move. Marcus and Magda Cohen, surprisingly, contacted her as soon as they knew what had happened. Abigail doubted that they had been given the whole truth, but was heartened by the fact that they didn't hold her responsible and did not excuse their son's behaviour. *'We have seen his degenerating lifestyle,'* they wrote, *'even though he tried to hide it from us. Nevertheless, he is our son and we will make sure that he does not disgrace our family further.'* After that, they had kept a discreet distance, but not before saying, *'We would like to be informed when our grandchild is born. We are Jewish and our family is very important to us.'*

On that, Abigail kept an open mind. Her own views were clear, though. *I will decide later whether or not I should respect the religious beliefs of the father of my child. Religion, to me, is treating others as you would expect to be treated yourself. My attitudes are essentially Christian, but I'm sure that Christian and Jewish values are intrinsically very similar. The fact that I accept Jesus Christ provided the world with ideals upon which to base one's life, does not, in my opinion, devalue what the Cohens believe. I would like to tell the Cohens that I believe how one lives one's life should be acceptable in the eyes of all mankind. I really ought to tell them it is a pity that David has not adhered to those ideals as a husband and as a man, but it is probably more prudent not to get involved in a discussion on such matters.*

Working with sick children gave Abigail such satisfaction. The Children's Hospital was situated on the outskirts of Manchester, but it was open to all children from a wide area. Although it was only a small hospital, children from Cheadle and Chester, Middlewich and Macclesfield, from areas all over Lancashire, Cheshire, Cumberland and even Yorkshire came for the specialist treatment on offer there and were given the best.

One could rarely be prepared for the unexpected. The nursing staff had been extremely busy as usual and Doctor Hawthorne had been on Surgical Ward One all day. A child with a ruptured appendix had become gravely ill and his parents had been at his bedside. Abigail had administered the medication herself to treat the peritonitis. For a while it had been touch and go with him and his parents were obviously very distressed. The boy's mother had stood up in order to go out for some fresh air, but the strain of watching her sick child had become too much and she keeled over, causing Abigail to lose her balance and fall awkwardly and heavily over an oxygen cylinder at the side of the bed. Ordinarily, this would not have been too much of a problem, but as she had not yet informed her employers of her pregnancy, she forced herself to carry on as though nothing had happened. She hoped that her anxiety for herself was not apparent to those around her, particularly the Ward Sister who, in Abi's opinion, missed nothing.

"Whoops!" she joked light-heartedly, rubbing her abdomen, "Here I go again, falling for my patients!" Nobody noticed her concern and busied themselves making sure that the boy's mother was all right and ensuring that she was taken out of the ward where she might recover quickly. Abi knew that she ought to have given herself time to recover from the fall, but typically, she ignored her own welfare and continued with the job in hand. When the boy's condition improved, she was able to take a break and went to have a cup of coffee in her office. No sooner had she sat down than her pager went and she was off again to tend another sick child whose condition had deteriorated, the coffee once again left to make cold, congealed rings round the inside of the cup. Only after she had been on duty for fourteen hours was she able to settle in her bed to catch up on some well-earned rest. "Am I glad to see you," she greeted Tom O'Mara as he arrived to take over for the night duty.

"So bad, eh?" he asked, knowing full well that every day was demanding, tiring, sometimes irritating, but always rewarding.

"Well, y'know..." Abi smiled wearily. She liked Tom. He was well into his fifties with a wealth of experience behind him and he had never lost his enthusiasm for his work. He was an Irish gentleman, a gentle man and he charmed the nurses with his soft brogue. If ever there were a typical doctor, Tom was just that. He opted to do the night duties as that was what he liked best. He was a widower.

"My nights are lonely since my wife died. I much prefer to go to sleep during the day when I can hear the birds singing and children playing outside. That way I feel I'm not alone," he told her. Abi thought it a very touching scenario, but she knew that Tom wouldn't want her pity and he loved being able to make his colleagues' working lives a bit easier by taking over the night shifts occasionally.

Back in her room, Abi got ready for bed and no sooner had her head touched the pillow than she was asleep. Despite the recent upheavals in her private life, she had managed to sleep well. There had been times previously when she had lain awake all night, listening to the deep breathing of her husband. She had listened to his ramblings in his sleep when a woman's name had frequented his somnolent groans. She had lain as close to the edge of the bed as she could with only the tucked in sheet preventing her from falling on the floor. She hadn't been able to bear David's touch any longer and needed as much space between them as possible as they paradoxically lay together. She was unable to relax for fear of his waking and abusing her verbally and physically as he had done during the latter part of their marriage. All that was in the past though and she found she was now able to sleep uninterrupted...

"Doctor Hawthorne! Doctor Hawthorne! Come quickly!" The loud knocking on her door woke her with a start. She jumped out of bed, threw on some clothes and ran to see what all the fuss was about. She didn't usually find an emergency call too stressful, but that night, she felt irritated that her sleep had been disturbed.

"What is it?" she asked, hardly disguising her annoyance.

The bewildered nurse hurried her down to admissions where the problem had occurred. "There was a man here demanding to see you. He said you owed him and he would not leave until he had seen you!" The nurse's voice was rising in a crescendo and she could not hide her panic.

"Did you ask Doctor O'Mara to deal with it?" Abigail thought that the nurse hadn't adhered to the correct procedure.

"He's on the ward, Doctor Hawthorne, and I was here alone. You know there is only a skeleton staff on the reception desk overnight." The poor nurse was becoming distraught.

"Don't worry. Where's the man then?" she enquired as she surveyed the empty room, incredulous that she had been raised from her bed for a hoax.

"There *was* a man here, honestly," the nurse assured her. "At first I thought he was drunk, but then he seemed all right and he asked for you, 'Urgently' he said."

Abigail was bemused. "Well, he isn't here now, is he?" She was too tired to argue. "I'm going back to bed and please don't call me again unless it's a matter of life or death!"

"I'm sorry, Doctor Hawthorne," the nurse apologised, embarrassed that she had made a fool of herself and evidently had not endeared herself to the clearly irritated doctor.

Sleep evaded Abigail. She was too tense to relax so she wandered about her room drinking hot chocolate in a vain attempt to make herself feel tired again. It was then that her mind drifted back to what the nurse had said... *'I thought he was drunk...'* She cast her mind back to the time when the old tramp had been admitted to Westerton. That night she had seen a part of her past that she would prefer to forget. Surely it wasn't rearing its ugly head again. She had been tired then as she was now, but she had come face to face with James on that night. "No!" she told herself, "You are just being paranoid. Snap out of it, girl!"

Abi lay in bed and stared into the darkness. She was unsettled and she felt tense. She deliberately tried to relax, focusing her mind on happier events, but it was impossible. Her body ached and her head was beginning to spin. She had a gnawing pain in her back and she was finding it difficult to lie comfortably. When the pain moved to the pit of her abdomen, she began to cry, not because the pain was too much for her to bear, but because she realised what was happening. She was going to lose her baby.

Abigail miscarried the next evening after being taken to Hope Hospital as soon as she raised the alarm. Physically she felt empty; mentally she felt drained. Meg and Philip had rushed over to Salford to be with her, but she needed to be alone and they understood that. "We'll come again tomorrow," Meg told her. "Try to rest and then you can spend a few days with us. A bit of Belford air and Lancashire hotpot will soon have the roses back in your cheeks!" Meg knew that Abi needed her space and she kissed her baby sister and left. How sad it was to see her like that.

Days later, Abigail was in Meg's kitchen sitting at the breakfast bar and watching Meg making toast on the kitchen range. The fact that she was with her big sister helped to ease her pain. Meg instinctively knew when she needed company and when she needed to be alone. With each new day, she felt stronger and her walks up Rivington Pike were providing her with the fresh air that was important to her recovery and the spiritual sustenance she desired. When she had been a teenager, she had climbed to the tower on the Pike, her dad's look-out point and there she had solved most of her problems. On occasions when she felt the need to reflect, she had visited her mother's grave and had talked to the woman who had given her life so that she might live. Now, as a woman who had lost a child, she knew her mother would understand her pain.

"Mother," she had said, "I wanted this baby so much, even though his father had rejected him. I longed to hold him in my arms and nurture him with all the love he deserved. Now, I can't do that, but I ask you to look after him in heaven. I know you will love him. I'm not a very religious person, but I do believe that lives continue after death in the hearts of those who are left behind. You and Dad are with me always and my baby has joined you now. Please take care of him." Hot tears coursed down her face and she knelt at the graveside for a while until she felt composed enough to face the world again.

After that day, Abigail began to look at her life more optimistically. It was as if a huge, black cloud had been lifted and she knew she had to be more philosophical in the future. Things happen for a purpose and she felt that she must start back to work and focus all her attention on her career. Working hard had never been a problem for her. Her life so far had presented her with numerous situations that asked for inner resources to surface in order to survive. She had not failed yet, and she intended to succeed again whatever life threw at her.

When she returned to the Children's Hospital, she felt refreshed and strangely invigorated. Her secretary was delighted to see her and hugged her warmly when she appeared in the office on her first day back. As soon as she drove through the tall gates, she had felt the warm welcome. The nurses waved excitedly to her and her colleagues, especially Tom O'Mara who had missed her desperately, greeted her with such enthusiasm that she felt an instant surge of affection that threatened to overwhelm her. "Welcome home, Doctor Abigail," Amy Sutherland had said, "We've missed you. How are you?"

Amy had been Abigail's Girl Friday from her first day at the Children's Hospital and whilst she had telephoned occasionally to ask about her recovery, she had sensitively realised that Abigail needed to isolate herself from the job and cut adrift for a while. "I'm fine now, thanks, Amy," she replied and knew at that moment that she really meant it. She could get her life back on an even keel.

Amy looked at her and grinned. "That's the ticket. I can see the Abigail that we all know and love emerging again. But just to bring you back down to earth, you should see the stack of mail there is waiting for you! I've dealt with a lot of it, but some of it is marked Private and Confidential so I've left that for you to deal with when you have the time."

"I'll sort it out later. My priority now is to see my patients. How is little Christopher? Has he improved?"

Amy's face changed dramatically and Abigail read the sign. "Oh no! We didn't lose him, did we?"

Amy nodded slowly and Abigail understood how the little boy's kidneys were so diseased that only a transplant would have saved him. He had deteriorated quite rapidly at the end and his little body could not take any more treatment. Christopher was only two years old. *God, if there is one, moves in mysterious ways,* she thought sadly.

Returning to the wards, Doctor Hawthorne was soon back in the old routine. She quickly regained her happy and competent manner with which she stole the hearts of patients and parents alike. Her natural way with people made her a favourite with everyone and hospital staff grew to respect her judgement and follow her example. Work was her keyword...work hard, work well was her motto.

The mail sat on her dressing table for days. She saw it every night as she went to bed; she saw it every morning when she awoke. She promised herself that she would go through it on her day off. Amy had sorted all the important stuff, so another couple of days would do no harm.

The pile of letters appeared to be just a normal set of insignificant envelopes, some white, some brown. Abigail flicked through them, noting that there were indeed a few with the words private and confidential written on the front. Others were obviously from her bank, from her solicitor and there was one from Patty. The rest were hand-written, perhaps half a dozen in all and in writing she didn't recognise. She opened Patty's first and delighted in hearing that she was planning a trip north in a few weeks. It would give them all something to which they might look forward. It had been ages since the Hawthorne girls had been together.

Her solicitor informed her that her Decree Absolute was due in four weeks and her bank was offering her yet another credit card. The other six letters remained unopened and she looked at them closely, curious and yet uncertain about revealing their contents. Taking the paper knife, she deftly sliced through the envelope and removed the neatly folded letter from inside. It was not the usual type of letter. It had been made up of newspaper print and in bold letters it said - *'HELLO AGAIN. GOOD TO BE IN TOUCH'*. Her first reaction was, "How odd!" but then when she opened the others and each one became more and more sinister, she became quite unnerved. *'I'LL SEE YOU SOON, YOU CAN BET ON IT,'* said one and *'SORRY TO MISS YOU THE OTHER NIGHT,'* said another, until the worst of the lot stated, *'WATCH YOUR BACK, DOCTOR HAWTHORNE. I AM ALWAYS BEHIND YOU WHEREVER YOU GO.'*

"My god," Abigail said out loud, "What have I done to deserve this?" She felt her heart thumping in her chest and her natural instinct was to run and bolt the doors and close all the windows. Stupidly, and hating herself for doing it, she looked cautiously under the bed and inside the wardrobe. She wanted to laugh at herself, but her panic-stricken thoughts wouldn't allow it. She wondered if she ought to inform the police and yet she thought that perhaps it was all a sick joke. "What are you doing, Abigail?" she asked herself, realising that she didn't have an answer. *Who on earth would play a joke like that on me?*

She deliberated for a while about informing the police and eventually, albeit reluctantly, she decided that for her own safety and that of the other women staff at the hospital, she should at least talk to somebody about the situation.

The investigating police officer was Vivien Burton, an extremely homely person with a keen sense of decency about her. She sat comfortably on Abi's sofa and read the offending mail several times before she made comment.

"It seems you have an admirer, Doctor Hawthorne," she observed with a wry smile. "a very persistent admirer from the look of it. I think we'll have to begin by taking a look at your friends and acquaintances in order to eliminate them from our enquiries."

Abigail was confused. "Are you really going to investigate?" she asked, amazed. "It might just be a prankster."

"We have to look into these matters, not only for you, but to cover ourselves, you understand. If we ignored it and something happened..." Vivien Burton looked Abigail straight in the eye. "...well, you can imagine the rest, I'm sure."

Abigail nodded. She couldn't quite believe it was happening. Surely, nobody could hate her so much as to make her life so uncomfortable. Why did such situations keep occurring?

"Think as far back as you can," DI Burton advised her. "Has anyone ever borne a grudge against you, however trivial?"

Now it was Abigail's turn to smile wryly. "How far back would you like me to go?" she asked the policewoman, who had an easy approach and a very pleasant nature. "There was a girl in my primary school who didn't like me,' she continued, "Betty West used to make my life a misery every time I gained one more mark than she did. Surely you don't need to know about her...do you?"

"We need every tiny detail, I'm afraid, if we are to find out who is vindictive enough to try to disrupt your life with these ominous promises, even though at this point in time, there is no evidence that this person intends to carry out the threats. Quite often, these people are cowards who hide behind bits of paper and postage stamps!"

Abigail related how Betty West had been the bane of her life from the first day at school to her leaving Great Moor Grammar. She surprised herself with how strongly she felt about it even then. Digging something out of one's subconscious produced shockingly deep resentment and she shivered at the intensity of her own feelings. She also mentioned how she had deserted her first 'love' because of the bet he'd placed on that first kiss. She couldn't believe that her past was so significant, but Vivien Burton appeared to be interested in all of it. When James Sylvester-Jones's name cropped up, the inspector raised her eyebrows. She had come across that young man and fairly recently, too, in a drunk and disorderly incident. "An arrogant pillock if I may make so bold."

Abigail sighed. "That's James," she agreed, "I have tried so hard to forget what he did, or almost did to me, but he keeps on turning up. I came face to face with him at Westerton a few years ago and then I think he might have turned up here drunk a couple of months ago, though I can't be sure. It's not my place to judge, but if anyone wanted revenge, it would be him." She became extremely uncomfortable when she related the episode with PG, but it had to be done. She didn't think for one moment that PG would be so stupid as to sully his reputation again. Finally, there was David... "Oh my god!"

"Oh dear, what is it, Abigail?" Vivien Burton had progressed to first names and Abi felt she had made a friend.

"My ex-husband was very bitter about my pregnancy. He also had a drink problem, perhaps still has, but it had never entered my head until now that it might have been him at the hospital. The duty nurse woke me late one night when a man was demanding he see me urgently, but when I got to Reception, he had disappeared. I really thought it had been James again after the Westerton incident."

Vivien was very sympathetic and reassured Abigail that she would get to the bottom of the problem as soon as she was able.

She took the letters for forensic examination and advised Abigail to carry on as normal. "These creeps usually want to disturb your way of life, but don't let him interfere with what you do. If he's around, he'll see that you are not put off by him."

"I don't think I like the sound of that," Abi whispered, feeling afraid to speak out loud in case she was overheard by the lunatic who was doing a brilliant job of totally unnerving her, but on Vivien's advice, she determined to carry on as best she could.

"I'll play this by the book," the policewoman stated. "I'll post somebody inconspicuously in the hospital, just to be sure that this mongrel isn't gaining easy access to you, or any of the other women, for that matter. It might appear to be drastic action, but I'll do it anyway." She couldn't help thinking that it might be an inside job.

There was a new white coated assistant on the ward the following day. Josie was assigned to watch Abigail at all times. The fact that she carried a notebook and pen round most of the day was part of her cover. She learned her duties quickly and fit in well with the rest of the staff. Only Abigail and the ward sister knew that Josie was undercover and the ploy worked well. The times when Abigail was off duty, Josie still did her job serving meals and straightening beds, making copious notes and telling the nurses that she was writing a thesis about hospital life, so as not to arouse suspicion. Abi agreed that she would make sure that either Vivien or Josie would know her whereabouts at all times and for a while, she didn't venture further than Meg's house on her days off. For weeks, nothing untoward happened. Vivien's investigations led nowhere, or so it seemed. She had interviewed the most likely people who could have tracked down Abi on the night in question, but they all had cast-iron alibis and the duty nurse had not been able to identify the person she saw on the night before Abigail had lost her baby.

~ * ~

Nobody had noticed the car without a permit parked in the staff car park. The driver sat in the dark, watching, waiting. For several nights, he had sat there until after midnight and then had driven away. His thoughts were not hostile. *Abigail Hawthorne is a beautiful woman and one day soon, I intend to have her for myself. I will bide my time.* Patience was vitally important to his ends and he would wait until the time was right to approach her. *Just recently, though, she always has an assistant with her. She never seems to be on her own.* He had been inside the hospital, too, and her friend was with her all day. *I don't understand that. Perhaps the other woman is a student or something. Still, I can wait.*

Flowers left on the doorstep of the residential quarters were for Doctor Hawthorne. There was no card, just her name on the label. She assumed they were from a grateful patient and arranging them in a vase, she placed them on the windowsill. The person sitting in the car in the car park was delighted that she had taken the trouble to display them in the window and he smiled to himself, thinking that he was getting closer to the woman of his dreams. Perhaps he might send her a message again. The flowers arrived regularly each week, sometimes left on the doorstep, sometimes delivered by the florist to her office. "Do you know who sent these?" she asked the girl who delivered them to her desk.

"I'm afraid I don't," the girl replied, "My boss takes the orders both in the shop and by telephone. I'm just the delivery girl. I could ask for you if you like, but I don't think my boss would take too kindly to my prying into that side of the business." She looked embarrassed and blushed slightly.

"Don't worry about it," Abigail reassured her, "I'll call in some time and ask her myself." She smiled at the young girl, who was obviously feeling awkward about her questioning.

"Him," the girl said, "My boss is a man."

"Oh, well, I'll call and ask *him* sometime then," Abi replied, thanking her for the flowers and her time.

She didn't think it necessary to tell Vivien Burton about the flowers. They weren't causing any harm and they were so beautiful, but she was nonetheless curious as to who was sending them. Work didn't leave room for her to dwell on the matter and she pushed the thought out of her mind as she went on her rounds and continued with her involvement in making sure that her sick children got all of her attention. When she wasn't on the wards, she was writing up reports, keeping records, dictating memos to Amy and listening to her colleagues' experiences, all part of their everyday routine. Each day she was relieved when she was able to wend her weary way back to her quarters, her own little world where she was able to relax and do her own thing.

As the weeks went by, Abigail grew calmer and more at ease. She received no more threatening mail and Josie seemed to think that it must have been a prankster as Abi had originally thought. Vivien Burton decided that it would perhaps be prudent for her to ease off surveillance and Abigail was happy with that. Much as she appreciated Josie's presence and the protection it afforded, she needed her space sometimes and, since there had been no recurrence of suspicious incidents, she felt there was no longer any need for a bodyguard.

She had grown to love her private suite and had managed to give it her personal touch. It was a one bedroom apartment on the first floor with a spacious dining kitchen, fitted with modern appliances including a large fridge/freezer and light oak units. The lounge/sitting room was small but cosy and she had enhanced the neutral shades of the walls and carpet by adding a gold coloured, comfortable sofa and one squashy, cushioned armchair in which she could curl up with a book, or watch television. She had a framed print of Monet's Water Lilies on the wall opposite the window that inspired a calm reflective mood when she needed to relax. A smaller print of Van Gogh's Sunflowers was there just because she liked it. On the coffee table by the sofa was a family photograph of her dad, Gran, Meg, Patty and herself as a baby when they had been in Moss Bank Park in Bolton. Abi loved that photograph, she simply loved it. The *Bolton Evening News* photographer had taken it during Wakes Week and they'd been in the paper with other photographs of holidaymakers in Blackpool, Morecambe and at various Butlin's Holiday Camps around the country. Her front door opened from the carpeted corridor on to an oblong entrance hall, large enough to house a telephone table and the hallstand that she had inherited from Hillside Terrace and which was one of her most treasured possessions.

It was when she returned to her quarters one evening that she had cause to panic as she went in. She had opened the door and thrown her keys on to the telephone table as usual when she noticed something odd. On the table was a single red rose and she knew it hadn't been there when she had left that morning. *Who has access to my rooms when she I'm not here? Only Mrs Collier, the hospital cleaner, whose duties extended to the residential quarters and even though she's a lovely lady and a first class cleaner, I doubt she would be inclined to leave tokens of endearment for me.*

She picked up the phone to call Josie. She had been given an emergency number for just such an occasion. She tried to dial the number quickly, but as she did so, a hand reached out from behind her and pressed down the hook. She spun round instinctively and came face to face with a stranger, an unknown man who was smiling sickeningly at her and signalling her to go into the lounge where he had poured two glasses of wine. Speechless, Abigail obeyed his bidding, her mind in turmoil. *Should I scream? Should I make a run for the door? Should I try to humour this man who is invading my privacy?* She tried to appear calm, but she was anxious that the stranger would see her heart thumping in her chest and realise she was afraid. *Afraid?* she silently asked herself, *I'm bloody terrified!*

The man seemed to be quite at ease. He smiled at Abigail who made a feeble effort to return an expression that would hide the fear she felt inside. "Who are you and what do you want?" she asked, her voice hardly audible.

"Don't you recognise me, Abigail?" the stranger asked, displaying an unusual kind of measured control that Abigail noted with knowledgeable awareness.

"I'm sorry, but no I don't. Should I?" She dared to look at his face more closely. He wasn't a bad looking guy, perhaps a little strained around the eyes, but he could pass for quite a handsome bloke under different circumstances.

"I went to the same school as you, Great Moor Grammar. I asked you to go to the cinema with me once and you turned me down. Now, nobody turns me down and gets away with it. You owe me, Abigail Hawthorne."

She searched her mind for some sort of recognition of this man who was suddenly becoming rather agitated. "I'm Alan Jackson," he spat. "I was Head Boy at the time and you didn't want to know," he explained further. "Thought you were too good for the likes of any of the boys in school, did you?"

"My goodness!" she exclaimed, "That must have happened almost twenty years ago." She delved into the deepest caverns of her memory and vaguely remembered this boy asking her to go to see Elvis Presley who was on at the Odeon. "I didn't refuse your invitation for that reason at all. I was only fourteen years old then and I'd never been out with a boy. You were eighteen and way out of my league both in age and experience. Surely you must have realised that. It wasn't that I didn't find you attractive..." She added the last bit in an effort to placate him in some way, however small.

"Ah yes, but all I know is that you were absolutely gorgeous, every boy's dream date and you set me back," he continued, "and now we can make up for lost time."

Alan Jackson was becoming more threatening and Abigail knew she had to act calmly in order not to aggravate the situation. She stood up from the settee and tried to walk slowly towards the door, all the time trying to keep the conversation light and distracting, but Alan Jackson was too quick for her and he jumped in front of her to block the way. Abi's mind was racing. *Not again,* she thought, *It's James Sylvester-Jones all over again!* There was, however, one very big difference this time. She had not been stupefied with illicit drugs and she was able to draw on all her resources to deal with this man, a man possessed with demons of the past. She saw that his agitation was increasing and realised that he must be on medication to stabilize his moods. He was displaying symptoms of mental illness and although she wasn't totally equipped to deal with such cases, she thought that she held the upper hand in that she recognised the problem. She talked to him about school, about university and asked him to tell her about his life at Cambridge. It seemed that he had only completed one year before he was advised to give up the intense course of study. He didn't actually explain why, and Abi felt it prudent at this point not to ask him to elaborate. He appeared to be very disturbed when he had told her of the enforced ending to his academic career and she was overcome with sadness in seeing this young man in a state of mental collapse.

There was a sharp knock on the door that startled them both. "Abigail?" It was Josie. "Are you all right?"

Alan Jackson reacted nervously. "Don't answer it!" he barked. "It's the devil!" He grabbed at Abi and held her close, quite gently really for a man in such an agitated state. "I'm here to protect you. Don't worry, dear Abigail. My voices have told me what to do." And then facing the door, he called, "Go away, Satan! You can't have her! She's mine now...mine forever."

Abigail called out. "I'm okay, Josie," hoping against hope that she wouldn't go away. "Let's go back into the lounge and finish our wine," she said to Alan and easing herself away from his grasp, she took his hand and led him back into the sitting room in a bold attempt to simulate an atmosphere of calm. She felt that if she were able to keep him occupied, she was in control, but suddenly, there was an almighty, shattering bang. The door flew open and two burly policemen bounded across the room and overpowered the unsuspecting Alan Jackson. The poor guy was no match for the two officers of the law and he was unceremoniously frog-marched out and into the waiting police van. "Please don't be too hard on him," she whispered to herself. "I'm sure he didn't mean to harm me," and flopped into the security of her squashy chair as Josie walked through the door.

"How did you know I needed you?" she asked Josie after Jackson had been taken away.

"You dialled my emergency number," Josie told her.

"Yes, but it didn't ring out before he put his hand on the hook."

"Wrong!" Josie explained, "It rang only once, but it was enough for me to know that you needed me. No one has access to that number."

"Thank god for that," Abigail said, relieved that yet another episode in her life could be laid to rest. Surely nothing else could happen to her. She was beginning to wonder if her life had been destined to combat one drastic event after another. It certainly appeared that way.

"You owe me a cup o' tea!" Josie demanded, "I had to leave mine at the station when my phone rang!"

"No problem," Abi laughed. "A small price to pay for saving my life!"

It transpired that Alan Jackson's parents owned the florist's shop near the hospital. By chance, he had seen Abigail in the hospital grounds and had taken to watching her daily. The notes had been his way of revenge for her refusal to go out with him all those years before. His schizophrenic tendencies had been diagnosed soon after he had gone up to Cambridge, but with the help of medication had lain dormant until recently when his obsession with Abigail had taken over his life.

Eventually, Abi discovered how a stranger had managed to gain access to her quarters. It seemed that Mrs Collier had opened the door to leave and then had gone back inside to find her gloves, leaving the door ajar. Jackson had been lurking outside, watching, waiting and in those few seconds had slipped in unnoticed. He hid himself behind the hallstand as the pre-occupied Mrs Collier had left, locking him inside to wait for Abi's return.

Working all hours to focus on other people's problems rather than her own had once again been Abigail's way of alleviating her stress. It was remarkable how she found peace in hard work, solace in single-mindedness, consolation in healing a sick child. *One of these fine days*, she thought, *I shall lead a normal life. But is normal just another word for mundane?* she wondered. Inwardly, she did yearn for a peaceful life, a life without the traumas she had suffered in recent months. *Is that too much to ask?*

Twenty-two

Her work at the Children's Hospital gave Abigail the incentive and motivation to go after her consultancy. It was a long haul, but she was totally committed to her calling. During some of her more trying times, she had questioned her own sanity in taking on such a daunting task, but on more rewarding occasions, she knew in her heart of hearts that the decision was right for her. Her vocation was her guiding light and she would succeed in spite of the intermittent self-doubts.

It wasn't often that she took time off, but she felt that she needed to recharge her batteries and she decided to go to Meg's in time for the long-awaited visit of Patty and Steve. She had two weeks' leave due and her room at Meg's was always ready for her. Meg had kept it just as she had when Abi was at university. Even when she had married David Cohen, the room stayed the same. Perhaps it was instinct, but Meg preferred to call it feminine intuition. She had to admit to herself, *I did like David regardless of the odd occasion when he was a bit of an enigma. He left me with confused feelings concerning his character on more than one occasion. He did have some admirable qualities, but hindsight makes me question why I actually instigated their first meeting. In spite of that, though, I always felt Abi had married too quickly, even though I would never have said so. Abigail is an adult who must make her own decisions and make her own mistakes. Hadn't Dad said so often enough?* "Mistakes are vitally important to our development. If we don't make them, we never learn," she quoted. *Abigail doesn't make many mistakes, but that marriage was certainly one gargantuan mistake from which she must have learned the lessons of a lifetime.*

~ * ~

Patty and Steve had arrived on the Friday night and Abigail was there first thing Saturday morning before they'd had breakfast. Patty and Steve were only able to stay up north for the weekend, so they all decided they would do something special, something outrageous for grownups, something that allowed them to relinquish adult restraints for a while. "We'll go to Blackpool and let our hair down on the Pleasure Beach," they agreed, gleefully laughing at the thought of it. They had not made such a trip since they were children. John had scraped together the fare and a bit of spending money to take them on a day trip during Wakes Week in 1947. They had gone on the train and had taken sandwiches and cake with fizzy pop for the children and a flask of tea for Nellie and John. They had gone on the Big Dipper, the Dodgems and the Waltzer until they felt sick and, in a fit of nostalgia, they intended to do it all over again in memory of their dad and grandmother. This time the trip included Philip, Steve and Nicky, who were only too happy to re-live the girls' past.

They left their cars at home. Going on the train was all part and parcel of retracing their journey. The fact that it was a diesel train and not the wonderful steam locomotive that had hissed and puffed and chugged along the track in the 40s, did not deter from their enjoyment. It was indeed a day to remember from the moment they arrived at Trinity Street Station in Bolton. An hour later, they had pulled into Central Station in Blackpool and the memories came flooding back—the cry of the seagulls, the whiff of the salty sea, the roar of the waves, the scent of candy floss, waffles and fish and chips all merging into one sickly, yet inviting smell that was Blackpool. They strolled down the Golden Mile, past the sideshows, the penny arcades and the Blackpool rock stalls until they came to South Shore and the Pleasure Beach, crowded, lively, noisy, bustling and wonderfully entertaining for day trippers. They took advantage of their anonymity, becoming very silly and extremely childish.

"Come on!" shrieked Patty, all inhibitions left behind long ago. "Shoes and socks off and into the sea. Let's get the sand between our toes."

They hastily removed their shoes and socks and left them in a pile next to the concrete wall. Rolling up the legs of their jeans, they hobbled across the pebbles, reached the compacted wet sand and raced to the edge of the water.

"Eek! It's freezing!" Abi exclaimed as each one in turn let out a well-tuned scream, men included, as the icy Irish Sea lapped over their feet and inched its way up unaccustomed calves. They laughed and shrieked, kicking and splashing around in the shallow water until they were wet through and exhausted and nobody seemed to mind apart from little Nicky who tried desperately to hide his embarrassment at the thought that his parents and his aunties were stark, raving mad. "Do you have to be so childish?" he asked haughtily and the adults shrieked even more with laughter.

All too soon, the weekend came to an end and Patty and Steve had to return to London. A moment of sadness reigned as they left the Wilkinson house, but they promised to visit again on condition that the others travelled south sometime in the not-too-distant future. That arranged, Abigail decided to spend the rest of her break catching up with her friends, especially Janet. They had lost contact for a while and with a little bit of research into Janet's whereabouts, they resolved to make a special effort to meet for lunch.

Janet turned up at the Pack Horse in Bolton in all her pregnant glory and both she and Abigail burst out laughing when they came face to face after so long. They hugged each other warmly. "You look great, Jan," Abigail complimented her old friend.

Janet grinned and patted her bulging stomach. "Literally!" she said, still laughing loudly and remembering the time when she was distraught about her shape being ruined by the unplanned pregnancy years ago. "How are you, Abs?"

"I'm fine... now," she replied, intending to fill in a few details later when she and Janet had ordered lunch. They had so much to talk about that it would take much longer than one lunch date to catch up on their lives since Great Moor Grammar. Still, they would be able to pack in as much as possible over lunch and then spend the afternoon walking around their old haunts.

Janet had not married Robin Baker, her first sexual encounter. When she went up to Oxford, she realised that he wasn't the boy of her dreams after all and, whilst they remained friends, they each went their separate ways. She had married Gary Everitt, whom she had met on the first day of her new teaching post in Bury. They were living in Greenmount and were excitedly looking forward to the birth of their first child. Nothing out of the ordinary had happened to Janet. Abigail's life thus far made Janet's look like a Sunday school outing. Fate had dealt them very different hands in the card game of life. Before they parted, they agreed to meet again after Janet's big event. "Perhaps we might arrange a grand reunion," Abigail suggested. "The Class of 1958."

"That would be brilliant," Janet agreed, "But do you really want to encounter Betty West again?"

"Well…" Abi was thoughtful, "She did me a favour in a roundabout way, I suppose."

"How do you work that one out?" Janet asked, knowing full well that Betty West had made Abigail's life a misery on so many occasions.

"She made me aware of male chauvinism, at least, and no doubt she has a man of her own by now and several little Betties tied to her apron strings. Good luck to her and I really mean that."

Feeling refreshed and happy with her lot, Abigail returned to work after spending the last few days of her break in The Lakes. She had rented a tiny cottage on the edge of Coniston Water and was able to go for long, peaceful walks and indulge herself in cream teas whilst she freed her mind of all the stress and strain that had weighed heavily upon her during the past few months. The Lake District was an ideal location for her to unwind. She had wallowed in the quietude, found peace in her solitude. She had felt a strange, spiritual affiliation with poet William Wordsworth in her lonely wandering, imagining the golden daffodils, long gone now, as the hills and dales unfolded before her. By the end of her break, she felt totally rejuvenated and when she arrived back in Salford, her enthusiasm for her work was fully restored. It didn't take long for her to fall back into the old routine. After only a few minutes, it was as though she had never been away. Each bed seemed to be occupied by a new child…children with pale faces and wide, appealing eyes made Abi's heart melt and her resolve all the more earnest. As a doctor, she knew she was serving mankind; as a woman, she felt all the compassion necessary to do her job well.

The autumn months were forecast to be cold, wet and miserable. People hurried about their daily tasks with heads down to avoid Mother Nature's icy fingers grabbing at their faces. Gone were the jaunty steps of summer. Movements were heavy laden with the burden of approaching winter weather. There was no doubt about it, the seasons definitely affected one's outlook on life.

Abigail was the duty doctor on the night when Rob Lawrence burst into the hospital with a very sick little boy in his arms. The man was distraught and for a few wild moments, didn't make much sense. The child was wrapped in a blanket, his face pale and damp, his little body limp and almost lifeless. "Help him, please help him," the man cried desperately. "He's hot and sweating and I can't hear his breathing. *PLEASE HELP HIM!*" he implored.

The duty nurse went to take the child from the gentleman's arms, but he held on to him as though he daren't let go for fear of losing him. "Please, sir," she coaxed, "We need to take a look at him. What's his name?"

"Joshua... he's my son, Joshua Michael Lawrence. Please help him," Mr Lawrence pleaded again. "He's all I have in the world."

Abigail was called to admissions immediately where she found Rob Lawrence almost in a state of collapse. Joshua was four years old and had become unwell earlier that afternoon. His father had comforted him and given him junior aspirin before putting him to bed. He had stayed with him until Joshua had gone to sleep, but had been disturbed by his son's coughing and his high temperature at about eleven o'clock that night. By midnight, the child had become delirious and the panic-stricken Rob Lawrence had wrapped him in a blanket and driven the twenty miles or so from Altrincham to the Children's Hospital in Salford. The child's breathing was very shallow and as he had gone to bed that night, he had tearfully told Rob, gasping and almost inaudibly, "I have a giant tummy ache in my chest, Daddy. It really, really hurts."

Abigail tried to reassure Mr Lawrence that he had done the right thing in bringing Joshua to the hospital. She instructed the student nurse to make a cup of tea for him whilst she examined the sick child. The medical team sprang into action and they transferred Joshua to a private cubicle, made him comfortable and gently continued to reassure him that they would make him better as soon as possible. Early indications were that he had pneumonia and tests would have to be done quickly to determine the strain. That done, they would be able to treat him, but he would have to be admitted and a close watch kept over him. In the meantime, they would transfer him to a side ward where he would be given round the clock attention. Once settled, they would try to lower his temperature.

Joshua Michael Lawrence was the only son of Rob Lawrence, a local architect. Rob had inherited his father's acumen for business and owned the renowned Premier Building Design Company. He was a very unassuming, gentle man and a devoted father. His dark, classical good looks came from his Italian mother, Rob being the diminutive of Roberto. When his young wife was killed in a road accident, Joshua was only a few months old. Rob had divided his time between his company and his son with remarkable success. He had declined the offer of accommodation with his parents and, although they looked after Joshua occasionally, Rob's strong paternal instincts made sure that the child knew that his father loved him and would be there for him at all times. His ability to organise his routine appropriately made him aware of Joshua's needs and appreciative of the little things in a close relationship between father and son. He had delighted in Josh's first tooth, his first steps, his first words. The baby's ability in vocalising, "A-Da-da-da," had meant more to Rob than it would have to most fathers. Abigail had listened to Rob's story and was able to empathise with the child. Hadn't she been deprived of a mother's loving touch and yet had been sustained within a loving family with a father whose devotion knew no bounds? Little Joshua Lawrence deserved the best treatment they had to offer and she would see to it personally that he survived.

Once settled in the side ward B1, the charge nurse carefully wiped him down with a cool napkin to help reduce his temperature. He was covered with only a thin sheet and an electric fan was placed by his bed in an effort to return his little body to normal as quickly as possible. He would be carefully monitored throughout the night and the nursing staff would keep a close watch over him to note any change in his condition. Abigail attached a drip to administer fluids intravenously and avoid dehydration. The little boy just lay there, hardly breathing, looking deathly pale and lying so still that Rob became agitated. Trying desperately to remain calm, his eyes appealed to Abi to give him some little hope, however small, which would help him to cope with the trauma of seeing his only child apparently clinging to life by a thread.

"I know how you must feel, Mr Lawrence," she said gently, sincerely hoping that she didn't sound patronising. Rob Lawrence did not take his eyes off his child, but nodded slowly to show that he understood what she had said and had obviously detected the concern in her tone. "I shall do everything in my power to make Joshua better," she whispered, "I promise."

Rob Lawrence held on to his child's hand and closed his eyes tightly to prevent the tears from running freely down his face. Abigail put her hand on his shoulder as a reassuring gesture and then left him to spend the next few minutes regaining his composure. *A promise is a promise,* she thought, *and come hell, or high water, I shall be true to my word.* She felt a strange affiliation to this child and a strong sense of dedication to duty. She would not fail him. Somehow, she felt that his life so far had mirrored her own and she would do her very best to show him that he could survive and succeed in this competitive world. She would do it for him, for his father and also for herself.

Twenty-three

Twenty-four hours can seem like a lifetime when you are watching the clock every step of the way, but forty-eight hours are like eternity when every bleep on a monitor is the only sign you have that your child is alive. Rob Lawrence remained at Joshua's side and refused to leave. He, himself, looked pale and drawn, his eyes heavy and dark through keeping them open too long. Sleep was the last thing on his mind, although it was only sheer willpower that prevented his eyes from closing. He held the boy's hand gently, willing him to get well. He mopped the child's fevered brow and whispered to him so that Joshua would know that he wasn't alone.

The nursing staff came and went; intravenous drip checked, temperature taken, pillows plumped up so that Joshua was half-sitting, half-lying and his airways would not become blocked. Throughout the night, there was a constant stream of comings and goings, but Rob took little notice unless they intimated that there was a change in his son's condition. No words were exchanged and he felt he might accept that no news was good news. Frequent cups of tea were left by his side. Some he drank, others were left to go cold. Abigail hovered in the background. She ought to have gone off duty hours ago. Tom O'Mara had looked in on her charge and offered to take over, but there was something in her expression that told him that she needed to be there for this little boy and he didn't argue.

"I'm here when you need me," he said to her. "Don't let your heart rule your head with this one, Abi. I can see that you are involved up to your neck. What's so different about this child from all the rest? Dedication is one thing, obsession is another."

"You'll have to trust me on this, Tom," she answered, firmly in control of her emotions. "There is so much I need to clear out of my system and I know that coping with it will help me come to terms with my past. I hadn't realised it was an issue until now and this child needs me. Please don't judge me until I've seen it through. If I mess up, I'm all yours!" she grinned and Tom recognised the stubborn determination which had endeared her to him when he had first met her.

"Okay, Doctor, but you know where I am if you need me."

"Thanks Tom." She couldn't leave this sick child and she needed to be there for him every second, every minute, as long as it took. She knew that the next forty-eight hours would be crucial. Tests had shown that Joshua had bacterial pneumonia, hence the quick deterioration of his condition. His high fever and rapid respirations were typical of the disease and his grey pallor had told her what she needed to know at the outset. The routine tests had confirmed her diagnosis and the antibiotics should start to take effect in twenty-four hours. After that, they should begin to see an improvement as Joshua woke up. The second twenty-four hours would confirm that they had caught him in time, before pleurisy had aggravated the situation.

Not wishing to intrude too much, nor interfere with the nurses' necessary attendance at regular intervals, Abigail opened the door quietly and went to sit next to the exhausted man. She wanted to reassure him that she was there and available at all times. She gently touched his arm and whispered, "Why don't you take a break? I'll stay here with Joshua. Go to the rest room and freshen yourself up. Take a nap if you like. I promise I'll call you if there is any change." There was no immediate response. "Mr Lawrence?" she implored.

"Yes... Thank you, Doctor Hawthorne. I think I shall just slip out to freshen up," he agreed.

"Good and please call me Abi. I'm known as Doctor Abigail to the staff. I promise I'll call you if needs be."

With that, Rob Lawrence entrusted Abigail with his son whilst he wandered down the corridor

towards the rest room. He felt as though he were in a dream and everything was moving slowly. His head ached and it was all he could do to drag his feet to where he hoped he might collect his thoughts. He arrived at the rest room and found it to be pleasantly decorated and furnished to make convenient accommodation for the parents of sick children. He sat on the bed and, resting his weary head on the pillow, he was asleep within seconds. He did not intend to sleep and he awoke with a start, momentarily disorientated. He looked at his watch... five thirty in the morning. He had no idea what time he had left Joshua and, hastily throwing cold water on his face to revive himself, he caught sight of himself in the mirror, an unkempt, unshaven, worried man who certainly would not allow himself to be seen like this under normal circumstances. But these clearly weren't normal circumstances and he had no time to stand in front of the mirror contemplating his appearance. He rushed back to the ward, running down the corridor, passing nurses and cleaning staff, all of who had seen the same desperate actions of anxious parents many times before.

Arriving at the door of B One, he found Abigail changing the drip. "What's wrong?" he asked, hardly able to disguise his anxiety, "Why are you changing the drip?"

Abigail, looking very tired herself, explained that she wasn't changing it, merely keeping sufficient fluids there to prevent possible dehydration. The antibiotics were included and Joshua needed the full prescribed amount in order for them to take effect. "Mr Lawrence...?" she said.

"Rob, please."

"Okay, Rob, come closer and look at Joshua. He hasn't wakened yet, but he's looking different. His colour is improving slightly, but I'm still not happy about his breathing." She didn't want to raise his hopes too much just yet. She needed to see more definite signs before she could reassure him that the crisis was over.

Rob still couldn't relax. His mind was still full of anxious thoughts. *Abigail is trying to be positive, but I can't be happy until Joshua wakes up and speaks to me and that just isn't happening and that worries me more than anything.*

They sat and watched as the little boy lay still in the bed and the bleep, bleep, bleep of the monitor invaded the silence with welcome regularity. They talked in whispers and Abigail learned about Rob's life as an architect; about his Italian roots and how his mother insisted that a bowl full of pasta was the cure for everything; about his wife and how he had coped since her death. "It's at times like these when I realise that I'm alone. I miss Yvonne, of course, but I know I have to carry on and I do. Joshua is the most important person in my life and I need him as much as he needs me."

Abigail listened intently and then told Rob about her father...how he had brought up three very lively girls with the help of their grandmother, how he had been their guiding light in everything they had done, how, eventually, he had been stricken with the cruellest of diseases and died an old man at the age of fifty-five.

The intermittent silences were not awkward. They sat with their own thoughts and watched the little boy who was struggling to hang on to his young life as the clock on the wall ticked away the seconds, the minutes, the hours and still it was only six thirty in the morning. Both were physically exhausted, mentally fighting to stay strong and focused. Neither would rest. They had their own reasons for their battle with the forces of tiredness that were ultimately very different, and yet the same, culminating in the desire for the well-being of Joshua Michael Lawrence.

Daylight came and went unnoticed in the darkened room. Nursing staff changed at regular intervals and Abigail's day off became a non-event. Whilst the hospital buzzed with activity, the two people inside ward B One remained stoically on guard, watching, waiting for any slight change in the boy's condition. Outside, the sky was black and rain pelted the windows to add to the desolate mood inside. It had been nineteen hours since Rob had rushed into the hospital with his very sick son and there was very little change. There was nothing else to do, but wait. When dark clouds threatened, there was a real sense of foreboding. Nothing seemed to take that away.

Twenty-four

The young doctor had certainly gone way beyond the call of duty, Rob had thought, as she went to make coffee for them both. He had persuaded her to take a break as she had him a few hours earlier. He had slept for two hours and he had felt refreshed afterwards. She had only managed to doze for a few minutes. It was as though she had a built-in force which drove her to fulfil her duty. She had an extraordinary sense of commitment. Rob had never seen it in anyone and certainly never in a woman. As the earnest nurses had made Joshua comfortable, sponging him down, changing his bed linen and his pyjamas, he watched in admiration of their dedication to their work. They carried out their duties with the minimum of fuss and, whilst they were mindful of the needs of the patient, they were also respectful of Rob's situation. Some asked if he were all right and others merely smiled and said they hoped Josh would soon be better. None of

269

them intruded on his privacy, although he felt instinctively that had he needed to talk, to unburden himself of his anxieties, they would all have given their time freely to ease his concern.

Joshua had not wakened, although his breathing was slightly improved and the fever had subsided. Rob leaned on the bed, resting his head on his folded arms. Closing his eyes, he drifted into an uneasy sleep, his mind tormented with visions of unrecognizable weird faces whose expressions taunted him with accusing eyes. In the distance he could see Yvonne, dearest Yvonne, whose spiritual presence reduced the torment and made him feel more at ease. Within seconds, he felt an overpowering sense of panic. "No, Yvonne! NO!" he cried out in his dream, "Please don't wait for him. He's not ready to join you yet. Let him live. Let him stay here. He has so much living to do." His words were lost in his dream, but it wasn't necessary to convince Yvonne that she shouldn't take Joshua away. Instinctively he knew that Yvonne was not there to take Joshua, but merely to watch over him in his hour of need. Her smile reassured Rob that he had no need to worry. *How could I doubt her? She had been the gentlest, kindest, loving person when alive. Why should she change in death?*

When he opened his eyes, Abigail was standing in the doorway with two mugs of hot coffee. As she offered one to Rob, he told her that his mind seemed to be less tormented now that he had had a rest. He didn't divulge that he had seen Yvonne in his dreams for fear that Abi wouldn't understand. He had occasionally dreamed of Yvonne before and had thought little of the significance, but today, her spirit had affected him greatly and given him strength to cope.

As if by telepathy, Abigail asked, "Do you know what I often do when my problems seem to be insurmountable?" Rob eyed her questioningly. "I go to my parents' grave and I talk to them. I always find some spiritual guidance even though it may not be immediately apparent. When I lost my baby and my errant husband at the same time, my mother's strength shone through. I never knew her and yet I felt that when I talked to her, she gave me the courage to face the future with renewed optimism. Strange, isn't it?"

Rob looked at the young woman and marvelled at her sensitivity. "I know what you mean," he told her, "No one could ever understand that unless they had lost someone very close to them," and he chose not to expound further. Tacit understanding would prevail and they both knew it.

There was an easy silence between them and the clock on the wall ticked away the minutes and the hours, every exactly measured tick, tock, tick, tock, stressing the importance of their watchfulness. Moments when the time went quickly passed by unnoticed, untouched by human hand. Minutes when the time went slowly prolonged an agony, engaged by destiny. Fate had brought these people here; people whose lives had been touched by similar circumstances. Abigail's whole life was devoted to making children well and this child needed all her skill and dedication to help him through this crisis. Rob, on the other hand, was his father, a father whose devotion was moulded purely of love for his son. Both adults, in their respective roles, were willing the child to pull through.

Rob sat still holding Joshua's hand to let him know he was there. Abigail sat opposite and gently held Joshua's other hand in order to feel any signs of change in his condition. It had been a very long night and once again daylight was breaking as the nursing staff went off duty and a new shift began to take up their posts. Rob had dozed intermittently, each time waking with a start and a feeling of intense guilt that he had neglected his duty in watching over his son. Abigail reassured him in an effort to convince him that he had already gone beyond the call of duty and he need not feel unnecessary guilt.

"You are the one who has gone beyond the call of duty, Doctor Abigail," he said and reached across to touch her hand in a gesture that said he appreciated her presence.

Abigail smiled, a tired smile, but nonetheless genuine. "I can't leave until I see Joshua through this," she told him and he squeezed her hand appreciatively. She looked into his tired eyes and nodded slowly. "We're in this together," she said quietly, "I made a promise to you when you brought Joshua in here and I intend to keep it."

For the past forty-eight hours, they had watched and waited for any little sign from the sick child that his condition was changing. There had been moments when total despair and desolation had consumed them, but as the child's breathing became more normal and his temperature lowered, they were encouraged and allowed themselves to relax a little. Their moods fluctuated from sheer anxiety to uneasy optimism; from anxious, nervous concern to expectant anticipation. Abi stood at the window and looked out on to a hazy autumn day. As she stared into the watery sun, she heard a deep sigh and a little cough which caused her to turn quickly. Momentary panic hit her and she ran to tend the sick child. Rob had jumped up and was standing motionless by the bed, still hanging on to his son's hand.

Beautiful, sleepy, brown eyes opened. "Daddy?" a tiny voice whispered, "Daddy?"

Rob dropped to his knees and gently cradled Joshua in his arms. "Hello, Tiger. How are you?" and the tears unashamedly coursed down his cheeks. He looked up at Abigail, whose eyes filled with tears of joy as she went to join the man who had been her companion during the past two days. Rob stood to face her and as if it were the most natural thing in the world, he took her in his arms and kissed her lovingly whilst the little Joshua smiled contentedly as he watched them.

~ * ~

Abigail Lawrence stood at the window of her Cheshire home gently rocking her sleeping baby as she watched her husband playing football with six year old Joshua. Two years before, they could never have envisaged this scene. Fate had led Abigail to a wonderful, peaceful existence. She silently thanked God for all the strength and resilience that had sustained her during the bad times. She silently blessed Rob, her husband, who had walked into the hospital where she worked one cold and wet Saturday afternoon in October 1972 with a very sick Joshua. Destiny had brought them together, of that she was certain.

She looked down at the beautiful blonde child in her arms—Sophie Marie Lawrence—and bent to kiss her gently before placing her in her crib to sleep in a world so different from the one into which she, herself, had been born. Abigail smiled as she thought of the mother she had never known. *Friday's child is loving and giving. Who could ask for better than that?*

Twenty-five

The Wilkinson kitchen was buzzing with activity. The outside caterers were unobtrusively going about their tasks with experienced efficiency and Meg's ability to lead without interfering, made their work easy. The marquee had been pitched in the garden two days before and the wooden decking was in place so that if the British summer weather should decide to take a typical turn for the worst, the guests would not be wading through wet grass and squelching mud.

Meg's organisational prowess was imperative to the smooth running of the event. It had taken all her powers of persuasion to convince Patty that she and Steve should bring their first child home for the christening. "We've waited so long for this event, Patty Ross, so don't deprive us of the pleasure of being present at my godson's baptism. You know how difficult it would be for us all to travel south. Please Patty, pretty please! I'll do you all proud.

After all, it will be a wonderful opportunity for you to introduce Jonathan Hawthorne Ross to his extended family."

"Meg Wilkinson, you are a right chip off the old block. We'll be there so long as you promise to do the night feeds while we're staying with you."

"Oh, well, that puts a different slant on things," Meg laughed.

"Only joking. Steve does the night shift anyway and I don't think he'd hand over his son. I actually think he enjoys waking up at two o'clock in the morning!" Patty told her. "Do you remember Abi's early feeds when Dad tried his best not to wake us? Poor Dad. We didn't realise what he was going through at the time, did we?"

"No, we didn't," Meg agreed. "I wish I could go back and give him more help."

"No, you don't, Meg. Don't get maudlin, as Gran would say. This is a happy occasion. Jonathan and Sophie christened together. I hope they don't cry, but I think *we* might!"

Abigail and Rob needed no persuasion at all to have a joint christening for the babies. Family was important to them both and they valued the time they all spent together. Josh had integrated well with the Hawthornes, and Abi was overcome with love for him when he had put his head on her bulging tummy to listen to Sophie's heartbeat before she was born. She was surprised when he announced, "You'll be the baby's mummy, won't you, Abi?"

"I will, but I'll still love you, Josh. I will always love you," she reassured the little boy.

"I know you will and we'll love the baby together, won't we?" Josh continued, "but..." He looked incredibly and beautifully pensive.

"No buts, Josh," she assured him. "You are the most important little boy in the whole world to your daddy and me. We love you very much."

"But…" he hesitated. "Will you be my mummy too, as well as the baby's?"

"Of course I will," Abi could hardly speak.

"I know I have my mummy in heaven and I'll never forget her, but she'll understand, won't she?"

"Understand what, sweetheart?"

"That you're my mummy too."

"I know she'll understand and I know she'll be happy about it. Does that help?" Abi asked him gently.

Joshua nodded. "Thanks, er…Mummy." And he skipped off without another word.

~ * ~

Meg had surpassed herself with the christening arrangements. The old Vicar of Belford had agreed to conduct the ceremony at Bromley Cross and a temporary font had been set up by the florist on the dais in the centre of the marquee. Patty and Abigail stood together cradling their babies, Jonathan in a white romper suit and Sophie in the flowing gown that Abi had worn at her own christening many years before. Meg was godmother to both babies; Abi to Jonathan and Patty to Sophie with Phil, Steve, Rob and the teenaged Nicky sharing the godfather duties among them.

Looking on was the matronly Jane Markland, now well into her nineties, but very aware that she was witnessing a remarkable achievement in the lives of the Hawthorne family. She had brought Meg and Patty into the world and had been filled with unfathomable foreboding when Mary had been moved to Townley's for Abigail's birth. Today however, together with the Reverend Anderton, she remembered how they had both seen the family through the good times and the bad times and she was so proud of them. Her thoughts were with Mary, with John and with Nellie. "Look at these three now," she whispered up to the heavens. "They're a real credit to you."

Much to everybody's surprise, Nicholas John Wilkinson stood in front of the congregation and spoke with confidence.

"Today, we have officially welcomed the two newest members into our family."

Meg looked at Phil for an explanation, but he shrugged and smiled proudly.

Nicky continued. "I have something to say to my mum, Margaret Elizabeth Hawthorne , and to my aunties, Patience Christine Hawthorne and Abigail Marie Hawthorne, but I think they'll forgive me when I say that most of all, it's for my grandmother, Mary Walmsley Hawthorne. He took a deep breath and began. "*Monday's child is fair of face, Tuesday's child is full of grace*...Meg...er..." he looked momentarily embarrassed, but recovered quickly, "I mean Mum, that's you." He paused. "And our very special nephew and cousin, Joshua Lawrence."

Joshua beamed with pride and looked lovingly at his daddy and new mummy.

Nicky winked at Josh then continued, "*Wednesday's child is full of woe* and thank goodness none of us was born on that day, but *Thursday's child has far to go* and that's baby Jonathan and me!" He grinned at Meg and Patty who both had handkerchiefs at the ready for when the tears began to flow.

"Baby Sophie... *Friday's child is loving and giving* and Auntie Abs... *Saturday's child works hard for a living.'*

Abigail nodded slowly, a knowing smile on her still lovely face.

"And last, but not least, Auntie Patty... *The child that is born on the Sabbath day is bonny and blithe and good and gay.*"

Patty smiled and winked cheekily at her adoring sisters.

"This was Mary's legacy to us all." Nicholas looked around at his wonderful family and knew that more than anything in the world, family matters.

Meet

Vera Berry Burrows

Vera Berry-Burrows is a UK-born former teacher of English Language and Literature, living in Queensland, Australia with journalist husband, Alan. She has a son and two grandsons living in the UK. She has been writing for a number of years and has had numerous non-fiction articles published in the UK and in Australia. She was educated at Farnworth Grammar School in Lancashire, trained as a teacher at St Katharine's College, Liverpool and gained a Bachelor of Arts degree with the Open University.

Since she took early retirement in 1994 having been in the teaching profession for thirty one years, writing has become her compulsive hobby.

Works by Vera Berry Burrows

Tomorrow Never Comes - Marriage, a new home and a new baby, Joel Thomas, all make up a perfect life for Nell Winston until suddenly her husband is no longer there and she turns into a woman possessed of compulsion to rule her son. Her strength is drawn from her unwavering sense to control until the young Joel decides to make a stand against her. Her domineering, self-absorption, along with egotistical stubbornness, takes her into a life that becomes her worst nightmare.

Joel's apparently selfish show of independence leads him along an extremely rocky road to eventual success in the Swinging 60's and with a complete reversal of roles, he takes charge of his mother's life. Will the new start in a different country bring the fulfillment they are both seeking?

Regarding Kimberley - Show business executive Kimberley Mason always felt something was missing from her life. She forms an association with a theatrical agency in Australia and uncovers a secret kept by her parents for thirty years. Revelations about her birth shatter her world. Discovering her real father is Australian television celebrity Joel Winston, she cuts herself off from the family she had always thought to be perfect

Leaving behind her past in England, she moves to Australia to be with the man she loves, her business partner, Simon Obertelli. Will running away ensure her future happiness or will the complications of accepting her famous father only lead to heartache?

Connections - Jane O'Connell did not envisage that her early retirement would completely disrupt her life. With too much time on her hands, she finds it difficult to adjust to her new existence. In her obstinate selfishness, she alienates herself from her family and friends. Running away from all things familiar appears to be her only option, but is it? Will the connections she makes really solve the problems she encounters in her life after work?

Family Matters - For three children left without a mother in the middle of World War Two, survival was all they could hope for. Their father struggled as a single parent, but instilled into his children, determination, ambition and self-respect so that they might succeed in post-war years and achieve everything which he was denied during his life.

This is their story.

My Name is Aphrodite - Rodi Bartlett sits on a plane taking her to the land of her conception. She can't call it the land of her birth because when her mother was sixteen years old, she had flown back to England from Corfu at the end of two weeks in the sun, unaware she was pregnant. When her mother, Adele dies young, details of the father, Cory Demetriou are exposed in her will and he has never been told of his daughter's existence.

Rodi's relentless search for the father she has never known, takes her to Corfu, mainland Greece and beyond. Filled with determination, setbacks, hope and love, this is the story of a young woman's quest to fulfil her mother's dying wish, but will Cory Demetriou accept her as his daughter twenty-six years on?

Dare To Dream - Left on the doorstep of St Anthony's Catholic Orphanage in Bolton, Northern England, Anne Marie O'Shea is placed in the guiding hands of another orphan named Bella Jones. As the years pass by, Bella accepts her lot for what it is; Annie dreams of a wonderful life, that special bit of magic that everybody deserves. When Bella is killed in a road accident at the age of twenty, Annie is left to fend for herself, to make decisions about her future and combat all the fears she has about forming lasting relationships. With numerous ups and downs, nurse training and emigration to Australia, a series of unbelievable co-incidences eventually puts the magic in her life that she could previously only dream about.

Payback - Julietta's holiday becomes a nightmare when she is swept up in the frenzy of other people's abhorrent need for revenge.

www.ingramcontent.com/pod-product-compliance
Lightning Source LLC
Chambersburg PA
CBHW061018120726
47910CB00006B/2002